D1226663

PRAISE FOR MELANIE DICKERSON

"The Piper's Pursuit is a lovely tale of adventure, romance, and redemption. Kat and Steffan's righteous quest will have you rooting them on until the very satisfying end!"

—LORIE LANGDON, AUTHOR OF *OLIVIA TWIST* AND THE DOON SERIES

"Christian fiction fans will relish Dickerson's eloquent story."

—*SCHOOL LIBRARY JOURNAL* ON *THE ORPHAN'S WISH*

"The Goose Girl, a little retold fairy tale, sparkles in Dickerson's hands, with endearing characters and a charming setting that will appeal to teens and adults alike."

—*RT BOOK REVIEWS*, 4$^{1}/_{2}$ STARS, TOP PICK! ON *THE NOBLE SERVANT*

"Dickerson is a masterful storyteller with a carefully crafted plot, richly drawn characters, and a detailed setting. The reader is easily pulled into the story."

—*CHRISTIAN LIBRARY JOURNAL* ON *THE NOBLE SERVANT*

"[*The Silent Songbird*] will have you jumping out of your seat with anticipation at times. Moderate- to fast-paced, you will not want this book to end. Recommended for all, especially lovers of historical romance."

—*RT BOOK REVIEWS*, 4 STARS

"A terrific YA crossover medieval romance from the author of *The Golden Braid*."

—*LIBRARY JOURNAL* ON *THE SILENT SONGBIRD*

"When it comes to happily-ever-afters, Melanie Dickerson is the undisputed queen of fairy-tale romance, and all I can say is—long live the queen! From start to finish *The Beautiful Pretender* is yet another brilliant gem in her crown, spinning a medieval love story that will steal you away—heart, soul, and sleep!"

—JULIE LESSMAN, AWARD-WINNING AUTHOR OF
THE DAUGHTERS OF BOSTON, WINDS OF CHANGE,
AND HEART OF SAN FRANCISCO SERIES

"Dickerson breathes life into the age-old story of Rapunzel, blending it seamlessly with the other YA novels she has written in this time and place . . . The character development is solid, and she captures religious medieval life splendidly."

—BOOKLIST ON THE GOLDEN BRAID

"Readers who love getting lost in a fairy-tale romance will cheer for Rapunzel's courage as she rises above her overwhelming past. The surprising way Dickerson weaves threads of this enchanting companion novel with those of her other Hagenheim stories is simply delightful."

—JILL WILLIAMSON, CHRISTY AWARD-
WINNING AUTHOR, ON THE GOLDEN BRAID

"Dickerson spins a retelling of Robin Hood with emotionally compelling characters, offering hope that love may indeed conquer all as they unite in a shared desire to serve both the Lord and those in need."

—RT BOOK REVIEWS, 4¹/2 STARS, ON THE
HUNTRESS OF THORNBECK FOREST

"Melanie Dickerson does it again! Full of danger, intrigue, and romance, this beautifully crafted story [*The Huntress of Thornbeck Forest*] will transport you to another place and time."

—SARAH E. LADD, BESTSELLING AUTHOR
OF THE CORNWALL NOVELS

CASTLE of REFUGE

Other Books by Melanie Dickerson

The Dericott Tales
Court of Swans

Young Adult Fairy Tale Romance Series
The Healer's Apprentice
The Merchant's Daughter
The Fairest Beauty
The Captive Maiden
The Princess Spy
The Golden Braid
The Silent Songbird
The Orphan's Wish
The Warrior Maiden
The Piper's Pursuit
The Peasant's Dream

A Medieval Fairy Tale Series
The Huntress of Thornbeck Forest
The Beautiful Pretender
The Noble Servant

Regency Spies of London Series
A Spy's Devotion
A Viscount's Proposal
A Dangerous Engagement

CASTLE *of* REFUGE

MELANIE DICKERSON

THOMAS NELSON
Since 1798

To Aaron.

The one I love.

The one who loves me.

Library of Congress Cataloging-in-Publication Data

Names: Dickerson, Melanie, author.
Title: Castle of refuge / Melanie Dickerson.
Description: Nashville, Tennessee : Thomas Nelson, [2021] | Series: Dericott tales ; 2 | Audience: Grades 10-12. | Summary: In medieval England, nineteen-year-old Audrey, the daughter of English nobility and facially scarred by her abusive, mentally ill sister, seeks God's protection when she runs away from an arranged marriage proposal, to find true love, safety, and purpose in her life.
Identifiers: LCCN 2021004049 (print) | LCCN 2021004050 (ebook) | ISBN 9780785234043 (hardcover) | ISBN 9780785234050 (epub) | ISBN 9780785234067
Subjects: CYAC: Love--Fiction. | Knights and knighthood--Fiction. | Nobility--Fiction. | Runaways--Fiction. | Sisters--Fiction. | Disfigured persons--Fiction. | Christian life--Fiction. | Middle Ages--Fiction. | Great Britain--History--Medieval period, 1066-1485--Fiction.
Classification: LCC PZ7.D5575 Cas 2021 (print) | LCC PZ7.D5575 (ebook) | DDC [Fic]--dc23
LC record available at https://lccn.loc.gov/2021004049
LC ebook record available at https://lccn.loc.gov/2021004050

Printed in the United States of America

21 22 23 24 25 LSC 5 4 3 2 1

ONE

SPRING 1378

ENGLEFORD CASTLE, HAMPSHIRE

AUDREY HID BEHIND A TREE AND WATCHED A KNIGHT AND his squire riding down the lane. The knight was nothing to look at—bushy beard and paunchy belly—but the squire had gentle eyes, a smooth face, and a slight smile on his lips. She would guess he was a few years older than her own fifteen. Tall and slender, his back as straight as a spear, he had dark hair and his skin was appealingly sun-browned.

They were riding toward her father's castle, no doubt to spend the night. Twilight was falling and travelers often chose to stay, as her father owned the only castle within a half day's ride in any direction.

She glanced down at her dress, noting the mud stains across the skirt. She'd get quite the scolding when Sybil, the head house servant, saw her condition. "Still a rambunctious girl-child at the age of fifteen. How will you ever get a husband?"

Her father would scowl and say, "You're too old for such mucking about. Don't let anyone see you looking like that."

And her older sister, Maris, would snort and laugh at her. Or scream at her and call her ugly names. One never quite knew how Maris would react. She was so changeable, smiling one minute, rageful the next.

Audrey passed the pond where she sometimes went fishing with the stable boy, continuing to the meadow where the wildflowers grew so thick she could pick an apron full in no time. She found one particularly dark pink flower and another unusually deep purple one. She held them up to the sun, pressing their tiny stems between her fingers. The light shone through the petals, lighting them up like a colored star, or like a burst of flame in pink and lavender.

That was what Audrey wished for her life to be—a burst of light. An intense color. Something unforgettable.

Her mind pondered this dilemma—how to make her life extraordinary. Some might say she was an insignificant girl, that she could not make her life a flash of intense light. Perhaps she could not, but God had made these wildflowers beautiful, which were here today and tomorrow would be food for the sheep. Could He not do much more for her, even though she was only a girl?

Besides, she liked being a girl. All the better to surprise people when she did something important.

And as a girl, and while she remained unmarried, she had

more freedom. If she were a boy, her father would have sent her to train as a knight when she was a young child. Instead, she had been allowed to study all manner of interesting things, read all sorts of books, and Father had even provided her with a tutor. But today her tutor was away visiting his sister.

Now that Audrey had learned all the languages her tutor knew—Latin, French, German, and English—she was worried her father would send him away. He was not the most genial fellow, but he did enjoy speaking other languages with her, and certainly neither her father nor Maris would ever practice with her or discuss the other things she was learning.

If she were to marry well—someone powerful and wealthy— she might have the means and opportunity to make her life meaningful. And yet she also did not want to marry some who didn't love her or whom she was unable to love. Love h, always seemed to be the highest ideal, a noble goal, since th opposite of love was what caused so much evil in life. Besides, the Holy Writ said, "God is love." That alone must make it of great importance.

Nevertheless, love alone did not seem to be enough. She wanted to do something extraordinary. Maybe she could teach girls to read. After all, the girls in the villages of England never learned to read. They learned sewing, and if they weren't too poor, they might learn embroidery or learn how to play an instrument. But if girls could read, they could accomplish many of the things men were able to do. They could become an alchemist who could turn iron into gold, or a physician who could make sick people well. At the very least they would be adept enough at mathematics that they could own a shop and cipher ways to make a larger profit.

But she kept these thoughts to herself, for she knew people would laugh, scoff, or even get angry with her for such thinking. Maris certainly would, and she imagined Father giving her that severe, confounded look he often gave her. Then he would turn away and ignore her, even though she'd just shared the desires of her heart.

She did not know what lay ahead of her, what her life would become, but she wanted to be a bright light, a shooting star, but one that shot up high into the heavens instead of falling to earth.

When she arrived back at Engleford Castle, she went in through the Great Hall, slipping through the door behind her father's dais. In her apron skirt she carried daisies, johnny jump ups, buttercups, and the pink and purple flowers that grew along the rocky shore.

Audrey stepped from behind the partition. Her father sat at the table with the knight and his squire.

Her father turned, his eyes roving from her head to her feet. He scowled, a harsh look in his eyes. He jerked his head toward the door, and she quickly went back the way she had come, her heart pounding.

He must be angry at the prospect of his guests seeing his daughter looking like a servant girl with mussed hair, muddy skirts, and wildflowers in her apron. She hurried toward the kitchen. Perhaps Sybil would appreciate her wildflowers.

Audrey turned the corner and reached for the kitchen door.

"Child! You look like the ditch digger's daughter!" Sybil cried.

"I picked some wildflowers and—"

"Go get changed, quick!"

"Why? What—"

"Your father's all in a fit to get you in front of that knight and his squire."

"What? Why?" Audrey's heart pounded against her chest.

"Come." Sybil took her arm and pulled her forward. It was all Audrey could do to keep from spilling her wildflowers.

In Audrey's bedchamber Sybil allowed her to spread her wildflowers on her windowsill to dry so she could press them later, while Sybil found her best dress, then helped her change her clothes.

Her stomach trembled as she managed to look Sybil in the eye. "Father's not going to marry me off to that knight, is he?"

"Not the knight. I think he has a wife. It's the s the oldest son of the Earl of Dericott."

An earl. And he was close to her own age. But she wasn't ready to answer to a husband or to have children. She'd miss her wildflower meadow, her dogs, her lessons with her tutor, and her horseback rides to the sea. And what if her new husband turned out to be as cold and angry as her sister, Maris? Or as unfeeling as her father, who rarely looked at her, even when he spoke to her?

Sybil brushed her hair so aggressively, Audrey cried out.

"Forgive me. Hold still."

Sybil pulled Audrey's hair back into a circlet and covered it with a sheer veil. Then she came around to look at Audrey's face. Her own expression relaxed, and she even smiled.

"You have grown into such a beauty. Just like your mother."

"Maris is prettier than I am." Her sister had flawless skin and large green eyes. Maris had often told her how ugly she was with a disgusted expression and tone in her voice, but then Maris was always saying cruel things, things Audrey wasn't sure she even meant. And she had seen the way the few young men she had met had looked at her. She was not ugly. But Maris was the beauty.

"You are very plain," Maris would say, scrunching her whole face, as if she could barely stand to look at Audrey. "Your nose is crooked and your eyes are that insipid color of blue that no one likes."

Maris's eyes would go wide as she burst out laughing, an ear-piercing sound, and say, "You look like a villein!" She meant the poorest of the poor, the people who were bound to her father's land and must toil very hard from sunup to sundown just to have enough food to stay alive.

"Your sister is pretty," Sybil answered, bringing her back to the present, "but not as fair as you. Besides . . ." Sybil's face clouded over, and she raised her brows and sighed. "Your sister does not have your patience for learning, nor does she have your sweet disposition."

Father often said, "Your sister is not right in the head, and it will be your responsibility to take care of her when I am gone." Then he would raise his brows and stroke his beard.

Father, who often laughed at other people's misfortunes, never punished her sister for her violence toward the servants nor her loud, rageful outbursts. But then Audrey could never quite condemn Maris either. Her sister had been treated cruelly by their nursemaid when she was a child, and Audrey believed that had affected her mind and was the reason she was often angry, with Audrey and everyone else. She was still her sister, and Audrey could remember times when they were very young when Maris would play with her and even take care of her when no servants were nearby. And yet . . . Maris often seemed to plan mischief against people who had never done her any harm.

Sybil hurried Audrey down the stairs.

"Do I have to do this? Do I have to meet them now? Perhaps Father wants me to wait until later."

"No, no, he wants you. Come, come. Don't dawdle."

Audrey took the last step rather awkwardly as her skirts got tangled around her legs and she almost tripped. Sybil grabbed her arm, and Audrey paused to get her balance again and shake her skirts free. She walked slowly toward the main door to the Great Hall, which stood open. Inside her father was regaling his guests with a familiar story about his own days as a knight's squire.

As she walked in, all three men turned to look at her. As did Maris.

Audrey's sister was sitting on the other side of her father. Her stomach trembled inside her. Would Maris embarrass her with stories about some misstep or other? No doubt she'd talk about something Audrey did in their childhood with the intent to humiliate her.

"And here is my younger daughter, Audrey." Her father

smiled at her, that peculiar flat smile of his, and held out his hand for her to come join him at the table.

Audrey hurried forward and sat on the bench beside Maris, facing the knight and his squire.

Audrey was too afraid to make eye contact with her sister. Instead, she smiled briefly at their guests, then looked down at her food. The knight was chewing, a tankard of ale in one hand and a large roll of bread in the other. He paid her little notice, but the squire stared her in the eye. Even when she purposely looked away, she could feel his eyes lingering on her face.

He was a handsome boy with a lean face and gentle eyes. Why she should think his eyes were gentle, she wasn't sure, but they made her wonder what he was thinking, what sort of person he was, and if her father might actually make an agreement with his father to match them.

The servants brought out more food while her father talked with the knight, a Sir Clement of Nottingham. Audrey was not hungry, so she nibbled on the cheese and dried fruit and sneaked quick glances at the squire. While listening to the conversation, she discovered that his name was Edwin Raynsford.

"You are to be the Earl of Dericott," her father said, looking hard at Edwin.

It seemed improper to bring this up, since it would require Edwin's father to die for him to inherit the title, but her father was rather impolite at times.

"Yes, my father is the Earl of Dericott, and I am his eldest son," the young man said. There was neither undue pride nor censure in his statement. His demeanor was calm and forthright.

And as she stared at him, for the first time in her life, she wondered if she might like to be married. She believed she would—if she could marry someone gentle and good, someone who looked like Edwin Raynsford.

While Father conversed with Edwin, Sir Clement ate his food and glanced back and forth between Audrey and Maris. Finally, Audrey chanced a look at her sister. Maris was sitting tall and straight, her hands folded in front of her. And she was staring at Edwin, her gaze unwavering.

Maris was seventeen, so she must think him handsome as well. But Audrey had heard Father say in a pique of temper that Maris would never be married, that he couldn't have her bring shame to the family by letting the world know his daughter was lunatic. Maris had been angrier than Audrey had ever seen her, and she could tell her father was sorry for what he'd said. He had tried to calm her down by saying, "There's no reason for you to marry. You are needed at home and can be free to do as you please."

"You're ashamed of me," Maris had breathed.

She had stormed through the house, slamming doors, and shut herself in her room for almost an entire day. Audrey had steered clear of her sister for several days after, carefully avoiding her for fear that she would take her wrath out on her.

As her father talked to Sir Clement, Edwin addressed both Audrey and Maris. "Do you ever go to the coast to see the ocean?"

His voice was lovely, like a stream shot through with a warm ray of sunshine. But Audrey did not answer him, lest Maris get angry and lash out at her.

"I adore the ocean," Maris said with a broad smile.

Audrey had never known her sister to profess any affection for the sea.

"I would love to go there with you." Maris gazed at Edwin with her eyelids lowered halfway. Was she trying to appear alluring?

Edwin's expression changed, and he cleared his throat. "We are on our way north tomorrow, I'm afraid."

"We can sneak away tonight. Meet me at the stable after dark."

"I am sorry, but I cannot." He shifted on the bench and turned to look at Father and Sir Clement, as if he was interested in their conversation.

Was the young man determined only to do good things, or did he have sharp enough instincts about people to be afraid of Maris? But perhaps Audrey was giving him too much credit. Maybe he was only afraid of his master finding out he'd run off in the night with their host's daughter.

Either way, Audrey kept her head down so Maris wouldn't look into her eyes and read her thoughts.

When the main dishes were brought out—pheasant and wild boar—they all got quieter, except for her father, who rarely had guests of similar rank, and he seemed pleased to have someone to converse with.

"And your father was the Marquess of Donwell?" Father said, still talking with Sir Clement. "I met him once on a trip through Nottingham." Her father went on with another of his tales, all of which highlighted something he could brag about.

She'd never really thought about it before, but her father loved to boast of his good deeds and the important people he had met.

Suddenly, Audrey felt a sharp pain in her side, and she gasped and flinched away from Maris. She looked down to see Maris holding a knife in her fist, pointed at Audrey under the table. Audrey scooted farther away from her sister, who had just stabbed her with the knife, though not hard enough to puncture the skin. Maris was giving her a look of surprise, pretending she had no idea why Audrey reacted the way she did.

Edwin turned his gaze on her.

"What is wrong with you, daft girl?" Maris laughed. "To suddenly jump away from me?"

"You hurt me."

"Hurt you? You truly are mad." She laughed, then smiled at Edwin. "She is mad, poor thing. We cannot tell what she might do next. She's been this way since birth."

Audrey felt her face starting to burn. She did not want Edwin to think such things about her, but she knew from experience that to argue with Maris or dispute her word would only make her more hostile. So she sat silently staring down at the food on her trencher.

What would life have been like if her mother had lived past her birth? Would she have defended Audrey? Her father almost never did. She felt like the sacrificial lamb sometimes, her life offered up to keep Maris from attacking anyone else.

But she also knew that her father hoped and expected her to marry well. Since he had no sons to inherit his title and property, if he did not remarry and produce any male heirs, his property and title would go to a nephew, her aunt and uncle's child in Derbyshire.

When she glanced up, Edwin was gazing at her with a questioning look on his face. No doubt he was wondering if she was lunatic. Or did he realize Maris was the mad one and he was sorry she had been forced to live with such a sister?

Again, she was probably giving him more credit than he deserved.

And once again, her father did not even seem to notice anything was amiss. He was still talking with Sir Clement. Neither of them even glanced their way.

Maris tried a few more times to engage Edwin in conversation, but he only responded minimally. And he seemed to address Audrey more than Maris. Audrey could almost feel the fury building in Maris.

Finally, the meal was over and her father dismissed Audrey and Maris. He and the two guests would stay and talk and drink some more before retiring.

Audrey stood and looked Sir Clement in the eye and then Edwin, as her mother's longtime house servant, Sybil, had taught her. "It was my pleasure to make your acquaintance."

Edwin met her gaze for a moment. "The pleasure was mine."

Audrey was well aware of Maris's cold stare, and she hurried from the Great Hall, praying her sister wouldn't catch up to her and hit her from behind, as she was wont to do.

Audrey made it to the stairs. Glancing over her shoulder, she did not see Maris following. Was she lingering behind to try to impress Edwin? Audrey didn't care. She lifted her skirts and ran all the way up to her room, closing the door and locking it. There. She had escaped from her sister and been spared any more embarrassment in front of the handsome Edwin.

Would he be her husband one day? He was destined to be knighted and to become the Earl of Dericott. She might do many good things as his wife. God would be able to use her life for many bright and remarkable purposes if she were the wife of a good and kind earl. She only hoped she would not be married off for a few more years. She wanted to pick wildflowers, visit the seaside, and reread *The Song of Roland* and her other most treasured books before succumbing to adulthood.

The next day as Audrey was making her way down the stairs, she heard her father talking in the Great Hall. Walking by the door, she peered in and saw him with his steward. Father dismissed him and called out to Audrey.

"Come in, my child. I wish to speak with you."

"Yes, Father?" Audrey approached him where he sat breaking his fast with some pasties and stewed fruit.

"Sit. I have something to tell you."

Audrey sat and chose a plum pasty, taking a bite and letting the sweet flavor spread across her tongue. Plums were her favorite fruit. She often picked them from the trees and ate them right there in the orchard. If any of the servants caught her, they would scold her. Only cooked fruit was safe to eat, they told her, but she had never sickened from eating them.

13

Audrey was reaching for her second pasty when her father finally spoke.

"I hope you made a good impression on that young squire, the future Earl of Dericott. I shall write to his father and make him an offer so that he will choose you as a wife for his son."

Audrey choked as some filling went down the wrong way. She coughed and took a swallow of her father's boiled fruit drink. "But we will not be married very soon, will we, Father? I am only fifteen."

Her father talked over her as if he had not heard her. "I can offer him a nice dowry, your mother's jewels, and even that property in Hertfordshire that belonged to your mother's family."

"Father, I am too young." Audrey's stomach flipped at the thought of the handsome Edwin discovering that her father had offered her to him in marriage. Of course she knew she wasn't actually too young. Many young women were married off even younger than she.

"Well, I daresay it will be at least a year before he marries. I want to ensure his father keeps you in mind, at least. I might even pay him a visit. An earl is a great match for you, and he was young and handsome to boot. You should be thanking me."

Truly, Audrey had always known she would be married off to someone. And Father was right. Edwin seemed much better than any other man she'd ever been introduced to.

"He did have kind eyes," she said, feeling herself blushing.

Her father did not reply, only stuffed half a pasty in his mouth.

"You don't think your sister frightened him off, do you?" Her father spoke with his mouth still full of food. "She's forward and aggressive. Men don't like that. They like women like you—quiet and docile."

Audrey did not like being called "docile," as if she were a horse. But Edwin did not seem anything like Father. All the better.

"Did he seem taken with you? Did he look at you very much?"

"I don't know." Audrey shrugged.

"You are very fair of face. I don't see why he would not have noticed. You will make a fine wife. I shall write to him today."

A movement caught Audrey's eye. She turned toward the open doorway and saw Maris glaring at her. But when she saw that they had spied her there, Maris moved away from the door and was gone.

"You've made her angry." Audrey's voice was hoarse as she imagined how Maris might retaliate against them both.

Her father waved his hand. "She probably didn't hear me. Besides, I've told her she will always have a home here. She doesn't need to marry. She should thank you for getting married so she doesn't have to."

Surely her father knew. Maris would never see herself as the fortunate one as long as Audrey was living her life, getting married, and having children, while Maris was forced to remain at home, with nowhere else to go.

Audrey could certainly see the situation through Maris's eyes. If she were told she could never marry and never leave her home, she would be grieved at having to miss out on having a family and home of her own, and she would worry about what would happen to her after her father died. But to some extent, Audrey might also feel relieved. After all, the woman who never married had a measure of freedom that the married woman did not. But freedom to do what? She imagined she would one day get tired of reading and gathering wildflowers. After all, she wanted to do something significant in the world.

Maris . . . she certainly had hopes and dreams too. Surely she wished to love and be loved, as Audrey did.

When Audrey's mother died soon after Audrey was born, her father acquired a nursemaid named Hattie to look after Audrey and Maris, who was only two years old. When Maris was about five years old, Sybil discovered that Hattie had been abusing Maris—slapping her, pinching her, even beating her. Sybil had found bruises on Maris's body and began secretly observing Hattie. Hattie was tender toward Audrey and showed her favor, but she was spiteful and violent toward Maris. Sybil reported the matter to Father, and he immediately dismissed the woman.

Knowing of the abuse her sister had endured for three full years, Audrey could never hate Maris. What evils her poor sister had suffered, and as a small child, she must have blamed Audrey, at least in part. She had to have resented Audrey for being the pet, the loved one, while Maris was mistreated. Such a thing must have deeply affected her. And Audrey, though she knew she was not responsible for such evils befalling her sister, still felt a weight of guilt about how her very existence had caused Maris such harm. And it was never very far from her mind.

Yet Maris was unrelenting toward everyone around her,

ragefully hitting and spitting and pulling hair, playing tricks on people and punishing them when they had done nothing wrong.

In spite of her father's dismissive attitude regarding whether Maris had overheard him, Audrey's heart was in her throat most of the morning, wondering how Maris would avenge herself over Father's words, over how he was slighting her and favoring Audrey. But after only seeing a glimpse or two of her sister, by nightfall Audrey had ceased thinking about it.

She sat by the fire in the small upstairs solar with a couple of candles beside her, studying her lessons for the next day. When she finished, she would read a bit of *The Song of Roland* in French. She had learned that language almost as well as she knew English.

Lying next to her was a tapestry she'd been embroidering. It was a garden scene with flowers and birds. She generally tried to work on it when Maris was not around. Maris never embroidered or sewed, as she had not the patience to remain still that long.

The sound of the crackling fire drew a long sigh from her as she nestled deeper in her chair with the book on geography her tutor had assigned her to read. She was imagining herself in one of the faraway countries on the map when she looked up and saw Maris staring at her.

Audrey quickly closed her book and folded her hands on top of it.

"What is that you're doing there?" Maris had a strange look on her face, her voice oddly quiet.

"Nothing."

"Nothing. Then you won't mind getting up and fetching me something." Maris sat down on a bench near Audrey.

Audrey took a breath. Why should Maris ask her to fetch her something? But it would be easier just to do whatever her sister wished. So Audrey waited to hear what her sister needed.

"Do you remember that small embroidered thing you gave me for my birthday?"

"The tapestry you laughed at and said looked like a small child had made it?"

"I did not like it at the time, but now I want it. I want to hang it next to my bed. Will you get it for me?"

Audrey's heart thumped hard. What was her sister scheming? But perhaps she truly did want the tapestry. Audrey could not refuse her. It would seem unkind. Besides, even if Maris just wanted to insult Audrey's work, she couldn't hurt Audrey anymore with her criticism. Audrey no longer needed her older sister's approval. She had surely grown that mature after all Maris had done. At least, that was what she told herself.

Audrey stood, taking her book with her, lest Maris wished to cut it up into little pieces, as she had done with some of her other books.

Audrey went to her bedchamber, laid her book on her bed, and went to her trunk. She found the small tapestry that Maris was referring to and took it back to the solar. But a lump had formed in her throat. Maris didn't actually want the tapestry Audrey had made for her. Audrey cast about in her mind, trying to think where the nearest servant was, where her father might be, in case she needed protection.

She passed by her father's bedchamber. The door was open, and he was talking to his steward about estate business. And a glance behind her showed Sybil walking toward her down the hallway. She felt some measure of relief, knowing if Maris tried to harm her, she could cry out and someone would be near enough to come to her aid.

She hated that she was so suspicious of Maris. She was her older sister, after all.

She walked into the solar. Maris had pulled her chair closer to the fire. She looked over her shoulder at Audrey and smiled. Audrey held out the small tapestry to her sister.

Maris took it from her hand, but as Audrey walked to her chair, Maris thrust out her foot. Audrey tripped over it. She couldn't stop herself.

She grabbed for her sister's hand, but Maris snatched her hand away. Audrey flailed desperately. But it was too late to put out her hands to break her fall.

She was falling toward the fire, face-first.

Audrey twisted her body so that she landed on her side. Her head hit hard, right in the edge of the fire. Searing pain was the last thing she remembered as her vision went black.

Two

FOUR YEARS LATER . . . SUMMER 1382
DERICOTT CASTLE, BEDFORDSHIRE

"You will not be required to pay your labor duties in the lord's fields or furlongs for one year."

Edwin faced the villeins who lived and worked on the demesne that his family had owned for over a hundred years—all the land round about Dericott Castle. The villeins had gathered at his request, and now he had their full attention.

The people looked quite scrawny, their skin browned from the sun. Their clothes, which were made of rough wool, were ragged and stained. Many of them stared at him for a long time, while others cast furtive glances, hardly daring to lift their heads for more than a moment or two.

"Do you mean no plow work? For a fortnight?" one brave soul asked.

"No plow work, that is correct, but I mean for the rest of the year."

The people exchanged glances with one another.

"Think of it as a year of Jubilee. Your debt of work has been canceled."

Edwin was not sure what reaction he had expected, but he had anticipated some show of joy or relief or celebration. But instead they were mute and still.

"You may use this year to work your own furlongs and your own crops, and you do not need to give any part of your crops to me. I give you leave to keep it all for yourselves. You have earned a respite. I have servants to till my furrows and to plant and sow, and what they cannot get to will lie fallow. You are to do for yourselves only, all year."

They all continued to stare at him and exchange glances with one another, as if confused and seeking confirmation that they had heard correctly.

"You are free to go."

A few of them began to smile. Several nodded and bowed and backed away. But as they walked down the dirt lane, they began to clap one another on the back, to laugh and talk.

One young man turned around and said, "Thank you, Lord Dericott. May God bless you for your generosity." He bowed and went on his way.

A few others did the same, thanking him and blessing him. But most simply hurried on, still appearing astonished, some mumbling to each other as they walked.

This . . . this felt good.

After such a long time of feeling heavy inside, weeks of lying in bed recovering from the removal of his arm by a London barber five months ago, he finally felt . . . better. His life had not turned out as he'd expected or wanted, and there was nothing he could do about that, but now that his father was dead and Edwin was the new earl, he had the power to lighten the burden of the people around him.

He couldn't remember his father even mentioning the peasants who labored on his family's demesne more than once or twice in his whole life, and certainly his father would not approve of Edwin giving them a year off from their labor tax, which tied them to the land and made them, for all intents and purposes, his slaves for a certain portion of every year.

His father seemed to think of the villeins as property, not living people with hearts and souls. But after what Edwin had been through, he'd had a lot of time to think. What was man that God should be mindful of him? Did God care more for an earl than for a villein? If he'd learned anything from his study of the Holy Writ, he'd learned that the same God who made one also made the other. And just as a villein could fall prey to injustice and misfortune, so could an earl.

The captain of his guard came toward him. "This missive just arrived for you." He held out a rolled-up parchment.

The seal and colors belonged to the Earl of Essex. He took it, his heart beating faster. Had Lady Ophelia, the Lord Essex's daughter, finally written him?

He broke the seal and unrolled the letter.

Dericott,

Thank you for your letter. All is in good order here, with only a few ill effects of Wat Tyler's Rebellion. A recent rain washed away a bridge. Other than that all is well in Essex and with my family. My prayer is that you and your family are in good health.

I wanted to express my condolences on your injury sustained some months ago when you and your brothers were wrongly imprisoned. I pray God will avenge you on those responsible.

I am yours respectfully,
Essex

Edwin read the letter again. The mentions of Wat Tyler's Rebellion, and Edwin's injury and those responsible, felt like a renewal of the weight their memory brought to his shoulders, bringing back the cloud of gloom that had been over him for the better part of a year.

But the worst part was that there was no mention of Lady Ophelia, whom Edwin intended to marry.

Just over a year ago she'd whispered into his ear at a ball at her father's castle, "I will marry you."

He'd asked her to marry him without even consulting his father. She had smiled at him so beguilingly that he'd instantly fallen in love that night at the ball. He loved everything about her—her dark hair and light eyes, the way she moved so gracefully she seemed to float, the way she smiled and laughed—all of it drew him in.

Father had been pleased at the match and had written to Lady Ophelia's father to negotiate the terms of the marriage. A few weeks later, Lord Essex had promised her to him with the benefit of property and jewels.

It was a good match for both of them, as Lady Ophelia and Edwin were wealthy, he destined to be an earl, she an earl's daughter. But shortly thereafter, Edwin's father was dead and he and his brothers were accused of murder and treason. Then he lost his arm, maimed for life.

Edwin had not seen Lady Ophelia since the ball. After his acquittal of all charges, he had written to her not once but twice without a reply. He'd finally written to her father, a vague missive inquiring after his health and whether he and his family had weathered the uprising without mishap, knowing already that they had. And this was his answer. It was strange that Essex would take the trouble to write and send a courier without insisting his daughter also include a reply to her future husband.

Was Lady Ophelia simply a poor correspondent? Did she still want to marry him after hearing that he was now lame? Would she be ashamed to be his wife? Honestly, he did not know her character all that well.

Leaning back in his chair, Edwin stared out at the rain that had just started falling from the gray sky.

The right thing to do would be to tell her that if she could not face being married to a man with one arm, then he would let her out of her pledge. But such delicate information would best be conveyed in person rather than a letter. He should go to her and speak with her. And he would. But not until he was more confident in his ability to keep his balance and not fall off his horse.

Audrey's looking glass told her the ugly truth: her dream of being a bright light in the world, of doing something significant, was lost forever. Most of the time she avoided looking at herself, but last night she'd had a particularly disturbing nightmare. In the dream, one whole side of her face had literally melted off. Gone. In her dream she'd started screaming, which had her pushing herself up in bed, a hoarse sound coming from her aching throat.

Gazing at her reflection now, she could see her face was still there, though the burn had deformed her ear and the scar extended over a small section of her face about two fingers wide. Hideous, to be sure, but thankfully not half her face.

She touched the alternately smooth and puckered, reddish skin, remembering the terrible pain that had lasted for weeks until the burns had finally healed. She had been so frightened in those days that she had entreated her father to protect her from her sister.

"Send me away," Audrey had begged. "I cannot bear to be in the same house with her. Please, Father. I cannot bear it."

"It was not intentional," her father had said. "She said you tripped over her foot. She did not purposely send you into the fire."

"She did, she did." Audrey had covered her eyes with her hands, reliving the horror of what her sister had done. Over and over the image haunted her, the moment her eyes had met Maris's, the cold, malevolent smile on her face as she stuck out her foot to trip her.

The one time Maris had come into her room—to comfort her, she had said—Audrey screamed. She couldn't help herself. She screamed until the servants put themselves between her and Maris. Audrey's mind had gone back to the moment Maris had tripped her, and she couldn't seem to separate that event from the present moment. She'd screamed until the servants and her father convinced her sister to leave the room.

Then her father turned on Audrey. "What's the matter with you? Screaming like a mad woman. There is no peace in this house."

Peace? How was she ever to have peace again?

Her hands shaking and her heart racing, she cried, "How can I have peace when I'm not safe?"

A few days later, Maris was gone. Her father sent her to a convent.

Father said little about it and seemed cross for several days afterward, so Audrey did not ask him any questions. She was only too glad to have her sister gone.

Despite not having seen her sister in four years, Audrey's memory still seemed so vivid. She recalled a dream she'd had several nights before.

Audrey was lying in her bed when she opened her eyes and saw Maris standing in her doorway. Audrey's throat constricted. She tried to ask Maris what she wanted, to tell her to leave her alone, but she couldn't speak. Her throat was too tight and dry.

Suddenly, Maris was holding a torch, fiery and glowing orange.

No! Audrey struggled to scream, desperate. She opened her mouth but no sound came out. She'd awakened gasping for air, her heart pounding.

She still felt shaken by the vivid dreams, but the four years since Maris left had been good, despite her father sending her tutor away soon after the accident. She had cried bitter tears, knowing he did it because he no longer thought she had a chance to wed anyone wealthy or powerful and therefore would not need any further education. She would miss having someone to speak to in French and German and to teach her various other subjects.

But in the following months and years, Audrey spent her days doing the things she loved and continuing her education on her own—studying her books and practicing her languages by reading books in French and German, gathering wildflowers, and embroidering tapestries. She began to feel safe, and how good it was to no longer feel beaten down and oppressed. She could be herself, laugh, speak her mind without someone deriding and criticizing her, hitting or pinching her.

Four years had not changed her very much, though perhaps she was less dreamy and she worried more about the kind of man her father would marry her off to. Her father made it clear he had much lower expectations—and standards—now that she was scarred. She was ugly, people saw her as ugly, and she had to get used to it.

The servants behaved differently toward her—less deferential, no longer jumping when she asked them to do something for her.

They treated her more like an equal, which, strangely, did not bother her. She rather liked it. But the people in the village stared very rudely at her, as if hoping to catch a glimpse of her scars.

Audrey was nineteen years old, and the older she got, the more she craved the society of other young women her own age. As her father hardly paid any mind to what she did, she'd made friends with a girl who worked in the candle shop in the village. Her name was Helena, and she was fortunate enough not to have any sisters.

Helena was slow to speak but quick to laugh. She had clear blue eyes that danced when she was happy and sparked when she was angry. She always smiled when Audrey walked into her shop.

After sighing in relief, again, that none of the dreams she'd dreamed were true—her face was still intact and Maris was still away at the convent—Audrey prepared to go for a walk to see Helena. She finished putting on her dress, and as she came around her dressing screen, someone knocked on her chamber door. Sybil came inside.

"You are already dressed," Sybil said. "I am late, but I have some news for you." Sybil's hands were clasped together, and she was avoiding looking Audrey in the eye.

"What is it, Sybil? Is something amiss?"

"Amiss? Not at all. Do you recall your father's friend Sir Clement of Nottingham?"

"Yes, I know who he is." A feeling of dread came over her.

Audrey would much rather remember his former squire, Edwin, who became Sir Edwin, and then just recently, the Earl of Dericott.

"Well, Sir Clement's wife has passed on to heaven and he has taken a notion to marry someone younger this time. As it turns out, he has a lot of wealth and wishes to build his new bride a large manor house. In fact, he has already begun the work. You would like to be mistress of a large new home, would you not?"

Sybil told the news so fast, her voice rushing through it so quickly, it took a moment to sink in.

"The new wife he wants is me." Audrey's stomach sank.

Sybil nodded.

"Father wishes it?"

Sybil nodded again.

Audrey's mind raced as she tried to imagine being married to the paunchy Sir Clement, a man more than twice her age.

"He seems a good sort of man."

Audrey dropped down on a stool.

"If it weren't for my scars . . ." She didn't finish the thought. They both knew her father had intended to use her beauty as a means to attract wealthy and powerful suitors. Sir Clement was not very wealthy. He had no title other than his knighthood, and he served in the king's guard part of every year. Had her scars made her unsuitable for anyone better than a knight old enough to be her father? Truly, her father must be anxious to marry her off to almost anyone. Of course. She was damaged now. Just like Maris. Audrey might not be changeable and vengeful, but she was scarred.

"It will not be so bad," Sybil said. "And you can take a few servants with you—I will be coming with you when you go. There. Isn't that a happy surprise?"

"Yes." But Audrey could not stop thinking of the sharp contrast between the old Sir Clement and his young squire, Edwin. Though it had been four years since she'd seen him, and he, also, had fallen into some very painful circumstances—he'd been accused of treason, he and his brothers, and in their escape from the Tower of London, he'd lost his arm, the poor man. But having been proven innocent, he now enjoyed the king's particular favor. But she was no longer good enough for Edwin, the Earl of Dericott. She was no longer fit for anyone young, handsome, and titled.

Sir Clement had come to Engleford Castle a couple of times lately—she now realized why he had visited so often—but she'd probably never see Edwin again.

"You will be better off there," Sybil said, her brows starting to draw together as she lowered her voice. "Maris is coming home."

Audrey's chest seized up and she couldn't breathe. She saw Maris's face from her dream, glowing in the orange-red of her torchlight.

She could have sworn her scars were burning. She pressed one hand to her ear and her other hand to her chest, forcing herself to breathe.

"Do not behave that way. You shall soon be a married woman, with a beautiful home to manage. You will feel like a queen. Besides, your sister will have surely learned to control her destructive impulses while at the convent. She may have become quite saintly in her absence. Four years is a long time."

Why was Sybil's voice so calm? How could she say such things?

"She tripped me so I would fall into the fire."

If Audrey could control her voice, she would have said that Maris ruined her face and her chance to marry Edwin, or someone else of equal rank. Everyone knew this, including Sybil. Did her father not care about her at all? Did no one realize how the very thought of seeing Maris again made her hands shake and brought back the terror as if it had happened yesterday?

"Why is Father letting her come home? Did something happen?" Audrey did her best to keep her voice calm and even.

"The convent asked him to take her back. Your father would not say why."

No doubt Maris had shown her jealousy and spite to someone who also did not deserve it. But Audrey said nothing. She did not wish to draw Sybil's criticism, Sybil, who always turned a blind eye to wrongdoing in anyone she felt a loyalty to. Such dogged loyalty was a trait Audrey could not understand, not when she was desperate for someone to protect her from Maris.

"You are still quite beautiful, my dear," Sybil said softly. "The lovely vision of your mother, in fact, though I do believe you are even fairer than she was."

Audrey's habit for the past four years had been to pull a lock of her hair over the side of her face to hide her scars. But sometimes, when she was home and comfortable and knew no one was around but the servants, she forgot. Now Sybil reached out and smoothed the hair down over her scarred ear. "There. No one can even see any scars. You are as beautiful as ever, and more so, as you are beautiful in your heart as well as outwardly."

But she was damaged, as far as any husband would think of

her. Many men would even consider her cursed. Scars were not from God, they thought, but were a curse of the devil. And in her case, it was certainly true. She'd been cursed to have a sister like Maris as well as being cursed permanently with the visible consequences of her sister's viciousness.

"When is Maris coming?" Audrey had to get away. Perhaps she could go to live with her aunt and uncle in Derbyshire. Maybe she could find work in a candle shop like Helena, or some other shop, where she could earn enough to support herself. She thought she had let go of her longing to become something remarkable, to do something important in life, but thinking of marrying Sir Clement made her dream seem more impossible, though she wasn't exactly sure why. And it was breaking her heart.

"She is expected in a few days, and Sir Clement is arriving today."

"And Father arranged it that way, I suppose. Did he ask you to tell me?"

"Yes."

"He's a coward."

"Don't say such things about your father, Audrey. It is disrespectful."

Was it respectful to one's daughter to endanger her? But to her father, she didn't matter. She was only a girl, not worthy of respect. Audrey had learned a long time ago that she might be a viscount's daughter, but she had no power over her own life.

She had to take care of herself. Her father had not protected her from Maris when they were children, so how could she trust him to protect her now?

Audrey left Sybil and went to find her father, her hands suddenly clenching into fists. She had to confront him, to say something. How could she not object to her father bringing Maris home after what she had done to her?

She soon found him in the Great Hall, eating and talking with his steward.

"Father, may I have a word in private with you?" Her voice shook.

Her father stared as if sizing her up. "Fitz-Herbert," he said to his steward, "you may leave. I shall speak with you later."

As soon as the man had passed through the doorway, her father frowned at her. "I do not like that expression of anger on your face. It does not become you."

"And I do not like being forced to live with the woman who changed my life forever, who took away my hope of marrying well." Truly, she did not care about marrying well for its own sake, but Father did not know that. He had never understood that she cared more about being loved and about living her life to help others. And if she had married well, she could have done more good in the world. Now what hope was there?

"Are you truly going to bring her back here after what she did to me?" Audrey's voice cracked as the tears flooded her eyes.

"I am not 'bringing her back.'" Father spoke slowly and deliberately. "The convent is sending her away. She has nowhere else to go. Would you have me disown her and allow her to fend for herself? To die in a ditch somewhere?"

Audrey's breath was coming fast and shallow. She wanted to scream and yell, but what good would it do? Her father's face was hard and he was glaring at her. And if Maris truly had nowhere else to go . . .

"Cannot you send her to live with relatives, someone? Or another monastery? Surely there is somewhere else she could go." Was she being unreasonable to ask such a thing? But how could she bear to have her peace and freedom and tranquility taken away, after the balm of the last four years and not having to worry every minute about what Maris might do next to her?

Her father leveled another cold look at her. "You will be leaving soon to marry Sir Clement. Perhaps she will be less contentious once you are married and gone."

As if Maris's behavior was Audrey's fault. Audrey spoke from between clenched teeth. "I am not the problem. I've done nothing to cause her to treat me the way she does." It suddenly occurred to her, "You are sending me away this time, to marry a man I do not wish to marry."

"Just what would you have me do?"

"I cannot talk to you about this anymore. I'm going for a walk." She turned and hurried out, her father silent behind her.

Audrey had always been the good, quiet daughter, but not this time. She would defy her father, Sir Clement, and Maris. She would not allow them to choke the joy, the life, out of her.

The sun was high overhead and felt warm and good now that it was summer and the trees and flowers were in full bloom. She determined that she would go talk with her friend. Perhaps Helena would understand how she was feeling. Certainly Helena would not wish to marry an old man like Sir Clement. She would understand that Audrey must escape this fate.

She ran most of the way through the meadow, which was her shortcut to the road that led through the middle of the village. She headed straight for Helena's candle shop.

Before Audrey walked inside, the smell that always wafted from the butcher shop washed over her, and she covered her nose and mouth with her hand the last several feet before entering her friend's shop.

Helena was taking candles from a cloth bag and putting them in a wooden crate on a shelf. Audrey hurried over to help her. Soon they had finished.

"Did you not bring me any wildflowers today?" Helena asked.

"Forgive me! I did not think—"

"I am only making a jest. You do not need to bring me more flowers. See? The ones you brought me a few days ago are still fresh." Helena pointed to a pitcher of water on a table nearby.

"Truly, I would have picked you some, for there are many lovely ones in the fields just now, but . . ." Audrey couldn't push the news from her mind any longer.

"What is the matter?"

"My sister, Maris, is coming home."

Helena sucked in a breath and put her hand over her mouth.

"And that is not all. My father is marrying me off to a knight, a man more than twice my age."

Helena's eyes went wide and her mouth fell open. "A knight? Is he wealthy?"

"He has enough, but I would not call him wealthy. I don't want to marry a man so old."

"How old is he?"

"He must be forty or more. I know he has a son my age." Audrey's stomach felt sick. But Helena looked as if she did not think it so bad.

"As long as he has a good house and servants," Helena said, "you will not have to work hard. Besides, since he is so old, he will die long before you will and you can marry anyone you please. You shall be a wealthy widow then."

"I suppose it will be better than living with my sister." But speaking those words did not help.

"My only marriage prospects are the butcher's pock-faced son and the old man who makes candles for my father—when he's not drinking ale all day at the alewife's house." Helena crossed her eyes and stuck out her tongue. Audrey shook her head and Helena laughed.

"You have the hope of falling in love," Audrey said. "There is always hope." *Unless you marry a man who is forced on you.*

If Audrey married Sir Clement, what hope was there for her? She might one day love him, but could she hope to *fall in love* with him?

She'd always wanted to continue learning, to read as many books as she could, and since she'd taught Helena to read, lately Audrey had been imagining what it would be like to teach more girls to read. That was the whole reason she'd always hoped to marry an earl or a duke, for it was only men of such wealth and importance who had libraries full of books, as well as the power to allow their wife the freedom to do something some people would object to, like teaching girls. Was Sir Clement wealthy and powerful enough for that? She didn't think so.

She would also admit, at least to herself, that she wanted romantic love.

Since Maris had deliberately hurt her, Audrey had become more cautious with her heart, careful what she revealed about herself and her dreams. And even though she had Helena as a friend, she longed for someone with whom she could feel completely safe, someone she could tell her deepest thoughts and feelings to. Helena was sweet, but her life was so different from Audrey's. Helena desired children and a home away from her mother and father, who fought and yelled at each other. Audrey wanted more than children and a house. She longed for the love of a husband, a mutual kind of love that she had read about in stories and that the troubadours sang about.

Could Sir Clement give her that kind of love? It seemed very unlikely. And now that she was scarred and damaged . . . all her dreams seemed unlikely.

Perhaps she wanted too much.

Audrey talked with Helena for a long time, as very few people were coming into the shop that day. Helena told her all the happenings and goings-on of the people she knew, most of whom Audrey had never seen and certainly never met. And their problems were so different from Audrey's—a whiny child, a leaking roof, the pursuit of the best-tasting stew. But she enjoyed listening to Helena speak. Her stories were entertaining, and it felt good to see the smiles on her friend's face while she talked.

But today, the more Helena talked, the more Audrey's mind kept flitting back to Sir Clement and Maris. Finally, even though she wished she could stay with Helena and avoid seeing Sir

Clement, she bid her friend fare well and went back home, walking through fields and meadows from the village to Engleford Castle.

Sybil met her as soon as she came in the door.

"You must hurry and change your dress," she said in an urgent but hushed tone. "Come, come."

"What is it?"

"Sir Clement is here."

Audrey cast about in her mind where she might run away to, though she knew that was impossible.

By the time Sybil had finished helping her get into her best dress, Audrey's hands were shaking. But she followed Sybil down the stairs to the Great Hall.

Sir Clement said little to her as he and Father talked. His eyes flitted to her, but he seemed too nervous to hold eye contact with her. Toward the end of the meal, Sir Clement started to look at her more often. He had more gray hair than brown, and he ate with his face near the table, as if he were afraid it might not make it to his mouth if he did not lean down close. Could she love a man like him? Would he treat her well? Would she even be able to kiss him without gagging? His face was leathery and wrinkled, and though she knew he wasn't, he looked older than Father, as if being too much in the sun had worn out his skin.

Finally, he turned the conversation around to her. "Your father tells me you like to read and embroider."

"That is true." Audrey willed her voice not to tremble.

"Your sister was here the first time I met you, if I recall

correctly. Isn't she the same sister who burned your face? Do you mind if I see it?"

Was he actually asking to see her scars? She froze, her face growing hot.

"Go on and show him," her father prompted. He gestured to her with his hand, his eyes fixed on her.

Wishing she could disappear through the floor, Audrey lifted her hair to show the man her scarred ear and the scarred skin in front of it.

"It isn't so bad," Sir Clement said softly as he sat perfectly still.

Audrey couldn't meet his eyes. She let her hair drop over her scars again.

No one spoke for a long moment, then Sir Clement went back to his conversation with her father about horses and how much to pay for a good brood mare and stallion.

Audrey's cheeks continued to burn. How dare this man and her father treat her like horseflesh to be appraised, bought, and sold. Her dignity had been snatched away and discarded just as her sister had thrown her into the fire and ruined her face.

She should sit with her head held high, with her eyes sparking fire and threatening to ignite into a firestorm of spirit. Instead, she kept her gaze on the table while holding back the tears. After all, she did not care what this man thought of her. But if she was forced to marry him . . . She just couldn't imagine it. He could never love her the way she'd dreamed of.

When Audrey was finally allowed to go to her room, she fled, hurrying away as fast as she could. She entered the corridor and made her way toward the stairs. She caught a glimpse of someone standing at the far end, near the front entrance.

Suddenly, her stomach threatened to lose the dinner she'd just eaten. Maris was home.

She rushed to the stairs and took them two at a time, ran the rest of the way to her bedchamber, then closed and locked the door.

THREE

THE NEXT DAY AUDREY OPENED HER EYES AND IMMEDI-
ately remembered the horrors of the day before. She was to marry
Sir Clement, and her sister was home.

She simply would not leave her room. She could send for her
breakfast and dinner and spend her time reading. As long as she
stayed in here, she wouldn't have to see Maris or Sir Clement.

She stayed in her room most of the day, but she could not stay
forever. And when Sybil came to attend her before dinner, she
shamed her by saying, "You are behaving like a spoiled child. A
dutiful daughter does not act this way."

"I will go downstairs, but only if you go with me, to defend
me from Maris if need be."

Sybil softened her expression. "I will go with you. Of course."

The first person she saw when she came down was Maris,
chattering away with Father and Sir Clement in the Great Hall.
Her arms seemed to crawl with bugs and she wanted to turn
and run.

"Ah, there is my sister, at long last." Maris smiled as Audrey entered the room.

Could her sister have truly changed? Had she found goodness and invited it into her heart during her long stay at the abbey?

"Come and sit beside me," Maris said, patting the bench beside her. But she smiled at Father and Sir Clement, not at Audrey. In fact, her eyes never met Audrey's.

Maris told stories about being at the monastery, of the activities she'd engaged in there, of how much she enjoyed the piety of it all, the prayers and reverence and beauty of the chapel. She smiled often, but Audrey began to notice the smile was very flat, the corners of her mouth never curving up, and her eyes were cold, dark, and distant.

How good it would be if it were true—if Maris felt a love for God and others, if she had truly changed into the sister Audrey wished for. But the hollow feeling in her stomach told her that her wish had not come true.

The longer she sat there listening to her sister talk, hearing her feigned laugh and enduring her unnatural smile, pretending to ignore Sir Clement's curious stares, the more Audrey's legs fidgeted under the table. Would she be allowed to leave once the last course of food had been brought out?

Audrey waited, watching for the servants to bring out the sweetcakes. When they finally did and everyone had taken some, Audrey ate hers quickly, then said, "May I go? I am tired."

Her father grunted, then glanced at Sir Clement, and when he did not say anything, he nodded.

Audrey forced herself not to move too quickly or to look as eager to leave as she felt. As she passed through the doorway and out of sight of the occupants of the Great Hall, she breathed a sigh.

"Sister, wait!"

Audrey's breath caught in her throat at the sound of Maris's voice. Slowly she turned to face her.

"You must be so happy. He may not be a young, handsome earl, nor very wealthy or titled, but to be marrying at all . . . You are very fortunate. Father said he did not have to give a very large sum for your dowry either. You must be glad to bring our father so much happiness. I, of course, can never."

Audrey caught on to the backhanded gloating but decided to pretend not to understand. "Oh, I do not believe you will never marry. Someday you shall, I am sure." Audrey's feet moved toward the stairs though she never took her eyes off Maris's face.

Maris's expression was shrewd. What was she thinking? Was she jealous of Audrey? Or was she silently triumphing over her, happy that she had prevented Audrey from marrying Edwin, the Earl of Dericott?

"I am tired. Good night." Audrey fled to the stairs, praying Maris wouldn't follow her. But she grabbed her arm in a pinching grip, and Audrey spun around to face her sister, her heart thumping.

"Aren't you glad to see me?" Maris's eyes were hard and black. "You have not said a word about me coming home. I suppose you are just too excited about your upcoming wedding."

Maris reached out and flicked Audrey's hair up over her left ear. She smirked as she stared at the scars.

"I don't think you are happy to be marrying Sir Clement."

"Leave me alone, Maris."

Maris took hold of her arm again, squeezing until pain shot up her shoulder. She leaned in and said, "I've been waiting to get my revenge on you. I have had a lot of time to think about what I want to do to you. I suggest you run off with your new husband. Because if you don't, you will not like what I have planned for you."

Audrey pulled out of Maris's grip and ran up the stairs.

"I will see you tomorrow," Maris called after her in her most gloating voice.

Audrey turned as she reached the top of the staircase and caught sight of Maris, who was staring up at her with a twisted smile.

Audrey was shaking by the time she reached her room. Maris was taunting her. It brought back the horror of the moment Maris had tripped her, the look on her face right before Audrey fell into the fire. Audrey could hardly breathe. Her chest ached and she felt, actually felt, her skin burning. Would she do something even worse to her now that she was back?

A plan formed in Audrey's mind. Her knees grew stronger as she walked to the other side of the room and found her traveling bag.

The sun had gone down, but there was a full moon and plenty of light by which to see the road. But first . . .

She went to the door and stuck out her head. A servant girl

was walking by. "Please tell Sybil that no one is to disturb me. I wish to go to sleep early, so there is no need for her to help me get ready for bed."

"Yes, miss," the servant said.

Audrey locked the door and started throwing clothing into her bag and praying. "God," she whispered, "forgive me, but if I stay here, I'll have to marry that man, or I'll have to suffer Maris attacking me again. I cannot bear it, not after all she has done. I cannot, God. Please forgive me."

She threw as many articles of clothing as would fit into the bag, mostly her old clothes that she wore when she was picking wildflowers, but she added one of her finer dresses. Then she stared longingly at her books. There was no way to take them with her. The only one that seemed at all practical to bring was her Psalter. She tossed the small book inside, then wrapped a sash around the bag to prevent it from spilling. She hurried to the door, then remembered that she needed money, or something of value to trade for food.

She went to her trunk and found some silver coins in a small leather pouch. She wiggled the pouch into her bag, then closed it back up.

Audrey went to the door and peeked out. No one was around. Should she wait until she was sure Sybil wasn't coming to check on her? But all seemed quiet, as if the servants had retired to bed, although it was still too early for that.

Audrey slipped into the hall, her heart beating fast and hard against her chest, her mind racing. Was she doing the right thing? Certainly she was being impulsive. Where would she go?

What would she do, a woman alone and undefended? But the alternative was to stay here and marry Sir Clement, and everything inside her screamed that was not her destiny. And if her father allowed her to refuse the marriage, she'd be trapped here with Maris.

She tucked her bag under her arm as she made her way down the back stairs. She went through the rear part of the castle, through the servants' stairs and halls, then out near the kitchen. Once she was outside she ran to the stable.

"I need you to saddle my horse," she told the groom. He gave her a hard look but didn't argue. And soon Audrey was riding away with her bag in front of her on the saddle.

The candle shop was closed when she arrived in the village, so Audrey rode to Helena's house, which was nearby. Helena must have seen her, because she came out to greet her before Audrey could even dismount.

"I'm leaving home," Audrey said.

"Now? Alone?" Helena's mouth hung open. "But you cannot. Something bad could happen to you."

"Nothing bad will happen to me. If anyone tries to hurt me, I shall simply ride away on my horse."

"You cannot ride away if someone attacks you. There are bandits on the roads. Is Sir Clement so very bad?"

"I just cannot marry him," Audrey said. "I cannot explain it, but I know it is not my fate to marry him. And I'm afraid of what Maris will do if I don't and I have to stay in that house with her." She was close to tears, and she struggled to know what she was thinking and feeling.

"Maris was there?"

"Yes. And she still hates me."

"How do you know Sir Clement won't love you?"

"I don't know. I only know that I cannot bear to marry him when I feel there is someone somewhere who will see me as a person, not as an object to be bought or sold, not as scarred and damaged."

"You want the romantic love that's found in stories and songs. But what if that does not exist? What if the best a woman can hope for is to have enough money for goods and a house, and a husband who doesn't treat her unfairly?"

Her heart told her that true love did exist. There must be more, and she wanted it. She wanted the same love Solomon and his bride had in Song of Solomon. She wanted someone who would call her his darling and tell her she was beautiful, someone who cared as tenderly for her as the man in that holy book.

Helena looked very sorry for her. "If you run away, Sir Clement might not have you when you come back. What if you cannot find what you are looking for?"

She suddenly felt confused and conflicted. What if Helena was right? What if Sir Clement was the best she could get?

"It was not only that I did not wish to marry Sir Clement. Maris was gloating and threatening me, and I could not bear it. I could not stay there with her, knowing she . . ." Knowing she had ruined her hope of being loved by making her ugly, by scarring her forever.

"Every time I looked at her, it was as if I was there again, on the night she caused me to fall into the fire." Even speaking of it now she was having trouble breathing.

Helena shuddered. "She is mad, or she has a demon. Truly, if anyone I know is possessed by a demon, it must be her."

Audrey shook her head. Her voice was hoarse as she said, "She will never stop hating me, and there is no knowing what she may do to me. I must leave."

"Where will you go?"

"I am not sure. Perhaps to visit my aunt and uncle and beg them not to tell my father where I am." But her uncle would disapprove of a young woman refusing to marry a man to whom her father had betrothed her. And her aunt would scold her for leaving home alone. They'd surely tell Father she was with them. But she didn't want to worry Helena by letting her know she had nowhere to go.

Helena threw her arms around Audrey, and she embraced her friend, the best friend she had ever had, even though Helena was a village shop girl with a candlemaker for a father and Audrey's father was a viscount. That had never seemed to matter to either of them.

"You are beautiful, Audrey, truly you are. Do not let your scars make you feel as if you are not beautiful."

Of course Helena meant well, but her scars would never go away, and no one could see them without thinking how ugly they were.

When Audrey drew back, tears were running down Helena's face. Her own eyes watered. She couldn't bear to see so much emotion in Helena, who so seldom showed it.

"I will never forget you, my friend." Audrey pressed a silver coin into Helena's hand and quickly mounted her horse again.

"Audrey, wait! Do not—"

But Helena's voice faded quickly as Audrey rode away.

Audrey traveled north for a few hours, until she was so tired she was falling asleep in the saddle. She turned her horse off the road and tied him to a tree, then spread out the horse blanket, since it was a warm night and the horse didn't need it, and slept on it.

When she awoke, the sun was filtering through the leaves. It took her a moment to remember where she was. She rubbed her eyes.

A man was standing several feet from her. He was bent over, his hands in her bag.

A shot of panic went through her. She sat up and saw another man reaching toward her horse's bridle. Heat rose up to her face and sent her straight to her feet. How dare they touch her things?

"Get away! What are you doing?"

The men stopped and narrowed their eyes at her.

Her heart quivered, but she was too angry to be prudent. "That is my horse! And that is my bag!"

The man who was pawing through her bag frowned. The other one grinned and pulled on her horse's bridle.

"We'll be taking them," the frowning one said.

The other man swung up onto her horse. Poor Blackie. She'd

had that gelding since she was very young. And now he was being ridden by a wicked man. The other man started running behind him, and in moments they were out of sight.

Audrey's heart pounded so hard she had to sit down. *O God, why did You let them take my horse?*

She felt sick as she put her head in her hands. The vision of the two men leaving, one on Blackie and the other on foot, replayed in her mind.

At least she still had her clothing.

She crawled on her hands and knees to her bag. She rummaged around inside, trying to feel for the pouch of coins, but when she didn't find it, she pulled all the clothing out, one piece at a time. The pouch of silver coins was not there.

What would she do now?

She sat back on her heels and looked up at the fluttering leaves overhead. The slight breeze created a peaceful sound, and a bird twittered and chirped nearby.

The world seemed completely indifferent to her trouble, and she was alone.

I will never leave you nor forsake you. The words from her Psalter burst upon her mind. God would not leave her, but would He feed her?

She had not brought food with her, and she'd thought the coins would buy her anything she needed. But now she had nothing of value, except her clothing, to trade for food. And she had no horse. Now she'd have to walk.

What if those men had decided to harm her? She had no weapon, nothing to fight them off. The looks on their faces told her they were capable of quite a lot of evil. And they could change their minds and come back to harm her.

Her hands trembled as she grabbed her bag and stood to her feet. She started walking along the edge of the road. Her stomach twisted at the thought of the men mistreating her precious Blackie. As she walked, she felt a bit weak in the knees from lack of food. If only she had put her coins on her person, in a pocket, or tied to a belt around her waist. But then the men might have searched her. They still would have found the money, and she would have had to endure them putting hands on her.

Horrible men. Audrey wanted to call down a curse on them, but she didn't even know how one did such a thing. There was something in the Psalms about David asking God to smite his enemies. But what good would that do? Jesus taught forgiveness, after all. So she whispered, "God, help me forgive them. But most of all . . . help me. Send someone to help me, for I do not know where I am going or how I will get there."

She kept walking, listening for any indication that someone was coming for her—either the men who had taken her money and her horse, or her father's men come to drag her back home.

Soon she came to a crossroads. Not knowing which way to go, she closed her eyes and whispered, "Show me which way," and when she opened her eyes, she felt a tug inside her to take the road to the right.

Now that the sun was high overhead, she was beginning to feel dizzy from hunger. She was nearing a village, and she needed food. But how would she procure it?

She pulled out one of her dresses, a fine linen one that was soft and had pretty embroidery around the neckline, sleeves, and hemline. It was one of her favorites, but she'd be very happy if someone would give her food in exchange for it.

She entered the village and smelled the smith's fire and heating metal, heard his hammer beating the steel into a horseshoe or a plow blade. People walked around, moving from place to place, purpose in their steps.

Next she smelled the alewife's wares—the pungent scent of the fermented drink—and hurried past it, lest the drinking men sitting outside the establishment should notice her and call out to her.

The smell of ale did not tempt her at all. She'd never liked the taste of it. But when she caught a whiff of the baker's shop, she was drawn down the street after the beckoning smell of baking bread.

Audrey went to the door. Two women were inside buying bread from the woman behind the wooden plank that served as a counter. Audrey waited outside. Could she truly offer this baker her dress in exchange for some bread? But her stomach cramped painfully just at that moment. Yes, she could do it.

The two women left the shop, staring hard at Audrey as they went, as if they rarely saw strangers in their village. But then Audrey realized her hair had gotten pushed behind her left ear and they were staring at her scars.

She quickly pulled her hair forward to cover them. Her heart was pounding. She tried to take a deep breath but her chest was too tight to let it in. She should hurry, before someone else came and she had an audience for this interaction.

Audrey went into the shop and the shopkeeper turned to her. She gave her a curious look but didn't say anything.

When Audrey realized the woman was not going to talk to her, she cleared her throat and said, "I wonder if you will trade some bread for this dress."

Audrey held up the fine linen dress for the woman to see, showing that it fit Audrey. It looked too small for the woman, who was rather well-endowed in the bust and was possibly with child.

Audrey said quickly, "You could take the seams apart and make a bliaud out of it—put little ties on the sides—and wear it with a chemise."

The woman looked her dress up and down. Then without answering she turned and called out, "John! Can I give this woman some bread for her dress?"

"What?"

Audrey's knees trembled at the angry tone in the male voice. He emerged into the open doorway behind the counter. He stared first at Audrey, then at the woman.

"She wants to give me her dress for some bread."

"It is very fine material," Audrey said quickly. "Very soft. Would you like to touch it?" She held out the dress to them.

Neither of them reached for it. He looked at his wife, as Audrey now assumed the woman was, and she shrugged her shoulders. Then he looked back at Audrey.

"Very well," he said. "Take two loaves—or three, if you want."

Truly, the dress was worth more than twelve loaves of bread, but she couldn't bring herself to say so or to ask for money in addition to the bread.

"Thank you." Audrey's hand shook as she held out the dress to the woman. They watched as Audrey took three loaves of bread and stuffed them into her bag.

Audrey's hand was still shaking as she walked out of the shop and pinched off a piece of bread and put it in her mouth. She was hungrier than she'd ever been. Walking for hours, and the terrifying encounter with the two robbers, had made her famished.

But now she had enough bread for three days. If only she had some cheese or meat to go with it, or even some nuts or fruit. She kept walking, wondering how soon it would be before the two women who saw her scars told everyone in the village about her cursed ear, or the man and woman at the bread shop told everyone about the strange woman who gave them a dress in exchange for three loaves of bread.

She continued walking down the road and people stopped what they were doing to stare at her. If those men had not stolen her horse, she could have ridden through the village in no time. She'd never realized how good it was to ride, fast and high above the road, rather than having to walk everywhere she went.

She saw the well in the center of the village and was reminded how dry and parched her lips were, how her throat ached with thirst. Thankfully no one was drawing water at the moment. She took the communal bucket and sent it to the bottom, heard the splash, then drew it back up. She grabbed the dipper and used it to take a long drink of the cold water.

Perhaps she should trade something for a water flask that she could take with her. After all, one could live without food longer than without water, and she did not know how often she'd be able to find water.

She drank until she was afraid she might get sick, then put the bucket and the dipper back in their places, hanging from hooks on the side of the well.

She pretended not to notice all the people watching her as she walked away. An old man with a donkey pulling a cart loaded with hay was heading toward her.

"I don't recall seeing you before," he said, his gray beard trembling as he talked.

"I am just passing through," Audrey said.

"Where are you going? By yourself? Is no one with you?"

"I shall be well, I thank you." She smiled and nodded as she hurried past him.

But would she be well? She'd already been robbed. But she wouldn't allow worry to pull her down. She had bread in her bag and she would be at her aunt and uncle's house in a few days—she was not certain how long it would take to walk there. She could at least get some food and supplies from them even if they weren't willing to let her stay there without telling her father where she was. She could run away before her father arrived.

What she needed was a job. But she needed to get farther away from Father and Maris before she inquired about employment. And find a larger village where strangers weren't so rare and didn't garner so much attention and curiosity.

Audrey made her way outside of the village and sat down under a tree with her back against the trunk. There she ate her bread, still wishing she had at least some butter to spread on it.

She'd never thought about it before, but not having enough food was a terrible condition. How many people in the world didn't have enough? She'd never had that problem, living in her father's castle, with plenty of everything a girl could want—food three times a day, clothes, and a warm fire. What must it be like to be poor? Her father gave away food to the poor on Christmas and a few other holy days through the year—it was required by the Church—but she'd never thought about how those poor people found food the rest of the year.

Audrey stood, her legs aching, and stretched out her back. How soon would her shoes wear out? She could tell the soft leather soles were already wearing thin. Could she walk in bare feet?

"Lean not on your own understanding," she whispered to herself. "God, I will trust in You to take care of me."

She walked the rest of the day without finding a stream or another village. She began to wonder if she'd left civilization behind. But finally, just at sunset, she came to another crossroads at the outskirts of a village. If she went left, she would go through the village, and since she was parched, her throat as dry as sand, she went in that direction.

She caught sight of a well at the edge of the road. She went straight to it and drew herself some water, just as she had at the last village. This time fewer people were milling about. Most were probably eating the evening meal at home. So Audrey took her time, drinking a dipper of water, then another, before finally moving on.

As she passed a house, she heard laughter and voices. Through the windows she could see people smiling and talking. A mother and a father and several children of a variety of ages were sitting around a table together, eating supper.

What would it be like to have a family like this one? she wondered. A mother and father who loved each other, and siblings to laugh and play with? Brothers and sisters who would never dream of tripping her and sending her into the fireplace. Brothers and sisters who would care about her and protect her.

Audrey passed the house with a heavy feeling. She stopped, telling herself she would prop against the tree to rest awhile. She continued gazing at the family. Perhaps she should go and knock on the door and ask if they would give her a flask for carrying water. But they might think she was lunatic. After all, a young woman traveling alone? They might ask questions, might think she was a villein escaping her master, running away from her proper place in life.

And perhaps that was what she was doing—running away from being a viscount's daughter, someone with too many scars to be married for love.

No, it was better to keep walking. With one last look at the laughing brood inside the cheerful little house, Audrey headed down the road.

She was no longer sure which direction she was going. Was it west? Or north? At least when the sun came up tomorrow she would know. But did it even matter? Perhaps it was a bad idea to go to her aunt and uncle's house.

She nestled into a small grassy hollow just off the road and fell asleep, her head pillowed on her bag.

Four

AUDREY AWOKE THE NEXT MORNING TO HER STOMACH growling and her throat hurting. Was it caused by thirst or some kind of contagion? She went back to the village she'd passed through the evening before and drank more water. But the water did not soothe her burning throat, and her neck was beginning to ache as well.

She'd had nothing to eat except the bread she'd bartered for. She'd eaten two of the loaves, but the remaining one was so hard after only one night she could hardly bite it. So she soaked it, a bite at a time, in the water to soften it. The bread was very unappetizing, but at least it was something.

She'd hoped she might be able to find someone who would trade her some cheese or other food for another one of her dresses, but it was such a small village, she decided to continue walking.

The sun was still hiding behind the clouds after Audrey had been traveling for what seemed a very long time. She was so hungry, even after eating the soggy bread, but her stomach no longer growled. She just had a sick feeling, and her throat hurt worse than ever. She wondered if she had a fever, she felt so shivery, chills sneaking all over her upper body, her legs aching. But she just kept walking. If she made it to her aunt and uncle's house, at least they wouldn't turn her away. Surely they would give her a bed to sleep in and something to eat.

Some warm soup would feel good on her throat.

Someone was coming up behind her. She was so tired, but she needed to hold up her head so they wouldn't think she was an easy target.

She turned and saw that it was a man and a woman, about forty years old perhaps, with a pair of oxen pulling a cart.

"Pardon me," Audrey said, "but do you know how much farther it is to Derbyshire?"

"To Derbyshire?" the woman asked. "You are a long ways from there, bless your soul, child."

The man stopped and leaned his head to one side, frowning and squinting. "I would imagine you will have to walk two more days to get to the southern border of Derbyshire," he said. "Or three, if you're not accustomed to walking so much."

Audrey's heart sank.

"Where are you going?" the woman asked.

"To my aunt and uncle's house."

"You poor dear. Did your parents die of the Pestilence?" The woman said the word *pestilence* with a look of horror. No one was immune to the fear of the terrible sickness that killed whole families and even whole villages, the contagion that had killed, some said, more than half the people living in London a few years before Audrey was born.

The woman drew closer and seemed to catch a glimpse of Audrey's scar.

"No. That is, my mother died giving birth to me, but my father . . ."

"Did he cast you out?" she asked softly.

"No. I just wanted to visit my aunt and uncle." That wasn't entirely true. Audrey felt a pang of guilt.

"He should not let you travel alone," the woman said, still looking into her face with concern.

Audrey suddenly felt more feverish than ever, but the woman might not be so kind in her manner if she thought Audrey was sick. She might think she had the Pestilence and run away from her.

What if Audrey did have the Pestilence? Would she get the dark-colored buboes under her arms and on her neck? Would she die?

No, no. It was only a mild sickness that would go away in a few days. She must not lose her courage. Not now.

"The truth is, I'm going to my aunt and uncle's for a visit because I don't want to marry the man my father chose for me. I'm hoping if I stay away, the man might decide to marry someone else."

The man and woman both took a step away from her and lost the concerned expressions they'd worn a moment before.

"My dear, if your father thinks you should marry this man," the woman said, placing a hand on her hip, "then you should trust him. He is older and therefore wiser than you are." She raised her brows at Audrey.

"A young girl thinking she knows more than her father . . ." The man shook his head.

Tears stung Audrey's eyes for the first time since she'd left Helena and started this ill-fated journey. Their disapproval hurt, even though they were strangers.

"Thank you for your help," Audrey said, walking away from them.

When she was a few minutes down the road, she wished she had asked them if she was on the right road to Derbyshire. But surely if she kept going north . . .

The road had become so curvy, she wondered what direction she was going. The sky was too overcast to give any clues from the sun.

Audrey's neck was hurting worse and worse, and she was beginning to cough. But she had so far to go, she shouldn't rest yet. Her feet were almost numb after so much walking, but that was a good thing, was it not? She wouldn't feel pain if they were numb.

Her toe hit a rock and she stumbled. She was just so tired and sleepy. Perhaps she should take a rest.

Her body told her to stop, but she saw a flash of lightning ahead as the clouds were getting darker. She needed to find shelter. *Keep going,* her mind told her, as if arguing with her body. *You must keep walking.*

The road she was on had to lead somewhere. Surely there was a village ahead. She needed more water, although it was strange how she no longer felt thirsty.

The wind was starting to get unruly, gusting and sending her hair into a tangled mess, tossing it in front of her eyes. The air was suddenly colder, making her shiver and ache all over, especially in her shoulders.

She thought she saw a large structure through the wildly swaying trees. She kept walking until she came to a lane that led off the road, through the trees. And then she saw it more clearly, though it was getting quite dark now. It was a large, gray castle. Was she imagining it?

As she turned down the lane and went toward the castle, she felt the first few raindrops. They were cold and set her to shivering so violently she could barely walk. Holding her bag to her chest, she trudged up the hill toward the castle.

Where was she? She had never seen this castle before. Was she back home at Engleford Castle in Hampshire? But she was on a journey, was she not?

She was so tired, so hungry and weak, and she ached so much. If only she could reach the castle. But the hill was too steep. Perhaps if she just lay down and closed her eyes for a few moments.

The rain was falling hard now. The tree-lined lane kept the raindrops from stinging her skin, but soon her clothes were soaked through anyway, her hair dripping.

She would just curl up close to the tree there.

Audrey sank down and hugged her bag to her, partially covering her head with her arm. She would rest here. Just for a bit.

The rain was cold and the shivering was taking too much strength. She couldn't shiver and walk up a hill at the same time. She would sleep now.

Edwin was finally getting back more of his strength and energy, and he felt restless. He missed his six brothers, who were all either continuing their training or were on their respective assignments as knights in the service of King Richard the Second. His sister, Delia, was happily married and safe with her husband, Geoffrey, a day's ride away.

A lovely blue sky would have been welcome, but instead, there were only clouds so thick he could see neither sky nor sun.

But he didn't care. He could not sit at home, not today. He would go for a walk.

Edwin took his walking stick and moved along the beautiful grassy trail that led him through woods, beside fields, and he finally stopped on the hill about a mile from Dericott Castle.

The white cloud cover was quickly turning dark gray. A strong wind began whipping the trees, blowing up some even darker clouds. He'd better start back if he did not wish to be drenched. Indeed, the rain might beat him home, as he was nearly a mile away.

He carried his walking stick. It had been nearly six months since he lost his arm and he was anxious to be able to walk without needing something to lean on. He was tired of the looks from people feeling sorry for him, tired of them staring at him as if his lost arm were some kind of curse visited upon him. But was that not what it was? A curse?

He needed to stop thinking like that. He had saved his youngest brother from being struck by the sword that severed his arm. He should be thankful that he had been able to save him, since ten-year-old Roland likely would not have survived the blow. And Edwin would gladly have given his life for any one of his brothers or his sister.

As he made his way down the hill, he felt himself losing his footing, tilting precariously. But he refused to use his walking stick. He gritted his teeth and righted himself before he lost his balance completely and fell. He moved more carefully, concentrating on putting one foot in front of the other, holding his one arm across his chest rather than doing what he instinctively wanted to do, which was to hold his arm straight out to the side. His mind told him that his left arm was still intact, making him think the arm he knew was missing was also sticking straight out to steady him. But of course, it wasn't. It wasn't there. And it never would be again.

The wind continued to blow harder, turning into a real storm as it started to rain. The cold drops pelted his head and face, as he had not worn a hood, and it wasn't long before he was wet and cold. His feet were slipping on the wet leaves, and still he refused to use his stick.

It was beginning to rain a bit harder as his toe hit a root that was sticking up. He stumbled, then slipped about a foot down the incline. When he stopped slipping, he leaned his shoulder against a tree trunk and waited to get his bearings.

He never would have thought losing an arm could cause him so much trouble. And what kind of dignity can a man have if he cannot stay on his feet? He was twenty-three years old. He should be able to walk down a hill without falling.

The horrifying part was that he could still feel his missing arm, could still feel pain in it, and . . . he missed it. He missed his hand.

He clenched his right hand into a fist. He hated this weakness. He would defy it, reject it, refuse to be weak. And yet he couldn't quite dismiss the thought that kept repeating over and over: with only one arm, he was only half a man.

The wind and rain stung his face and clung to his beard. He slipped and nearly fell once, then again, but he did not slow down his pace. By the time he reached the bottom of the hill, the rain was pouring down so hard he could only see a few feet in front of him.

He saw the castle through the trees. He had to climb another incline to reach it, as it would take him too long to walk around to the bridge that spanned the ditch around the castle.

Finally, he reached the door at the rear near the kitchens. He stepped inside, cold and almost shivering, he was so soaked.

"Thank heaven you are home." Mistress Wattlesbrook was hurrying toward him.

"What is the matter?"

"Philip just came in and said he found a young woman lying on the ground outside the castle."

"He found a young woman?"

"He was afraid to touch her and see if she was alive, although he thought he saw her shivering."

He strode toward the front entrance. "Where is she?"

"She's somewhere out by the lane, he said." Mistress Wattlesbrook fell in behind him as he made his way down the dark corridor toward the front of the castle.

What was a young woman doing out in this weather, especially alone?

The groundsman met him as he neared the front door. "Lord Dericott, forgive me, but there is a woman—"

"Show me."

Philip looked as if he might object, but he turned and led the way out the front door.

Philip's thin brown hair was quickly plastered to his head as he strode down the lane toward a nearby copse of trees. And there, on the ground, lay a bundle. And the bundle was shivering and mumbling.

The rain was coming down hard and cold, but at least the wind had died down.

"Can you hear me?" Edwin bent down, trying to see the girl's face.

She didn't answer or move.

Philip also bent to look at her. Edwin wanted to brush her hair away so he could see her face and hopefully get her attention, but he was already losing his balance. He knelt abruptly on the ground beside her, then reached out and gently pulled her sopping wet hair back from her face.

His gaze fastened on her ear, which was disfigured. It was as if it had partially melted away, and the abnormality extended to a bit of skin on her face, red and puckered and strangely smooth.

Philip gasped and drew back, taking hold of Edwin's shoulder as if to pull him away as well. But Edwin leaned closer.

Her face was well-formed, and if her eyes were open, he

imagined she would look quite pretty. The abnormality, to be sure, was hard to look away from, poor girl.

"My lord, she is marked!" Philip said in a hoarse voice. "Take care. She could have a demon."

Still the girl did not respond to their voices and she had stopped shivering. He touched her forehead with the back of his hand. Her skin was burning hot.

His heart squeezed in pity as he looked up at Philip. "Those are likely burn scars, not the devil's markings, and she is very sick. Go and get two of the grooms to carry her into the house."

"Yes, sir." Philip hurried away.

Her clothing did not distinguish her as anyone wealthy. Though she was very young, she was not too young to be married. His stomach twisted in pity for her again. He knew what it was like to suffer the visible consequences of a terrible event. A moment of tragedy could mark a person for the rest of their life.

How well he knew.

Two of the grooms came running. They were sturdy fellows who easily picked up the girl and carried her toward the house. Mistress Wattlesbrook stood in the doorway. She would take good care of her, and if God was willing, she would survive her illness.

A cloth bag was on the ground, no doubt belonging to the woman. Edwin picked it up. It was dripping water, as the rain was still falling.

"Shall I put her in Lady Delia's old room, my lord?" Mistress Wattlesbrook asked.

"Yes, that will be good."

Edwin took the wet bag and set it on a table by a window. The rain was pouring down, but there was still enough light coming through to see by. He took out each article from the bag—a well-made hairbrush, two outer dresses and one underdress, an embroidered cloth belt, and some tooth powder and a toothbrush. Some of the articles made her seem wealthy, but the dresses were not fit for a woman of means. And at the bottom was a Psalter with a fine leather covering. Was she able to read?

Edwin took out the book and shook off the excess water. If she were to survive, no doubt she would not want this book, the most valuable thing in her bag, to be ruined. Water was the worst enemy of books—except, of course, fire.

He went and found a cloth and wiped and dried the book the best he could. Fortunately, the leather binding and wraparound covering, with its metal clasp, had protected the parchment pages better than he might have thought. Edwin carefully laid it out to dry on a bench beneath the window.

He went to his only sister's room—she was now married and in her own home—and stopped outside the closed door. He heard a muffled voice inside that sounded like Mistress Wattlesbrook's. The door opened and a servant girl rushed out. She drew back for a moment, as if startled.

"Pardon me, my lord." She closed the door and hurried away, no doubt on some errand for Mistress Wattlesbrook.

Edwin wanted to ask the servant how the woman was doing, if she had spoken, but he didn't want to detain her.

He stood outside the door, listening. After a minute or two

he had heard nothing, so he began walking from one end of the corridor to the other, pacing as he waited.

Becoming accustomed to the way his body felt, one-sided as it was, had been frustratingly slow and difficult as he learned how to keep himself balanced so he would not fall. He practiced holding his one arm close to his body while seeing himself in his mind with one arm, not two. And every time he did, he had to acknowledge that he would never be the capable swordsman and knight he once was. He would never be that strong again.

The servant girl returned, going back inside the room. As she closed the door he tried to peek in but only saw Mistress Wattlesbrook's back as she leaned over the bed.

He continued to walk up and down the corridor, thinking of the young woman's face. How had she come to be alone and sick and lying under a tree in the rain? She was obviously traveling somewhere. But why was she alone? And how had she received the scars on her face?

He paced awhile longer until finally the door opened and Mistress Wattlesbrook and the servant girl came out.

His eyes met Mistress Wattlesbrook's and she sighed. "The poor thing is very sick and chilled to the bone."

"Did she say who she is?"

She shook her head. "Didn't even open her eyes except to squint at me. And she just mumbled something about Derbyshire."

"What else did she say?"

"That was the only word I could make out. Derbyshire. I don't know if she was coming from there or going there."

"Do you think she will recover?"

"We won't know for a while, but she is young and looks strong."

"And the scar on her ear?"

"Looks like she was burned in a fire."

"Do you think she could have the Pestilence?"

"I don't think so." Mistress Wattlesbrook shook her head. "She doesn't have the buboes. She does have a cough and a rattling in her chest. We shall see if she improves after she's slept. I gave her some herbs, and she drank a good amount of my feverfew and liverwort tea, so I think she will wake up feeling better in a few hours. There's no knowing how long she may have been lying there on the ground."

"It is a good thing Philip found her." And a good thing Edwin and Mistress Wattlesbrook weren't as afraid of her scars as Philip was, as the man might have left her there if he'd seen her scars first.

"She is a pretty thing," Mistress Wattlesbrook said, taking a deep breath and letting it out, staring out the window at the rain. "I shall be curious to hear her speak when she awakens."

"Will you tell me when she does?"

"Of course." Mistress Wattlesbrook smiled, but the crinkle-eyes expression was a look he knew well.

Along with her husband, who had died a few years ago, she'd served in his household since before Edwin was born. He knew she was thinking that he was showing a lot of concern for a girl who could be anyone—a runaway servant, a married woman escaping her husband, anyone.

But Edwin was not interested in the young woman in that way. Mistress Wattlesbrook knew he was pledged to marry Lady Ophelia, though she had never met the lady, and for Mistress Wattlesbrook, out of sight was out of mind. Or perhaps she had taken note of the fact that Edwin had had no communication from the lady in almost a year.

Edwin did feel compassion for this young woman, but he was only concerned that she was well taken care of and looked after as long as she was under his roof.

If he was honest, however, it was more than that. Philip's reaction at seeing her scars had reminded him how it felt when people noticed his missing arm and stared in horror . . . or even fear. This girl probably understood better than anyone how he felt about being stared at. But in spite of her scars, her features were delicate, and she was quite fair of face and form. It was unjust for her to be treated as an object of horror. He would not allow it.

Edwin's heart burned to right wrongs and stop injustice in whatever form he saw it, whether the victim of the injustice was a poor villein, a peasant, or a princess. This was his goal for himself, his self-imposed purpose in life. And if Lady Ophelia did not want to marry him now that he had lost his arm, then he would leave marriage and children to his brothers and sister, and he would relinquish the duty of carrying on their family name to them. Upon his death his title and Dericott Castle would go to his nearest brother, Gerard.

Which reminded him . . . He still needed to pay a visit to Lady Ophelia.

Was he wronging her to think she would not want to marry him? Perhaps she would prove loyal to her promise, although he didn't want her to marry him and then be disgusted by him. Either way, they were still pledged to marry and he would not be disloyal to her, however she might feel.

FIVE

AUDREY FELT HERSELF BEING LIFTED BY GENTLE HANDS. Where was she?

She shivered, her body cold and wet. People surrounded her. She could hear their voices, but she couldn't open her eyes. She hurt all over, especially her head and her chest. Was she dying?

She was warmer now. Someone was pouring warm liquid into her mouth. She swallowed it obediently. She was thirsty, but her throat hurt so badly. Was she in Derbyshire? She didn't remember arriving. Was this her aunt, the woman who was tending her?

Audrey tried to talk and managed to ask if she was in Derbyshire. The woman told her no but said she was safe. The woman asked her questions, but Audrey couldn't quite muster enough strength to answer. The woman's voice was gentle, as were her hands when she lifted Audrey's head and helped her drink.

She fell back asleep, then awoke, this time realizing she was in a bed with a canopy overhead and curtains drawn on three sides. The fourth side revealed a room with a tall narrow window. There were tapestries on the wall, and a woman sat nearby, sewing.

"Pardon me." Audrey's voice sounded like a frog croaking.

The woman looked up and hurried over to her. "You are awake. I shall tell Mistress Wattlesbrook."

The girl hurried away before Audrey could ask her any questions.

She must have fallen asleep again, because a woman was suddenly standing beside her bed.

"How are you feeling? Are you in pain anywhere?" The woman's eyes were wide as she leaned closer.

"My throat." It hurt so much to talk. "May I have some water?"

"Of course you may."

The woman turned to the table behind her and produced a cup of water. She helped Audrey sit up and held the cup to her lips. Audrey drank several gulps before she started coughing.

The pain was so sharp when she coughed, it made her close her eyes and clutch at her chest.

"There, there, we will go slowly," the woman said.

She was still weak, her head as heavy as a boulder, and she could not even grasp the cup the woman was holding to her lips. She was almost as weak as when she'd lain down on the ground with the rain pouring over her. Which made her wonder . . .

"Where am I?"

"In a safe place, with good people." The woman patted her arm. "And I know all about healing herbs from some very wise nuns, so you have nothing to fear."

"Am I in Derbyshire?"

"No, my dear. You are in Bedfordshire." The woman pressed her hand to Audrey's cheek. "You don't seem to have a fever anymore. That is good."

"My chest hurts."

"You have been coughing for many days, then?"

She sat up a little higher, and her head seemed to spin around and around, so much so that it made her stomach threaten to heave. She had to close her eyes and lay her head back on the pillow.

"You're as pale as new snow," the woman said, gently removing a pillow from behind her back so she could lie flat. "Just rest now."

Audrey wanted so much to tell her she was sorry for being so much trouble, that she was thankful for the woman's help, but she couldn't seem to summon the strength to speak. Soon she felt herself drifting into darkness.

Audrey heard voices but couldn't open her eyes. How long had she lain like this, in and out of consciousness? The kind woman—or women, as she suspected there was more than one—had taken care to raise her up now and then to make her drink. Sometimes it was some kind of bitter herb drink, and sometimes it was watered-down wine or broth.

Occasionally drinking brought on a coughing fit, which hurt so much she wondered if she was dying. She wanted to wake up and ask questions, to stay awake long enough to pray for God not to allow her father to find her, but she was just so tired . . . so very tired . . . tired in her bones and tired in her thoughts.

Her mind wandered in from the darkness of sleep and heard voices, one of them male—a deep, manly voice. What was a man doing in her room? It must be her father.

"No." Her eyes flew open and she tried to sit up.

"What is it, child?" the kindly woman said, coming to her bedside.

She strained her eyes to see who the man was. He was a dark figure, a few feet from the foot of her bed.

"Who is that?" she asked, her voice raspy. She suddenly realized she had more strength in her limbs but not enough to push herself to sit up.

"That is only the master, Lord Dericott," the woman said, touching her shoulder as if to soothe her. "Do not worry. He will not harm you."

Her head was starting to ache and she regretted the effort to try to get up.

Lord Dericott? Why did that name seem so familiar? And then she remembered. The handsome squire, Edwin, who had spent the night at her home with Sir Clement, whom her father had wanted her to marry. He was now the Earl of Dericott. Edwin, the handsome boy whom she had thought might make a good husband. Had she ended up at his home?

If she knew his name, knew who he was, had seen his face, then that meant he knew her name and her face. Would he not recognize her and send word to her father? Had he already done so?

Audrey stifled a cry of fear. She had to get out of here. She had to leave before her father came and found her.

She pushed the blanket to the side and rolled off the bed. She tried to get her feet under her but her legs wouldn't co-operate. She hit the floor hard, pain emanating from every body part. She gasped, trying to get air into her lungs, which set off a coughing fit.

The coughing subsided, leaving her exhausted. The woman who had cared for her took hold of her shoulders.

"Help me," the woman seemed to say to the man.

Audrey's body ached, but she couldn't stay here. Her father might be on his way at this moment. Or worse, he may have sent Sir Clement to fetch her.

"I have to go. I have to leave." She wanted to get up, to will herself to stand up and walk, but the little strength that had returned had left her again. She couldn't even get on her hands and knees to crawl.

Someone was lifting her. She opened her eyes enough to see that it was Edwin. He looked a little older than he had four years ago, and broader in the shoulders.

He would tell her father.

"Please don't tell him," Audrey managed to say before her eyes refused to open and the darkness claimed her.

"What does she mean?" Edwin nearly lost his breath at how des-perate the girl had looked when she threw herself out of bed. He and Mistress Wattlesbrook managed to get her back on the bed, he holding her awkwardly with his one arm. Before the injury, he easily could have lifted and carried the girl . . . when he had two hands and two arms. But he mainly regretted not being close enough to prevent her from the hitting the floor. A purple bruise was already forming on her cheekbone.

"I don't know," Mistress Wattlesbrook said. "She's been a bit delirious with the high fevers. But at least she seems to be getting better, less fever—although pushing herself out of the bed was not the best way to help herself heal."

Edwin studied the girl's face. He was almost certain he had seen her before.

"Has she said her name?" Edwin asked.

"I asked her once. I think she said Audrey."

The name sounded familiar but he didn't know why. "I suppose Audrey is a common enough name."

"Yes, common enough." Mistress Wattlesbook placed her hand on her hip and stared at the wall as if deep in thought. "There was a girl in the village by that name. Her father is one of your villeins. Do you think she could be that girl?"

Something inside Edwin rebelled at the thought of this young woman being a villein's daughter, but why? He couldn't shake the thought that he'd seen her before, and not in the Dericott village. But he did not remember the scars on her ear and the edge of her face, and he would certainly have remembered such an unusual thing. But perhaps the scars had been covered when he saw her the first time. Or perhaps she had not had them then. Nevertheless, he couldn't help thinking he should remember her.

"She seems fearful," Mistress Wattlesbrook said, brushing the girl's long blonde hair off her forehead. "I think she must have been running away from someone."

"Seems likely." Why else would she be so desperate to leave, even in her weak, sick state? And why else would she say, "*Please don't tell him*"? She was afraid of someone. He wished he could tell her that there was no safer place she could be than here at Dericott Castle, as neither he nor his servants would ever allow anyone to harm her.

Audrey opened her eyes with the vague feeling that she was in danger. But a woman was lifting her head and helping her drink. Then she remembered everything, from getting sick, to being taken care of, to learning that the master of the house was Edwin, Lord Dericott.

She had to get out of here before he summoned her father. But what if he didn't recognize her, or didn't remember her? A breath of air filled her lungs at this thought.

Yes, here was hope.

"Drink it down, now," the woman said softly. "That's good."

Audrey stared at her. She was the same middle-aged woman who had been tending her from the beginning. This was the first time she hadn't been too feverish and weak to hold her eyes open for any length of time. The woman had gray hair and blue-gray eyes and the kind of wrinkled skin that looked soft to the touch.

"You are feeling better today, it is plain to see," the woman said with a smile. "What is your name, child?"

"My name?"

Once she told the woman her name, she would tell Lord Dericott, and then he would remember who she was, if he didn't already.

"I believe I heard you say it was Audrey. Where are you from? How did you get here?"

So they knew her given name. She must have said it when she was sick.

"Forgive me for asking so many questions. I am Mistress Wattlesbrook, and I am Lord Dericott's head house servant."

"Thank you, Mistress Wattlesbrook. My name is Audrey. I came here from . . . south of here, but I wasn't sick. That is, I became sick as I was walking. The illness came upon me quickly. I remember lying on the ground and closing my eyes, but I did not know where I was. I'm so sorry I've taken up so much of your time."

"Do not fret, my dear. I was pleased to attend you. The master insisted I turn over my other duties to care for you. It was no trouble at all."

"Oh." Did that mean Lord Dericott knew she was the daughter of a viscount? "I'm so sorry to have been a bother. I shall leave forthwith."

"Oh no, you shall not. You are too weak still." Mistress Wattlesbrook appeared quite adamant. "But where did you come from? You still have not said."

Mistress Wattlesbrook did not know where she was from.

That was good. Audrey hesitated, then said, "I do not wish to go back there. Please do not make me tell you."

"There now, all is well. No one will send you back where you do not wish to go, especially if they mistreated you there. Is that where you got your scars?" She pointed at her ear.

Audrey instinctively reached up to cover the scars with her hair. She thought about how Maris had tripped her and how her father had not believed Audrey when she said Maris had done it intentionally.

"Yes." Her throat tightened, making her voice raspy. "I don't want to go back."

"To Derbyshire?"

"Oh. No. No, not Derbyshire. I am from the south."

Mistress Wattlesbrook seemed to be thinking. She picked up the cup and turned toward the door. "I will fetch you something to eat. You must be famished. Are you?"

"I am a bit hungry." Truly, she could eat an entire roast pheasant. And with it some bread and butter. And several fried pasties.

"I'll be back very soon."

Audrey was relieved to be feeling so much better, but she couldn't help imagining Lord Dericott remembering her as the viscount's daughter that he had almost married. Or had he? Perhaps the hoped-for alliance had been all in her father's head and he had not mentioned it yet to Edwin or his father. If he did remember who she was, he would certainly feel an obligation to tell her father where she was.

She needed to be prepared.

She glanced around the room and saw her bag sitting on

a trunk in the corner. It looked as if all her clothing had been washed and folded and stacked up beside it. She would go put her things in her bag so she could leave as soon as she saw an opportunity.

Audrey lifted the covers to see what she was wearing. An underdress. She would put something over it and be ready to sneak out. Would they stop her if they saw her leaving?

She put out one leg, then the other. She stood on the floor and the entire room shifted. She held on to the bed. *Please let the room stop spinning.* Her face tingled and dark spots were closing in on her vision.

She climbed back onto the bed, collapsing on her stomach, her only thought about breathing in and out and not fainting. Finally, her vision returned and the stinging in her face subsided.

"Are you all right?" Mistress Wattlesbrook hurried over and helped her back under the covers.

"I thought I could walk, but I'm still a bit weak." Audrey tried to smile.

"I brought you some oat porridge. I think it's soft enough that you can swallow it." She spooned it up and placed it in Audrey's mouth before she could protest.

It wasn't roast pheasant, but it was warm and soothing and tasted like it was sweetened with milk and honey and cooked apples.

Mistress Wattlesbrook helped her sit up straighter, and Audrey was able to hold the bowl and feed herself.

"It is delicious. Thank you." After another bite, she said, "May I ask who found me and how long I have been here?"

"Our man Philip found you under a tree and came straightway and fetched the master." Mistress Wattlesbrook seated herself by Audrey's bed and talked while she ate. "A few of the grooms carried you inside and laid you in this bed. That was three days ago. You have been here ever since, and I have been tending you. You have been as sweet-tempered a patient as I have ever taken care of." She smiled.

"I am very grateful to you."

"Audrey is a lovely name." Mistress Wattlesbrook picked up a different cup from the table, with a tiny cloth ball floating in it.

Audrey took the offered cup and drank it. The liquid tasted like dried grass and honey.

"I know it tastes bad, but it is good for you and will help your cough. Just take tiny sips."

Audrey obeyed, sipping the warm concoction. She hadn't eaten solid food in so long, her stomach was feeling a bit sick. But sipping the herbal drink seemed to make it feel better.

"Pardon me while I go and let Lord Dericott know that you are awake and talking." Mistress Wattlesbrook left the room.

Lord Dericott had seemed like a kind and cheerful young man when he was Edwin, the knight's squire. But four years had passed, and though she didn't know all the particulars of the tale, she had heard that Edwin—Lord Dericott—had lost his arm in a fight with the king's guards as he and his brothers escaped the Tower of London. That had stuck in her mind, the thought that the handsome young man, trained as a knight, strong and brave, should have to go through life with only one arm.

But now she needed to make sure she kept herself safe, and

that meant leaving this castle immediately if there was any chance that Lord Dericott knew who she was. She gazed again at her bag and her things. She had to get her strength back as quickly as possible.

As Audrey was finishing her drink, the door opened and Mistress Wattlesbrook said, "My dear, Lord Dericott wishes to speak to you."

She came in and tucked the covers around Audrey, even though she was fully covered by her underdress. A moment later, Lord Dericott walked in. Mistress Wattlesbrook stepped aside.

Lord Dericott was no longer the nineteen-year-old squire who had shared a meal at her father's table. He was older and even more handsome, with his serious eyes and his face more filled out and less angular. Someone had taken great care to hem the sleeve of his fine white tunic and sew it down over the place where his arm should have been.

"How are you feeling—Audrey, is it?"

So he did not remember her . . . hopefully.

"Yes, Lord Dericott. Thank you. I am feeling much better today."

"I am glad. Do you need me to send word to your family that you are safe and recovering from illness?"

Her heart stopped beating for a moment. *Take a breath and be calm*, she told herself. It was a reasonable thing to ask. And it sounded as if he had no idea who her father was.

"No, I was . . ." She swallowed, taking a long moment, pretending her throat was dry. "I was on my way to visit my aunt and uncle. But they did not know I was coming—"

"In Derbyshire?"

Her heart stuttered again. "Oh. Yes. How did you know?" Her face burned.

"You mentioned Derbyshire before," Mistress Wattlesbrook said softly.

"Of course. Yes. So I will be on my way as soon as I am able to travel."

Lord Dericott continued to stare at her. As well he might. She had not answered his question.

"Shall I tell your aunt and uncle where you are? In case your mother and father begin to worry about you?"

"I do not have a mother. I am alone, as it were. My mother is dead." It was all true, although a bit deceptive. *Forgive me.*

"Poor dear," Mistress Wattlesbrook said. "But you did say something . . . I believe it was 'Please don't tell him I am here.' Is there someone you're afraid of?"

The air seemed to leave her and she sucked in a breath through her mouth, which brought on a coughing fit. She coughed uncontrollably, but the sharp pains in her chest were not as pronounced as they had been. When the coughing began to subside, Mistress Wattlesbrook handed her the cup of herbal water and honey.

"Forgive me for prying," Mistress Wattlesbrook said.

"There is nothing to forgive," Audrey said between sips. "And I am very grateful for all you have done for me, Mistress Wattlesbrook, and you, Lord Dericott. Thank you. I do not wish to trespass on your kindness overlong, so I will leave as soon as I get my strength back."

"You may stay at Dericott Castle," Lord Dericott said firmly. "If you wish, Mistress Wattlesbrook can find you something to do. One of our serving maids just married someone in a neighboring village, so we are in need of another servant."

Now she was certain he had no idea who she was. He'd never offer a servant position to a viscount's daughter. But she had been wearing one of her old flower-picking dresses, and she had traded her only fine dress for some bread. He would have no reason to think she was above becoming a servant.

But what could be more perfect? Her father would never imagine she was working as a servant at Dericott Castle, the home he had hoped she would be mistress of. He'd never find her here.

"Thank you. That is very kind of you." And it was. So very kind. Audrey's eyes filled with tears, and she had to blink them away. She took another sip of the herbal tea and cleared her throat. "I dare say I shall be well enough in a day or two to start work."

"You just rest. We are not so in need of servants that you should endanger your healing." Mistress Wattlesbrook smiled.

"You must recover fully," Lord Dericott said. "Rest and obey Mistress Wattlesbrook."

"Thank you. I shall. I promise." She stared back at her new master, realizing she would much rather be this man's servant than Sir Clement's wife.

Or Maris's sister.

Six

AUDREY CLIMBED TO THE TOP STEP BESIDE THE GIANT BED and yanked the fur covering. Dust flew up, making her sneeze, and she lost her balance, teetering to one side. She stared at the floor below, then leaned toward the bed until she was able to get her balance, planting her hands on the bed.

She let out the breath she'd been holding. If she had fallen off the steps, she might have broken her ankle, and then how could she work?

She tugged again at the fur covering and it slipped off the bed and onto the floor. But she'd swept and scrubbed the floor earlier that morning, so she let the covering lie where it fell and continued stripping the bed of its sheets. As she gathered them in her arms, her head started to spin again, but she focused her gaze on one spot on the feather mattress until the dizzy spell passed. Then she carefully backed down the steps.

Not fully recovered from her illness—although she'd assured Mistress Wattlesbrook that she was well enough to work—she was still a bit weak and wobbly. But she wanted to show that she was willing to work and that she knew how.

Truly, as the daughter of a viscount who owned lands and enjoyed peace and favor at the king's court, the only work she'd ever done was studying under her tutor. But she'd observed her father's servants, and even followed them around when she was a child, enough to have a vague knowledge of how household chores were done. She found she liked to be doing something with her hands, accomplishing tasks. Yet she was already certain she would tire of cleaning floors and stripping beds eventually.

Though she did like the feeling of being useful, what she wanted was to be safe and never have to worry about Maris wreaking her spitefulness on her. She also did not want to marry an old man she did not love. She wanted to fulfill a purpose, to be a bright light. It was a cherished dream she held in her heart, and though it sounded vague even to her, and she didn't know exactly how it would come about, she felt very strongly that there was something she was supposed to do, a good work God had planned for her to do since before she was born.

She used to think it would have been better to be a man. She would have had more opportunities to do good things. But she was not a man. She was a woman who loved flowers and poetry and playing with kittens. She would not have made a very good man, and she certainly did not wish to fight other men in battle like knights had to do.

A woman she was, and a woman she would always be. A woman could be a servant, a shopkeeper, or a wife and mother. Some women owned property and commanded their own estate and servants. If she were wealthy in her own right, it would be easier to do something significant. But she and Maris would never be able to inherit her father's property, and she wasn't sure what would become of Maris. If Audrey did not marry or find a life of her own somehow, she and her sister would both be homeless one day.

For now she was content to take these sheets to the laundry maid, who would begin work before dawn the next morning by boiling water for the washing. She could strip this bed a day ahead because it was no longer slept in, though it was very luxurious, with velvet bed curtains, a tall and sturdy frame, and ornate carvings in the bedposts. The walls were covered with intricate and colorful tapestries.

It was so dark, Audrey went to the window and threw open the shutters. The sun was shining and birds were singing. And down below, on the grassy area between the castle and the forest, Lord Dericott was walking.

He moved slowly, his head down. When she'd seen him four years ago, he had held his head high and smiled throughout the meal. He still looked strong and capable, but his face was often downcast. What could she do to cheer him?

Perhaps it was foolish even to think about that.

She carried the sheets down the back stairs that the servants used, trying not to trip on the bedclothes. Mistress Wattlesbrook met her at the bottom.

"Just put those down over there," she said, pointing into the adjoining room where clean sheets were kept on the shelves along the walls.

Audrey complied.

"Come here, child." Mistress Wattlesbrook waved her over and looked intently at her face, her brows scrunched together. "You look pale. Have you been coughing?"

"Only a little."

"But you are feeling a mite peaked, I dare say. Well, it is time to sit for a bit and eat the midday meal." She motioned Audrey into the kitchen where a trestle table and benches were set up at the back of the warm room next to the oven.

Audrey sat and then saw that the other servants were serving themselves their food. Audrey jumped up, and a maiden handed her a wooden bowl. She was a short girl a bit older than Audrey, and she smiled shyly.

"I'm Joan."

"I'm Audrey."

"I know you were sick. I am so very glad you're feeling better now." Joan spoke with a strange high-pitched, breathy voice.

"Thank you. I am grateful to Mistress Wattlesbrook and everyone who helped her take care of me. Were you one of the ones who sat with me?"

"Yes, but only twice, and not all night long." Joan's eyes were big and wide.

"Thank you so much."

Joan held out a hand as if to stop her. "I don't want you to think I did anything special, although I would have done more—I gladly would have, if Mistress Wattlesbrook had asked me to. You were so very sick, I could see, and suffering terribly. I wanted so much to help you." She had a pained look on her face.

"That is kind of you. You are very kind." Audrey had never met anyone like Joan. She was so childlike, both in her voice and in her manner, Audrey couldn't help but wonder if she was a bit addled.

"Can I get your stew for you?" Joan reached out to take Audrey's bowl, then snatched her hands back. "You will want to get your own stew. Forgive me. I'll just get your bread for you, since you are new and probably don't know where to get it." She hurried over to another table, lifted a linen towel, and drew out a fresh roll. She stood waiting for Audrey to spoon up a ladle of stew into her bowl and sit down, then she handed her the warm bread.

"Thank you so much," Audrey said, humbled by the woman's eagerness to help her.

She watched, making sure the woman got her own food and found a place at the table across from Audrey. Then they all bowed their heads and Mistress Wattlesbrook said a short prayer of thankfulness.

The stew was flavorful and even contained bits of meat. Overheard conversations between her own servants had given her the impression that servants were rarely given meat by her father except on holidays. But this was certainly not a holiday.

She ate the food quickly, suddenly realizing how hungry she was. But as she neared the bottom of her bowl, a wave of sickness crashed over her—weak arms and knees, foggy thoughts, and a queasy stomach. Audrey put down her spoon and her half-eaten roll and closed her eyes.

"Audrey?" Mistress Wattlesbrook's voice was low. "Are you well?"

"Just a bit of dizziness, but I am well."

The head house servant frowned. "Are you finished with your food?"

"Yes, I thank you."

"Wait here." She went into an adjacent storage room.

"Audrey, is it?" one of the servants said. "Tell us about where you came from." She looked younger than Audrey and her fingernails were stained purple and brown. Her green eyes were on Audrey, and she had tiny freckles on her nose and cheeks.

"It is not very different from here."

"Tell us something about it."

Audrey took a deep breath, trying to push away the fear that was rising up, fear that they would discover who she was if she told them about where she was from. But she could surely be vague enough. She wanted so much to be friends with the other servants here, but it was difficult not to worry or want to protect herself—the consequence of her deception.

The five other maids sitting around the table stared at her, waiting. She couldn't tell them that just a mile from her home was the sea, with its dramatic rocky coastline and vast blue waters. If she told them that, they might repeat what she said to Mistress Wattlesbrook, who would in turn tell Lord Dericott, and he might realize who she was.

At least her headscarf covered her scars, so they did not know about those—unless Philip or Mistress Wattlesbrook had told them. Did all the servant girls who had sat by her bedside know about the scars?

"It has green hills and trees and fields, just like here. The people look the same." Audrey shrugged.

"Are you from a city or a village?"

"A village. Near a village."

They looked curiously at her, as if she were different from them, all except Joan, who just smiled timidly at her. Was her speech different enough from theirs that they would notice? Her tutor had taught her to speak precisely and formally, but she did not always follow the rules of noble etiquette and speech.

Mistress Wattlesbrook raised her voice. "If you are finished with your food, get back to work. But not you, Audrey." She fixed her gaze on her. "You are not well enough to work a full day. You are to go back to bed."

Audrey followed her mistress from the room, grateful she was so kind. When had anyone treated her so well? Sybil was sometimes kind, but not always, and her friend Helena possessed a warm and loving heart. But this woman did not know Audrey, and certainly did not know she was the daughter of a viscount.

Mistress Wattlesbrook took her up the stairs and down the corridor to the bedchamber where she'd been sleeping.

"I know you will not want me to sleep in this room, now that I am a servant," Audrey said. "I must sleep with the others, in the serving maids' quarters."

"In good time," Mistress Wattlesbrook said, smiling as she set the cup in her hand down on the little bedside table and ushered Audrey into bed. She tucked her in and handed her the cup. "Not until you are well. Until then you will stay here, where you can rest in peace and quiet. Now drink that."

Audrey obeyed, sipping the slightly bitter herb drink. "Thank you. You are the kindest woman I have ever met."

Mistress Wattlesbrook opened her mouth but didn't speak. She blinked several times, staring down at Audrey. "I believe you have been treated with a lot of unkindness in your life," she said softly. "And I am very sorry for that. But you will find that our Lord Edwin—Lord Dericott, I should say—is as kind a master as you would ever want. Now try to rest, and I will come back before supper and see how you are feeling."

"Thank you."

After Mistress Wattlesbrook left and Audrey had drunk her tea, she sank down into the soft bed and closed her eyes. Soon she'd have to sleep on a small cot in a room with all the other maids, so she might as well enjoy this bed while she could.

Edwin hadn't sat on a horse since he'd come home to Dericott Castle from London over five months ago, and as he rode, he could feel himself continually slipping or otherwise losing his balance.

He'd been riding his entire life. He and his faithful horse, Shadow, had jumped, raced, and jousted with the best of the knights of England. But now he could hardly go faster than a walk without almost falling off. And he was only going around the grounds of the castle.

He rode up the rocky hill to the northwesternmost part of the Dericott demesne. Just as he was almost to the top, he started slipping to one side. He pulled on the reins, halting Shadow, then used the saddle horn to pull himself back into the middle of the horse's back.

He sat trying to get his breath. Was he so weakened that trying to right himself in the saddle would send him gasping for air? He clenched his teeth, held on tightly to the saddle horn, and let Shadow heft them over the last boulder to the top of the hill.

He surveyed the land below—fields and forests, a stream, a fish pond, flocks of sheep and geese, and herds of cows. He was responsible for this demesne, for its people, its animals, and its crops. And yet he felt like only half a man. He could hardly even sit a horse.

Before the injury, he'd rarely been beaten as a swordsman. Now, if someone attacked him or his family, could he defend himself or anyone else? Could he even fight back?

He did not blame the soldier who sliced his arm nearly off, causing him to have to have it amputated by the London surgeon. That man was only doing his duty, defending himself and his fellow guards. Edwin had been fighting for his freedom and the lives of his younger brothers. He would not be beaten, even if it cost him his life.

And he would not let this beat him. He would practice sitting his horse, practice his sword-fighting skills, but he had to admit he would never be as strong with one arm as he had been with two. And it was eating him up inside.

He guided his horse down the hill back toward the house. He could and would learn how to balance in the saddle with his left arm gone, and he would do his best not to let himself be humiliated.

The horse's movements going down the hill were even more jolting than going up. Edwin concentrated on keeping himself upright and straight. But the harder he had to grip the saddle horn with his hand and use his thigh muscles to stay in the saddle, the more he remembered how he never had to think about how to stay upright before he lost his arm. A knight didn't think about how to stay in the saddle. It was as easy and natural as dancing at a festival with a pretty girl—which, along with embracing the people he loved with both arms, was another thing he'd never do again.

He reached the bottom of the hill and set out at a trot toward home. But as they drew closer to the castle, Edwin pushed Shadow to go faster. He immediately began to slide to one side in the saddle again. Clenching his teeth and leaning forward, he held on—until Shadow dodged to the left. Edwin slid to the ground, landing on his right shoulder.

He almost welcomed the pain as punishment for his foolishness at pushing himself past his limit, but at the same time it fueled his resentment toward his own weakness. What earl can't ride across his own demesne without falling off? What kind of man was he? Lady Ophelia would never want to marry him now.

Right in front of him, a badger stood its ground, grunting and growling at him. The badger must have been what spooked Shadow.

Edwin pushed himself up with his one arm, but that movement made the badger bristle its fur, growl more ferociously, and start coming toward him, its teeth bared.

"Don't move!" said a girl's voice.

Audrey, the new servant, was running toward the badger with a stick. The animal turned on her.

SEVEN

EDWIN WAS BEING DEFENDED. FROM A BADGER. BY A GIRL.

He scrambled to his feet, but by the time he was facing the badger, it was running away.

"Are you hurt?" Audrey hurried toward him, still holding the stick.

"I am well." He brushed some dead leaves from his clothes. "Where has my horse gone to?"

Audrey pointed. Shadow was about forty feet away, grazing on some green grass.

"Shall I fetch him for you?" she asked.

"No need." Edwin started toward his horse, his shoulder aching and his pride aching even more. He took hold of Shadow's reins. He wouldn't be able to get back in the saddle without a step stool to assist him, but he was not that far from home now.

He looked over his shoulder at the young woman. "You are well now? From your sickness?"

"Nearly."

He waited, wanting her to go on but not wanting her to think he was ordering her to explain.

"Mistress Wattlesbrook is only allowing me to work half of each day. She says I'm not back to my full strength yet. I can imagine that seeing me out walking around might seem as if I am trying to take advantage of my mistress. I told her I was well, but—"

"You do not need to explain. I know Mistress Wattlesbrook, and there is no arguing with her, especially when she's trying to take care of you."

She laughed, then pressed a hand over her mouth to stifle the sound. When she tilted her head down, then looked up and caught his eye, he had the distinct feeling he'd talked to this young woman before. She was so familiar. And yet he couldn't imagine how or when he would have spoken to her. A young servant woman was not likely to be someone he had talked with, even before he'd inherited his father's title.

But perhaps she had not always been a house servant. She obviously had been escaping from someone or something. Could she be trying to escape a cruel husband? If she were being abused, he would not send her back. He could help her petition for an annulment. No one should be mistreated by the person who had vowed to love and cherish them.

Perhaps it was more complicated than that. Did he really want to get involved, after all the trouble he and his brothers had gone through? But perhaps it was because of all their trouble that he wanted to help her, to keep someone else from suffering injustice because of one or two ruthless, greedy, grasping people.

Or she could be the greedy, grasping one, running away from something bad she had done, away from those she had wronged.

But she had such an innocent air about her, a sweetness in her eyes and her smile. Surely she was not at fault. No, it was much easier to believe that something bad had been done to her.

He was letting his thoughts run rampant. He should take care not to romanticize her situation when he knew nothing of it and remember that his stepmother could also conjure up an expression of goodness when she was trying to be pleasing, while all the time she was plotting cruelties and injustices out of a heart of greed and malice.

"Where were you going?" he asked her.

"I wanted to explore the little stream I caught a glimpse of the other day." She glanced over her shoulder from whence she had come.

"I see you have a stick. For fending off badgers?"

"I had not thought of badgers. I was rather thinking of snakes when I picked it up and decided to use it as both a walking stick and a weapon, should I need one." The young woman's smile made him stare. He hadn't spoken to any woman near his age or with so cheerful a smile since his only sister, Delia, married and left two months ago.

And she was quite well spoken, which also reminded him of his sister. If Audrey were a servant, she must have been a titled lady's personal servant, intelligent enough to mimic her speech.

"That is clever thinking. I will show you the stream if you will allow me."

Why was he offering to show her? He should not encourage familiarity from the servants—his father had warned him against it more than once. But this girl had a transitory air about her, as if she might leave as suddenly as she had come. She was intriguing, a mystery as to where she had come from and what her life story had been up until Philip had found her lying on the ground, barely conscious. His suspicion that she had not been a servant before she had come here was growing. This could be a way to discover who she was.

He pulled Shadow after him as he started toward the young woman.

Her hair was unfettered and fell down her back in blonde waves. A breeze ruffled it, uncovering the scar on her ear. She grabbed the locks on her left side and pulled them down in front of her ear. Her cheeks turned pink.

"Do you mind if I ask how you got those scars?" They were both thinking about them, so he might as well ask.

"I fell into the fire." She said the words while pulling on her hair and looking down at the ground. Her voice was so sad and dejected.

"Was it a long time ago?"

"Four years."

Still she kept her head down. He shouldn't have asked her. Now her bright smile was gone.

A dark orange mushroom was growing not far ahead of them. Audrey fell back to walk slightly behind Edwin. He pointed at the toadstool and a bright blue dragonfly that had landed on it, its quivering wings catching the sunlight.

"Oh, that is lovely," she said quietly and standing still, as if afraid of spooking the dragonfly. "I've seen mushrooms like that before, but I don't think I've ever seen a dragonfly like that one."

"And certainly never together."

He was rewarded with a smile as she drew nearer to the brightly colored pair. But the dragonfly flew away before she could get very close. She sighed and they moved on.

They pressed through some trees and bushes and came out at a bend in the stream where wildflowers grew along the bank. A large, flat rock invited a person to sit and think. He inclined his head toward it.

"You can sit, if you wish."

She stood on her toes to get up on the rock. She was dainty and small-boned, with tiny wrists and narrow shoulders. But perhaps he was just accustomed to seeing his fellow guards and knights, and Mistress Wattlesbrook, who was rather round and plump. He rarely saw the young women servants who worked for him, as they stayed in the kitchen or otherwise out of his sight.

They both stared at the stream. The trees blocked out most of the sun, but a dapple of light here and there made the water shine and shimmer as it trickled over the rocks in the stream-bed. The sounds were so peaceful, and he stood between her and his horse, who started cropping the grass at his feet, adding a distinct crunching sound as his teeth sheared off the grass one big bite at a time.

Audrey leaned back, propping herself on her hands, and turned her face up to meet some shards of light streaming through the leaves overhead. Truly, her features were perfect . . . ethereal . . . almost fairy-like. Her small nose was perfectly formed, her eyelashes thick and darker than her hair. Her mouth bore a pink hue, with an adorable dent in the middle of the upper lip. Perhaps he was being foolish, but he didn't think he'd ever seen a lovelier girl.

Edwin looked away, his own face warming at the thoughts he was having about his servant girl. Such was not his way, and thank heaven she could not read his mind.

He stared at the water again, letting it cast a calming spell on him. He was surprised, shocked even, that he could so quickly move from thinking that if Lady Ophelia did not want him, he would never get married, never make a woman happy with his lame body, to thinking how lovely this young woman servant was, being aware of the perfections of her features and her peaceful expression. Did she realize her hair had fallen back and revealed the edge of the scar on her face? But she seemed to have forgotten she wasn't completely alone, as she kept her eyes closed and took deep breaths and let them out slowly. Was she also trying to calm her thoughts?

He would not stare at her but would listen instead to the way the breeze rustled the leaves, see how the sun shone on the water, the rocks glimmering underneath.

"You have a sister, do you not?"

Edwin turned to see Audrey sitting upright and staring at him.

"Forgive me. I don't mean to be impertinent. I was just

thinking that I heard she helped you and your brothers escape . . . from the Tower."

"Yes, my sister, Delia. She did help us. And we have been declared innocent by the king of all wrongdoing. We were falsely accused."

"Oh yes, I know. Forgive me for prying."

"Nothing to forgive." Would a servant girl ask such bold questions of her master? Not likely. He found himself staring at her again but forced himself to look away.

"Your sister, Lady Delia, does not live here anymore?"

"She married two months ago and moved away."

"I see."

There was silence again. If she could ask questions, he could as well. "Do you have any sisters or brothers?"

"I have one sister. No brothers." Her expression changed, clouding over.

"Is she older or younger?"

"Older."

"Were you and your sister close companions?"

"She is not the kind of sister one becomes friends with."

"I am sorry to hear that. My sister is a very kind and good person. I can't imagine anyone not liking her."

"You are fortunate indeed."

"Why is your family so small? Did your father die?"

"No, he is alive. My mother died."

"And your father did not remarry?"

She shook her head, looking down again.

"Forgive me if I am dredging up bad memories."

"Do not worry. I do not remember my mother."

"Was your sister cruel to you?" He said the words as gently as he could.

She did not answer right away. She took a breath and blew it out noisily, staring down at the rock she was sitting on. "Yes." She looked at him with a crooked smile. "Yes, she was."

They were both silent for a minute or two before she went on.

"Something bad happened to my sister when we were both very young. Our mother died in childbirth, so we needed a nursemaid. My sister was mistreated for several years by the woman, who was very cruel to her while doting on me. And my sister blames me. She's also blamed me, on occasion, for our mother's death."

Edwin's heart ached for Audrey, as a heaviness was evident in her voice and the way her shoulders drooped.

"I used to feel such pity for my sister that I would excuse her behavior by remembering all she had gone through. But she became jealous of me because our father planned to marry me off first and threatened to never allow my sister to wed. I believe Father thinks she is mad."

Edwin took a step back, almost colliding with Shadow. "Is she so bad?"

She looked down again. "She purposely tripped me so I would fall into the fire. That's how I got my scars."

Edwin drew in a breath. How could anyone be so heartless, especially to her own sister?

"I used to think there was something wrong with me that she would torment me so, telling me things that weren't true to try to confuse me and get me to doubt my own senses. Once when I was too little to know any better, she told me there was snow outside and I couldn't see it because I was bad. She constantly told me I was ugly, that no man would ever marry me, that my father only felt sorry for me. Then she caused me to get burned . . ." She shook her head and looked the other way, pulling on her hair to make certain it covered the scars.

The poor girl. He knew what it was like to have someone saying things about you that weren't true. His stepmother had done the same, though Delia had suffered her cruelties the most.

"Your sister was only jealous of you. That is why she told you that you were ugly."

She shook her head. "She found a way to make her words true. She made me ugly," she rasped in a whispery voice.

Surely she did not truly think she was ugly. But perhaps he knew what she was feeling, the sense that no one could ever see anything about you except your scars. He would always be the man with only one arm. And she would always be the woman with the scars.

EIGHT

AUDREY SHOULDN'T HAVE SAID SO MUCH OR REVEALED SO many things about herself. But there was something about Lord Dericott that made her feel safe and made her want to tell him her thoughts and feelings, to answer his questions and share even more with him than he asked. Perhaps it was because she sensed she could trust him not to look down on her but also not to feel sorry for her. He would feel compassion without contempt, give her dignity without dismissing her pain. He had been through his own share of injustice.

"Your scars don't make you ugly. I can't even see them."

"You are very kind."

Truly, he was kind. But to what purpose? It was strange that he would speak thusly to a servant. Did he recognize her after all? She should be more careful around him.

"I should go attend to the ledgers my steward wanted to review with me. Will you be all right?"

"Of course. I should go and see if Mistress Wattlesbrook will allow me to do something, if I can convince her that I am well." She smiled, remembering their earlier conversation about that woman's caring precautions.

They walked back together—although she walked a step behind him, as he was the master. When they came to a pretty little stone bridge that spanned the stream, he pointed at it and said, "My grandfather had that bridge built so the shepherds could bring the sheep over the stream to the pasture on this side. When the water level was high, the younger sheep would sometimes get swept away."

"It is a very pretty bridge." Maris would ridicule her for saying a bridge was pretty. Would Lord Dericott think her strange?

"I have always thought so too. That is, after spending more time away from home than I spent here, I was able to appreciate its beauty."

Once again she had worried about someone thinking she was odd or daft because of something Maris might say, when she should realize Maris only wished to be spiteful. But it was so difficult to completely dismiss all the things Maris had said, things Audrey had believed for so long about herself. She hadn't realized she'd had so many of Maris's thoughts in her head until she came here and met people like Mistress Wattlesbrook and Lord Dericott, people who were safe to open up to about her innermost thoughts.

"Are there many streams and bridges where you grew up?" he asked.

"About the same as here." Was he trying to find out where she came from?

They walked rather slowly, and he said, "I have liked all of the areas I have visited in England."

"Have you ever been to the Continent?"

"No. Have you?"

Audrey laughed. "Of course not." A servant girl would have had no opportunity to travel to the Continent. And even as a viscount's daughter, she rarely went far. It had been ten years since she'd been to her aunt and uncle's home in Derbyshire.

He could command her to tell him where she had come from. He seemed curious. But he refrained from ordering her to answer any prying questions. He was incredibly gracious.

Her mind flashed back to when Maris had asked her for the tapestry, feigning amiability when she'd actually planned to trip her and cause serious harm to her. Was Lord Dericott trying to lull her into a false sense of safety, only to betray her later? No, no, she should not think such things, not after he had taken care of her and allowed her to stay.

Would she ever be able to trust again? Would she ever stop remembering the horror of what her sister had done to her?

"Dericott Castle is very striking and grand. I like the windows and that some of the towers are square. My—" She stopped talking. She'd almost said, "My father's castle towers are all round." That would have been a serious blunder.

"Your?" he prompted.

"My . . . experience with castles is very limited. Oh, look at that beautiful swan." She pointed at the bird as they passed a small pond, eager to change the topic of conversation and relieved Lord Dericott stopped to watch the swan as it swam gracefully.

Why was Lord Dericott moving so slowly? It was taking so long to get to the castle. Not that she disliked his company, but she had come so close, multiple times, to revealing too much about herself.

"Delia once told me that she felt we were like swans, me and my brothers and her, trying to swim together and keep one another safe." He smiled slightly, his eyes taking on a faraway look.

What must it be like to have siblings who were not vicious, with whom one could have a close friendship? Audrey remembered the family she'd seen in the village having a meal together, smiling and talking, and she suddenly longed for that sisterly bond, so much that her chest ached. Was this envy? Or just a desire to have a connection and a sense of belonging with someone who would not hurt her?

The swan moved closer, and Audrey saw that several little cygnets were swimming along behind the tall swan.

"Oh, it's a mother. Do you see the babies?" she couldn't help saying.

"I do. She comes back each year to our little pond to hatch her eggs."

The cygnets were fuzzy and dark gray, much different from their snow-white mother. How beautiful and sweet they all were, each one perfectly formed and full of innocence.

The mother did not seem to like the two large humans staring at her, and she moved away, soon hidden from view behind some bushes along the bank.

Lord Dericott was watching Audrey as she observed the

swans. He moved along as well, and soon they were at the stables near the castle.

"I enjoyed our walk. Fare well," he said, nodding to her, then handing his horse off to a groom as he spoke to him.

Audrey's heart skipped a beat as she watched him leave. This was the man she might have married had it not been for Maris. She might have been mistress of this impressive castle and all the servants—instead of being a servant. But she could not think about that. The priest was always saying that God was sovereign, and she'd read in the Holy Writ that even a sparrow did not fall to the ground without God knowing about it. So God must have a reason for allowing her scars.

She hurried away to the castle to find Mistress Wattlesbrook.

Edwin sat in his library at the back of the castle on the ground floor. The roomy armchair that had once been his father's was lined all around with cushions. His father had been known to fall asleep in it.

Instead of sleeping, Edwin was reading. He'd studied French and Latin and, for a very short time, German, and as he had spoken only English for the last few years, he was reading a French epic poem to try and keep the language fresh in his memory. French was often spoken at court, and all the noblemen spoke it, so he felt it his duty to make certain he did not forget it.

A servant girl—Audrey—entered the room and began to dust the sheepskin- and leather-bound books. As he was sitting in a corner by the open window, she did not yet see him or know he was there. Perhaps he should clear his throat or make some other noise to let her know she was not alone.

The girl rubbed the spines of the books and looked to be examining them closely, leaning in as her dust cloth barely moved. Then to his surprise she pulled one of the books off the shelf. She held it in her hands, staring down at it for a moment before opening it.

She was so still as she looked down at it, she must be reading. And since most of the books on that shelf, he happened to know, were in French . . .

Did she know how to read? And in French? Surely not. Not unless she was the daughter of a nobleman, and no nobleman's daughter would be working as a servant.

She kept gazing down at the book. After two or three minutes she turned the page. And still she stared, motionless, at the page before her.

"*Parlez-vous français?*"

She jumped and slapped the book closed, spinning around at the same time. "I didn't know anyone was here," she said breathlessly.

"Forgive me for startling you. Do you read?"

"I'm so sorry." She started putting the book back into its place but fumbled so much she nearly dropped the book, and she did drop her dusting cloth. "I was wondering if there were any illuminations. I love to look at the drawings and colorful . . . Forgive me for disturbing you. I will come back when you are not . . ." She turned toward the door.

"You do not need to go. You were not disturbing me at all." He stood up from his chair to move closer to her.

"Mistress Wattlesbrook would not wish for me to be in here while you are working or reading, so I will go."

"Before you go, *montrez-moi le livre que vous lisiez.*"

She turned toward the bookshelf and reached for the book. So she did understand French.

She snatched her hand back and spun to face him. "I should go." She nearly ran for the door.

"Stop. Please."

She stopped, but she did not turn around.

"*Comment avez-vous appris?*" he asked.

She faced him, her eyes wide and her cheeks pale.

She must be a nobleman's daughter. But what terrible misfortune had befallen her that she should find herself here, among strangers, cleaning Dericott Castle?

Audrey's heart pounded sickeningly. What could she do? Lord Dericott was demanding to know how she learned to speak French. Or to read? She was not sure which he meant. But no servant girl should be able to do either.

She couldn't tell him the truth, but how could she lie? And how could she avoid answering him? Simply changing the topic of conversation would not save her now.

"Please forgive me, my lord. I should not have been touching your book." Her eyes filled with tears of confusion and fear.

She had nowhere to go if she had to flee again. What if she was robbed again? Or attacked? "Please do not send me away."

"No one is sending you away." His voice was deep but soft and quiet. "I only want to know how you came to be able to read and speak French. I am curious."

She tried to blink back the tears, but one leaked from the corner of her eye. She dashed it away with her fingers. Her voice was barely above a whisper as she said, "Please don't force me to tell you."

"I will not force you."

When he said nothing more, she said, "Thank you." She was able to blink the rest of the tears away.

Lord Dericott spoke in French as he said, "You may continue to dust the books."

Should she pretend she did not understand him? But surely it was too late for that. So she picked up her dust cloth and continued to clean.

"Which book were you reading?" he said, again speaking in French. "Forgive me, but it has been a long time since I was able to converse in French, and I would like to have someone with whom to practice."

"*Très bien. Je t'obligerai,*" she said, agreeing to oblige him. She pulled the book off the shelf that she had been reading and handed it to him, her cheeks burning.

"*The Romance of the Rose,*" he said upon seeing the cover.

"I was never allowed to read it." Indeed, her priest had told her it was profane and sacrilegious for anyone, especially a young unmarried woman such as herself. But she had not seen anything bad in it from the two pages she had just read. Perhaps she had not understood it, or it held some kind of additional meaning besides the obvious.

"You may read it now, if you wish." Lord Dericott tried to hand it to her.

"No, no, thank you. I don't want to read it." She shook her head, her cheeks burning even more.

He placed the book back on the shelf. "If you have time and wish to read something, please feel free to come and borrow a book."

"Thank you. That is very kind." She rubbed the spines of the books with her cloth. "And you may feel free to speak to me in French, if you wish."

"Merci beaucoup."

She glanced back at him to see if he was smiling. He wasn't, but there was a soft look about his eyes and mouth, and she suddenly remembered the boy he was four years ago at her home. He'd been less solemn then, but at this moment she could clearly see that same boy in his grown-up, more somber face. And her heart tripped over itself. Her thoughts, on that faraway day, had been of marrying him, of hoping the marriage would not take place too soon, of worrying what Maris would do to her, knowing her sister was jealous and angry. But that was just one day before the "accident," when Maris caused her scars.

She'd often thought of him in the days after when she'd lain in bed, crying from the pain of her burns. But at some time during the following years, she'd stopped thinking of him. In truth she had no reason to think of him, as she could never marry him.

But she was thinking of him now.

"Lord Dericott?" Someone was approaching the door of the library.

Audrey turned to face the bookshelf and continued cleaning, trying to look intent on her task, while Lord Dericott took a few steps toward the door and away from her.

"There is a messenger here from . . ."

The person's voice grew too faint to hear as he and Lord Dericott walked together down the corridor away from the library.

She remembered the compassion in the tone of her lord's voice, the kindness on his face. He had neither berated her nor ignored her. He'd been interested in how she learned French and even wished to speak it with her. But he had not forced her to tell him more than she wished to. He could have intimidated and coerced her into telling him exactly who she was. He would have been well within his rights to do so, as she was his servant living in his home. No one spoke of it much, but it was well-known, even to someone as sheltered as Audrey was, that masters often took advantage of their servants.

Such a kind and fair master as Lord Dericott would be very hard to find again, should she have to leave. But did she truly wish to be a servant all her life? To do mundane tasks such as cleaning? She did not mind helping; it was better than having nothing at all to do, with no purpose or way to be useful. But when she thought about her future, she saw only a fog. She knew something was out there, but she had no idea what it could be.

Edwin stared out the window. The rain had finally ceased, which meant the visitor he'd been waiting on for the last two days would probably be arriving today.

He cringed at the thought of his old teacher and trainer seeing him now. He had mostly good memories of him, and even thought of him as more of a friend than a superior, though he was so much older than Edwin. But the idea of him seeing Edwin in his current state, with only one arm, filled his stomach with dread.

He'd been Sir Clement's squire for years, had learned all the old knight had to teach him. They'd sparred with the sword, and Sir Clement had taught him riding tricks, sharing horsemanship wisdom that he'd gained from many years of experience.

Now Edwin could never be the swordsman he'd been before. He could barely stay in the saddle.

He heard the servant's footsteps approaching and turned from the window to wait for him.

"Sir Clement is here."

"Send him in."

Well, it would be good to see him after all.

Soon Sir Clement was coming in the door and crossing the floor toward him.

"Welcome," Edwin said.

"Old friend." Sir Clement walked straight up to him with a grim look on his face.

Oh no. Would he express pity and condolences on his lost

arm? Would he stare at the empty space where his arm should be and look sad? He wasn't sure he could refrain from anger if he was treated thusly.

Sir Clement clapped him on the shoulder and a small smile crossed his lips. "I must call you Lord Dericott now. You are looking well."

"You look well also. How was your journey?"

"Good, good. I am glad to see you, heartily glad you fought your way out of that mess with your stepmother and old 'Baldric the Sneaky.' Where did they end up?"

"The Continent, possibly. If they ever come back to England, they will be hanged."

"As well they should be. In fact, we might just go down and find them and drag them back, just for that purpose."

There were many things he could say to that suggestion. "I've thought about it." Many times, in fact. They should pay for what they did—for their greed and the terrible time they put his family through, his young brothers and sister who were completely innocent—not least of which was murdering their father.

But vengeance belonged to the Lord. And perhaps one day Edwin would stop dreaming about exacting vengeance himself. He knew he needed to let it go, but forgiveness was difficult when the offense was so great.

"It has been a long time since I've been to Dericott Castle," Sir Clement said. "I like the way it's situated—on a hill facing south. You tend to get the breezes and clear views that way . . ."

May God bless him for continuing to talk about inconsequential things, the condition of the roads and the trees and fields around Bedfordshire. It allowed Edwin to breathe a little easier and feel more relaxed and prepared for the inevitable questions and condolences that would come.

"I am heartily glad to see you," Sir Clement said again as they both sat drinking a tankard of ale. "But I have a specific reason for traveling about just now."

Edwin listened closely. Judging from the look on his friend's face, he had something important to say.

"I am searching for someone." His eyes clouded over, his mouth contracted into a thin line, and his brows lowered. "Do you remember when we stopped for the night, about four years ago, at Viscount Engleford's castle?"

Edwin's mind went back, trying to grasp hold of the memory.

"The viscount had two young daughters, both pretty, but one was exceptionally so. I believe the viscount had you in mind for a husband for her."

The memory was slowly coming back to him. He had no recollection of their names, but they had sat across from him during a meal in the viscount's Great Hall. He recalled the older one looking shrewd and saying unkind things about the younger one, who was very shy and barely looked up the whole time they were eating.

But something was making the hair rise up on the back of his neck, prodding at him like a thought inching its way from the recesses of his mind.

"That younger one has run away from home and vanished, and I feel partially responsible for it."

The prodding grew stronger.

"Her father had pledged her to me in marriage. We had agreed on the bride price, and I was to take her to wife in a couple of months." Sir Clement held up his hand. "Now, I know what you are thinking."

Audrey. Could she be the young girl he and Sir Clement had met at her father's castle four years ago?

"What am I thinking?" Edwin's heart beat hard.

"That she is much too fair and young for the likes of me. That her father would rather she marry a young handsome earl like you. But she got burned, you see." He lifted his hand and pointed to his ear.

Edwin's chest hurt.

"She has scars now on her ear and a bit of her face from falling into the fire. But you can't see them when she pulls her hair down, and her father vows that she is a sweet girl."

Why did it make him imagine hitting Sir Clement for talking this way about Audrey? Sir Clement was not a bad man. He would not be a cruel husband. Inattentive perhaps, but not cruel. But it seemed wrong to speak of her so disrespectfully, as if her scars were a thing to hide and be ashamed of.

"But she must not have wanted to marry me, since she ran away from home." He hung his head. "So I will not press her to do so. I have told her father I am letting him out of the arrangement. I do not wish to marry a woman who is so opposed to the union that she would run away from kith and kin and everything safe."

Audrey had said her sister tripped her so she would get burned, but . . .

"Could it be that she feared for her life? That her sister wished to harm her and she was afraid to stay in her home?"

Sir Clement frowned. "Her father said he sent the sister away to a nunnery after Audrey's face got burned, but the sister came back home. I think he may have been marrying her off to me to keep her away from the sister. But if you think the father may have been allowing the sister to harm her . . . that would be unlikely. He'd have nothing to gain and everything to lose from making her too ugly to marry a duke or an earl."

Ugly? Audrey was not ugly. Not in any way. But if her father had protected her from the sister, why had she been so afraid of being sent back there? He and Mistress Wattlesbrook had believed she had been abused and was fleeing something frightening. Had she fled her home only because she did not wish to marry Sir Clement? That would seem rather unlike a girl who would be willing to serve as a house cleaner and kitchen worker. Also, she had said, "Please don't tell him." To whom was she referring?

"I don't suppose you have heard of such a girl, with a scar on her ear and face? She is a pretty little thing, regardless of her scars, blonde hair. Her father fears some harm has come to her."

Her father must be very worried about her. Edwin should tell Sir Clement that Audrey was here now, that she was safe and unharmed. But something stopped him. If she was so desperate to remain hidden, perhaps she had a good reason.

"Surely you will be able to find her," Edwin said. "Or perhaps she will go back home on her own."

"I am only helping to look for her as a favor to her father, and because I feel partially responsible." He rubbed a hand over the back of his neck. "I will not be marrying her, and I should have known better. I never should have agreed. A widow more my age would be more suited to me. Perhaps even a rich widow, eh?" He laughed, but he didn't look or sound very mirthful. This business with Audrey running away had shaken him.

He should tell Sir Clement she was safe. But he couldn't bring himself to say it.

"Will you be staying a few days?" Edwin asked.

"I will stay one night, but then I need to keep looking, at least make a good faith effort. Though I suppose she may have run off with a lover, some young buck with a ruddy, handsome face. Not like mine." Again he laughed his mirthless laugh and rubbed his chin, which was covered in short white whiskers.

"Do not worry. I believe she will be found. She may be closer than you think."

Sir Clement looked doubtful but said nothing.

Perhaps it was time to have a talk with Audrey and ask some very pointed questions.

NINE

AUDREY WAS FETCHING TWO BUCKETS OF WATER FROM THE outdoor well to carry to the laundry maid, though they were only half full. It irked her that the other women could carry full buckets. But she was determined to get stronger so that she could carry full buckets too.

Audrey had felt lighter and more peaceful since coming to Dericott Castle. However, when she was working hard, and at night when her body was tired, she missed Sybil and Helena. Would she ever see them again? Though Sybil was sometimes cross and dismissive, how Audrey longed for an embrace from Sybil's motherly arms and a smile from Helena when she walked into her shop. And though she knew she might never see them again, she was saving up things to tell them, keeping a list in her head, just in case.

She saw Lord Dericott walking across the bailey with an-other man. Lord Dericott indeed caught one's eye with the way his torso looked with one arm missing, but he was still tall and muscular, his stride confident.

The man beside him also captured her attention. He was familiar, with his graying hair and the way he looked next to Lord Dericott. When he turned and showed a full view of his face, she gasped and dropped her buckets.

Sir Clement. He was here. He would take her back to her father and to Maris.

She snatched up the buckets, which miraculously had not spilled, and turned her back on the two men.

Her heart pounded and she had to gasp for breath. Had they seen her?

She walked as fast as she could without drawing attention to herself. She passed the stable and made it to the large oak tree under which the laundry maidens toiled over the linens.

"What is the matter?" one of the servants asked. "Have you seen a ghost?"

"No, no, I am well." Audrey smiled, but her thoughts were racing.

"Go on and strip the beds, then," the laundry maid said, shooing Audrey away with her hand.

Audrey hurried toward the servants' entrance. Just before she entered the castle, she glanced over her shoulder. Lord Dericott and Sir Clement were standing still now and seemed to be deep in conversation. Audrey went inside.

She climbed the steps. Were they talking about her? But Lord Dericott did not know who she was. She was safe, was she not? But how long would Sir Clement stay? He would surely see her. She would ask to work in the kitchens so that she could stay hidden. But what if he came in the kitchen to fetch some food? No, she wasn't safe here anymore.

She continued on up to the upstairs bedrooms.

Sir Clement would force her to marry him. Or perhaps he no longer wanted to marry her, after she'd been so disrespectful to her father as to run away from home. Regardless, Sir Clement would surely tell her father where she was.

She thought back to the evening when she ran away. Why had she done it? Yes, she'd been unhappy about having to marry a man who was more than twice her age. She hadn't realized until that moment when she'd been told she would have to marry Sir Clement just how much she wanted to marry for love.

But it was Maris, seeing Maris's taunting face and hearing her snide voice, that had pushed her to take such a desperate step.

And now that she might be dragged back to her father's castle and to Maris, she couldn't bear to let it happen. She liked feeling safe and being with good people like Mistress Wattlesbrook, Joan and the others servants, and Lord Dericott, feeling as though her father and Maris had no idea where she was and could not control her. She was happy at Dericott Castle.

Audrey ran to the room where she'd been sleeping since she arrived, where they had continued to allow her to sleep even though she had recovered from her illness. She would miss Dericott Castle, and she might never find a place so good again. But she had to leave, and quickly.

She knew what she had to do.

She threw her clothing into her old bag. Should she take the servant's clothing Lord Dericott had provided for her? It felt wrong to do so, so she changed into her own dress and left her servant's dress on the bed.

She took up her bag, her hands shaking. She did not feel good about leaving. In fact, her stomach felt sick and her chest heavy.

"God, am I doing the right thing? Tell me what to do," she whispered. But she couldn't hear a response from Him. Her thoughts were whirling around in her head, fearful, anxious thoughts. Her heart was beating so hard, and she kept imagining Lord Dericott and Sir Clement bursting into the room with scowls on their faces, saying, "You should not have run away from your father."

She imagined Mistress Wattlesbrook joining them, admonishing her with, "It was a childish thing to do," and shaking her head at her.

Their disapproval would crush her. And then they would send her back with Sir Clement. Or they would hold her captive here until her father sent his men to fetch her. She'd be back at home with Maris, who would laugh at her for failing to get away. What kind of vicious scheme would she devise next to torment Audrey?

Her father would be less inclined to protect her from Maris. He would probably accuse Audrey of also being mad. And perhaps she was, but her sister had driven her to leave. Just the sight of her after almost four years of her being away at the convent had brought back all the fear, all the pain of feeling as though her father had not loved her enough to protect her.

Leaving must be the right thing to do. She couldn't bear being forced to go back home.

She lifted her bag, which was light with her few belongings, her thoughts spinning in a frantic whirl.

Edwin hurried to find Mistress Wattlesbrook. She was in the kitchen talking with the cooks. Her eyes flew wide when she saw him. She rushed toward him, no doubt horrified that he, the lord of the castle, would be in the kitchen with the common cooks and kitchen maids.

"My lord, you should have sent someone to fetch me." She hustled him out of the workspace and into the misty midday air.

"I wish to know where the new servant Audrey is. That is, I need you to go with me to speak to her."

"Of course, but may I ask what the matter could be? Has she done something wrong?"

"You will hear it all when we find her."

"Oh dear." Mistress Wattlesbrook hurried back into the kitchen, and Edwin stood near the doorway as she asked the other servants where they had seen her last.

"She was on her way to strip the beds of their sheets," the laundry maid said. "But that was an hour ago and I haven't seen her since. I had to send someone else to do it. She has set us all behind on our tasks."

Edwin rubbed the back of his neck. Could she have seen Sir Clement and hidden herself? Or even run away again?

He left Mistress Wattlesbrook and ran into the castle, almost losing his balance when he reached the bottom step of the servants' stairs. He leaned his shoulder against the wall for a moment, until he could get his bearings, then hurried up the steps. He went down the corridor on the first floor, looking into each room and calling her name.

"Audrey."

But he did not see her. In fact, he did not see anyone until he went up to the next floor and saw a servant coming out of a bedchamber, her arms full of bedsheets.

"My lord," she said, bowing to him.

"Have you seen the maiden Audrey?"

"No, my lord." Her eyes were wide and she shrank away from him.

"You may carry on."

He looked through the rest of the rooms. Just as he reached the last one, Mistress Wattlesbrook came up the stairs, breathing hard.

"She has gone." Mistress Wattlesbrook continued to try to catch her breath.

"What do you mean?"

"Her bag and her clothing are gone, and she left her servant's clothes on her bed."

So she had run away. "She can't have gone far." He would send Sir Clement and the guards in different directions, and surely they would be able to find her.

He hurried down the stairs and found Sir Clement.

"She was here," he told him.

"What do you mean? Audrey?"

"She was here and has only just left. But I want to make it clear that she is under my protection."

"Why was she here? For how long?"

"She was sick and collapsed outside the castle. I did not recognize her, did not know who she was. After she recovered she stayed and worked as a servant here, and appeared to be running away from someone who wished to harm her. I assured her she was safe here."

"Very well. As I already said, I will not force her to marry me."

"Let us go and find her, then."

Edwin rounded up his guards and they quickly set out to search for Audrey.

Audrey passed the pond where she and Lord Dericott had observed the swan and her babies swimming, then the spot where he'd fallen off his horse because of the belligerent badger. If she had to choose one man she thought was true and kind enough to marry, she would choose Lord Dericott.

But it hardly mattered what she thought of him, because he wouldn't wish to marry her. She'd learned from the servants that he was marrying a Lady Ophelia, the daughter of an earl.

He would be disapproving of her now. Once Sir Clement told him about the girl he was supposed to marry, once he described her and explained that she had left home to avoid marrying him, Lord Dericott would surely guess that he was speaking of her. What would he think of her? It twisted her stomach to imagine him thinking ill of her.

She turned to stare back at the castle that was mostly gray stone but with some half timber and plaster sections in between towers. Most people would surely not describe it as lovely, but to her it was. It was majestic and mysterious and unique, unlike anything she had seen before, and she loved it. It reminded her a bit of some of the buildings she had seen in London the one time her father had let her accompany him there.

Perhaps she would never see it again.

She went north, hoping she was heading toward her aunt and uncle. Once she had put some distance between her and Sir Clement, she could ask someone on the road how to get to Derbyshire. For now she followed the stream.

After walking for an hour, she wished she'd taken the time to go to the kitchen and get some food. Lord Dericott was free with his food, and Mistress Wattlesbrook never scolded the serving maids for taking a small repast between mealtimes. She could have taken some bread and dried fruit and even some cheese, and no one would have thought a thing of it. But now as her stomach growled at her, she wondered from where and how her next meal would come. She had no money, as she had not been paid any wages yet, and she owned very little of value that she might trade for food.

Perhaps she had been foolish to leave Dericott Castle. She could encounter more robbers like the ones who stole her money.

Perhaps she should have gone to Lord Dericott and begged him to let her stay and work at the castle.

And what if Sir Clement never described her to him? Lord Dericott might not even realize she was Sir Clement's wayward bride-to-be or that he was searching for her. Sir Clement might leave without ever knowing she had been there.

The farther away she walked, the more uneasy she felt about leaving.

Was it too late to go back? Certainly the other servants would be angry with her for shirking her work, but though Mistress Wattlesbrook might scold her, she would not mistreat her for disappearing for a few hours.

Audrey had not only left without food, but she also had not taken the time to retrieve her walking stick. She was looking around the forest floor for another suitable stick when a movement caught her eye. About two feet from her, slithering through the leaves, was a snake.

Audrey screamed, then clamped her hand over her mouth.

The snake lifted its head and her stomach sank.

It was a dangerous adder.

The servants at home had taught her which snakes were poisonous, and this was definitely one of the poisonous ones. She'd only encountered one once before on her walks, and it had moved away from her before she had time to get very frightened. But this one was close.

"If it is within two feet of you, it can strike you in less than a moment," her father's groom had told her.

"You must not move, or it will strike," another had said.

Audrey held her breath, her hand still over her mouth. Was the thing staring at her? Its little tongue flicked out of its mouth, moving about, then darted back inside.

She couldn't stay motionless forever. It would surely strike her. And she had no weapon, nothing except the cloth bag she was clutching to her chest.

It moved its raised head slightly, its black eyes trained on her.

If she could just move back, out of its striking range, she would be safe. She would run and it could not catch her. Could it?

She took a step back. It jerked its head slightly and slithered closer. She took another step back, but her foot landed on something big and round. A fallen tree. She lost her balance and screamed, throwing her bag toward the snake as she fell backward. The back of her head struck the ground.

TEN

EDWIN HEARD A SCREAM. HE PUSHED HIS HORSE TO GO faster, weaving around tree trunks and ducking branches, holding on to the pommel and leaning forward to keep from slipping. Just when he wondered if he was going in the right direction, he saw Audrey standing among a cluster of trees, clutching her bag to her chest. Why was she so still? Then he saw the poisonous adder in front of her, its head up, coiled and ready to strike.

He slid off his horse and drew his sword.

Audrey screamed and fell backward, throwing her bag at the snake. The snake struck the bag, biting it, then pulled away. It coiled itself again, its head swaying as if trying to find its prey.

"Don't move!" Edwin kept his eyes on the snake, stepping between it and Audrey.

"Oh!" she cried. "It will bite you!"

The coiled snake was getting ready to strike. Edwin sliced his sword blade through the snake's body, cutting off its head.

He turned to find Audrey staring up at him with wide eyes. He held his hand out to her and focused on fixing his feet firmly enough not to fall as he pulled her up.

"Oh, thank you!" She peered around him to stare at the snake. "Is it dead?" She clutched his hand in hers and pressed her other hand over her heart.

"Yes."

"You saved me." She gazed up at him. In that moment, with the way she was looking at him, he felt as whole and strong as he had before he lost his arm.

She seemed to realize she was still holding his hand and let go. She took a step away from him.

Edwin bent and, careful not to lose his balance, picked up her bag and handed it to her.

"I suppose you know who I am now."

He simply looked her in the eye. What explanation would she make?

"In case you don't, I am the daughter of the Viscount Engleford and I was pledged to marry Sir Clement."

"Yes. I know."

"You will not send me back, will you? Please don't send me back."

"To your father?"

She nodded. Her bottom lip trembled just before she clamped her teeth on it.

So she was more worried about her father than about Sir Clement? But . . .

"Do you wish to marry Sir Clement?"

She shook her head vigorously.

More horse hooves drew near. Sir Clement was coming their way. Audrey seemed to shrink as she wrapped her arms around her bag and lowered her head.

"Is this Audrey?" Sir Clement dismounted his horse and addressed Edwin.

Why didn't Sir Clement speak directly to the woman? He walked toward them.

"You don't have to worry," Sir Clement said to her, even though she still hadn't looked up at him. "I will not force you to marry me. But I do have to tell your father that I found you and that you are safe."

"Please don't tell him where I am." She was staring right into Sir Clement's face now, her eyes wide.

Sir Clement rubbed a hand down his cheek and grimaced. No doubt he was thinking about the consequences of defying the viscount, who would demand to know where his daughter was living.

"I shall tell him you are under my protection," Edwin said. "And I will not allow you to be mistreated while you are at Dericott Castle, nor will I allow anyone, even your father, to take you away against your will."

Audrey's mouth fell open.

"That could get you in a lot of trouble," Sir Clement said. "It would be easier just to tell him I never found her."

"But that would be a lie, and you are no liar." Edwin could not let his friend violate his conscience.

"The girl does not want to go back to her father's house,

135

but why? I have said I won't marry her against her wishes." Sir Clement turned to stare at Audrey. "You should return to your father."

Perhaps now that no one else was around except Sir Clement, it was time to ask her some specific questions.

Audrey's hands still trembled from the terror of nearly being bitten by the snake, as well as the subsequent relief of being rescued by Lord Dericott. Seeing Sir Clement come riding up made her tremble for a different reason.

But hearing Lord Dericott say she was under his protection and that he would not allow her to be taken back against her will made her catch her breath. Her heart fluttered as she looked into his eyes. Could he be so kind, so protective of someone he hardly knew? He was so different from Father.

But now Sir Clement was staring hard at her. No doubt he resented the fact that she was causing so much trouble, she who was only a girl.

Her father had said that to her once. "You're only a girl. Why are you making such a fuss? You're hurting my ears."

Maris had cut a large hunk out of Audrey's hair, and Audrey had cried and yelled at her father for not punishing her sister for the act of meanness and jealousy.

Neither Lord Dericott nor Sir Clement looked as dismissive and annoyed as her father had looked that day. But her heart trembled in fear at being similarly dismissed now.

"Is it your sister?" Lord Dericott said gently, "Is that why you do not wish to go home?"

"Are you afraid?" Sir Clement added.

Perhaps they deserved an explanation. But how could she make them understand? It sounded so strange and foolish when she said it out loud. However, she had little choice but to try.

"I do not wish to go back to my father's house because of my older sister, Maris."

Both men continued to stare at her, but Sir Clement's eyes squinted and his forehead wrinkled.

"She is revengeful and jealous of me. I know it sounds strange and unbelievable, but I am afraid of her. As I told Lord Dericott, she is the one who tripped me—deliberately—and caused me to fall into the fire and get burned. And my father does not protect me from her, even though he says she is mad. He sent her to live in a convent for four years, but they refused to house her any longer. I ran away because she came back."

Pouring out the whole ugly truth created so many emotions that she had to blink back tears.

"I am sorry your sister deliberately burned you. It is terrible." Lord Dericott's voice was low and quiet.

"I know it is hard to believe. I thought if I could just say the right thing or do the right thing, if I could convince her that I would never do her any harm, that she would stop treating me and other people so badly. But after she tripped me and caused me to fall into the fire, I have been too afraid of her to hope any longer. All I know is that Father has allowed her to come back from the monastery, and I cannot go back there." Audrey's voice broke, but she took a deep breath and forced herself into numbness.

Sir Clement said, "Your father told me that he was glad you were marrying so you would be away from your sister."

Her father was trying to protect her by having her wed Sir Clement. But she did not want to marry Sir Clement. Would he and Lord Dericott think her spoiled and ridiculous for refusing his offer? But she did not care. She wouldn't marry Sir Clement just to get away from her sister.

"Why did you not tell me who you were?" Lord Dericott had such a compassionate look on his face.

"I did not know if you would allow me to stay if you knew who I was and that I had run away. I thought you would send me back to my father. Besides that, I am a bit ashamed of my fear. I don't want anyone to think I'm a coward."

"There is no shame in trying to protect yourself from a dangerous person. And I would not have sent you back there."

Lord Dericott's words were like balm to her heart, while his voice made her feel warm and safe—and ignited another feeling that made her uncomfortably aware that Sir Clement was standing there staring at her. The two men, both in appearance and in the feelings they created in her, formed a sharp contrast.

She did owe Sir Clement an explanation, perhaps, for running away and refusing to marry him. It was true, she could marry him and be safe from Maris. And Sir Clement did not seem like a bad person. But there were a few reasons, including the fact that something inside her rebelled at the thought.

Audrey would have been more than glad for her father to

marry off Maris instead of her. But Maris had always pitted herself against Audrey. It seemed she would never stop holding the grudge against her for being the nursemaid's—and then Father's—darling.

She faced Sir Clement and took a deep breath. "I am truly sorry, Sir Clement. Please forgive me for not honoring your agreement with my father." Her cheeks were burning as the two men gave their attention to her. "I am sure you will find a woman who will be very happy to marry you."

It wasn't an explanation, but she hoped it helped make amends.

"I have no wish to make anyone unhappy, so you are forgiven, of course." Sir Clement had a crooked smile as he turned to Lord Dericott. "Well then, I shall go home and see what prospects I can find—a wealthy widow here or a titled spinster there."

The jest made Audrey feel a bit better—at least Sir Clement wasn't heartbroken over not getting to marry her. The knight and Lord Dericott exchanged a few more words, then Sir Clement got on his horse and rode away.

Lord Dericott motioned to Audrey. "Come. You can ride my horse back to the castle."

"I don't mind walking."

"You are riding." It was a command, not a request, so Audrey let him boost her into the saddle.

Of course, she had ridden a horse many times, and she was an accomplished rider. Lord Dericott walked alongside her, and she couldn't help wondering what had happened to Blackie.

Her heart twisted at not knowing if he was being abused

or taken care of. She could hardly bear to think about it. She imagined her horse had run away from the robbers and was being loved by a nice family.

Would Lord Dericott really tell her father that she was under his protection, letting him know he would not allow her to be sent home against her will? He could easily write to her father and tell him that he could fetch her whenever he wished. But she did not believe Lord Dericott would renege on his word. He'd been nothing but good and gracious to her. It would be easier for him just not to tell her father anything.

"Will you let my father know I am at Dericott Castle?"

"Yes. And I will tell him he must allow you to come home as you wish, when you wish it, and no sooner."

"So you believe I will decide to go home?"

Lord Dericott did not reply right away. Finally, he said, "No one will force you to leave at all. You may stay at Dericott Castle as long as you like."

"Thank you." She was not hurt by the fact that he intended for her to continue working at the castle. He could not very well have a young woman of similar rank and station staying as a guest in his home, unaccompanied by anyone.

"But we must find something for you to do besides clean bedrooms and work in the kitchens."

"Why?" Audrey gazed down at the young earl, whose manner was so subdued.

"Because you are a viscount's daughter."

"But I was a viscount's daughter before, when you allowed me to work for you."

"But I did not know you were a viscount's daughter then. And now I do. And therefore it is unseemly for you to work as a common servant."

"What if I wish to work as a common servant?"

"It will not be allowed."

Audrey tried to think of an appropriate retort. She did not like anyone telling her what she was not allowed to do. But she could hardly complain. He was protecting her, forbidding her father from forcing her to go back home. If her father filed a formal complaint against Lord Dericott, it could go badly for him, as he had so recently been in trouble with the king's court.

They traveled in silence until they came to one of Lord Dericott's guards on horseback. Lord Dericott greeted him and gave him instructions to find as many of the other guards as possible and send them home, for the lost sheep had been found.

She had caused a lot of trouble by running away. But how was she to know that Sir Clement was not coming either to take her back to her father or to force her to marry him? Still, she regretted running away.

The time passed quickly as they made their way to the castle. Lord Dericott was rather talkative. He pointed out different types of trees and flowers, and told her the names of the streams and rivers they crossed. He asked her about the kinds of trees and flowers that grew near the sea and near her home, and they even exchanged a story or two about their childhoods.

"Are you always so calm in dangerous situations?" she asked him.

"What do you mean?"

"I mean when you killed that snake. I was terrified and you simply stepped up to it and cut off its head."

"You would not have been so frightened either if you had a sword in your hand."

"Perhaps not, if I knew how to use it." She smiled at him and he smiled back.

"I have been trained to be unflinching in the face of danger. And I think it is part of my temperament to remain calm when others are afraid."

She stared hard at him, examining his expression for arrogance, but saw no hint of undue pride. He was simply stating a fact he had observed about himself.

"And I have shown that my temperament is flighty and impulsive." She knew it was true, but why had she said it out loud? Her cheeks grew warm as she felt the sting of her own indictment. She suddenly didn't like him knowing that about her.

"Impulsive? Do you regret leaving Dericott Castle?"

"I . . . well, yes. I caused a lot of trouble, and as it turned out, Sir Clement simply wanted to find me and make sure I was safe. And you had to put yourself in danger to save me from that poisonous adder. If I had stayed, all would have been well."

"But you did not know that. You thought you were protecting yourself."

He was trying to make her feel better about her foolishness. "Are you always so kind? Do you never scold your servants for wrongdoing?"

"I am a newly appointed landowner and master. I am not

accustomed to scolding anyone. Although I suppose I have scolded a few soldiers in my two years as a guard captain. Besides, you are not my servant anymore. We must find something else to occupy your time."

"Something suited for someone who is flighty and impulsive, I hope." She was teasing him while deriding herself, curious as to how he would reply.

"I would not call you flighty or impulsive. You have worked hard—Mistress Wattlesbrook has told me so. And you have other good qualities. You are ever cheerful. You have a smile that others respond to and are drawn to. Anyone might appreciate that, in a servant or a viscount's daughter."

Did he mean that? It was true she had always tried very hard to be cheerful. After all, no one wanted to be around a person who was grumpy and frowned all the time, and Audrey had always endeavored to make people like her, perhaps because she felt a lack of love, having no mother to love her, her father and sister so deficient in their esteem of her. She always considered herself rather needy and was embarrassed by it. But Lord Dericott was the first person to notice or appreciate her cheerfulness and desire to please.

Was he also in need of love and esteem? But his new wife would provide that. She hoped so anyway, for his sake.

She could think of nothing to say except, "Thank you."

Perhaps Lord Dericott liked her cheerfulness because he himself was not the most cheerful person. His usual expression was rather somber. But he seemed a man of steady character, which was part of what made her content to be at Dericott Castle.

As for what he intended for her to do now that he knew she was a viscount's daughter, she had no idea what he had in mind. Her future seemed a hazy mist, a now-familiar fog, as she wondered if she truly had a grand purpose in life and what it might be.

She only hoped her future did not involve Maris. But she had a strange feeling Maris was not done with her yet.

The next day the sun was shining and the sky was beautiful, with several shades of blue and a few woolly white clouds. Audrey was helping Joan hang the sheets on the line when Mistress Wattlesbrook came running toward her—or at least trotting, as she was a bit old and heavy for running.

"You must stop that this moment and come inside with me." Mistress Wattlesbrook spoke in a breathless voice, which didn't seem to account for how quietly she seemed to be talking.

"What can the matter be?" Audrey asked.

"Mercy!" Joan cried, grabbing the bedsheet so it would not fall on the ground and get soiled. Her eyes were wide and she looked alarmed at the sudden summons.

Mistress Wattlesbrook was motioning to Audrey with a quick jerking of her hand for her to follow.

Audrey shrugged apologetically to Joan, who lost most of the alarm from her expression and smiled. "All is well. I can take care of this. You go on ahead."

When they were inside the castle, Mistress Wattlesbrook

said to Audrey in a whisper, "You must not be hanging clothes on the line."

"Whyever not?"

"Because Lord Dericott gave me strict orders not to allow it."

"Orders? Not to allow it?" Audrey put her hands on her hips. "If I am not allowed to do my work, then just what am I supposed to do?"

"That is just it. It is not your work anymore. We shall find another serving maid in the village."

Audrey crossed her arms over her chest and huffed out a breath. "I was helping Joan. I don't want to leave her to do the task herself."

"I will send someone else to help Joan. You go and read a book or do some embroidery." Mistress Wattlesbrook smiled. "I believe the light in the library is very good this time of day."

The urge to let Mistress Wattlesbrook know that she would rather be hanging out sheets with Joan and the other laundry workers than embroidering was strong—surprising Audrey. She enjoyed talking to Joan and the other servants, doing something that wasn't solitary and isolated. But Mistress Wattlesbrook was only doing as she had been told.

Audrey remembered how kind Mistress Wattlesbrook had been to her. No good would come from spewing her frustration over not being able to do what she wanted and being told what she could and could not do. The head house servant would tell her it was because Audrey was a viscount's daughter and therefore she should not be doing such work, but what good was being a viscount's daughter if one could not do what one wanted?

Mistress Wattlesbrook was not to blame, but Lord Dericott was.

Audrey excused herself and hurried away to look for Lord Dericott. She found him in his library, the very place Mistress Wattlesbrook had encouraged her to go. She didn't want to think what that woman's motives might be.

"Lord Dericott, I don't see why I cannot hang laundry if I wish to. I must have something to do, to earn my place here."

Audrey planted her hands firmly on her hips.

He gazed up at her and grimaced. Then he took a deep breath and let it out slowly before speaking.

"I have written to your father. I told him you are under my protection and that I am treating you as a woman of your station should be treated. And I pride myself on always keeping my word. What would he think of me if he knew I was working you like a common household servant?"

Audrey sighed. "What am I supposed to do, then? I need some way of repaying you for your kindness."

"I do not require repayment. It is my privilege to show hospitality to you, as your father showed once to me."

"Once, for only one night. It is not the same. I need something to do. I do not wish to spend my time being idle and unhelpful to anyone."

"Mistress Wattlesbrook and I spoke about this. You can read and embroider. I have many books here, the best household library in four counties, and I will supply you with all you need to embroider whatever you wish."

No doubt it was a thoughtful and generous offer.

"I enjoy reading, but I wish to do more. I need a purpose."

"You may go on walks, and you may take any horse from my stable that you choose and go riding—with a guard for escort."

Now she felt like a child who needed placating. Was that how he saw her?

"I want an occupation. I am not a child."

They continued looking at each other. Perhaps Audrey was coming across as childish. Lord Dericott was an earl, a man, her protector, and for all practical purposes, her provider, but she did not know him well enough to know his thoughts.

"Forgive me." She let out a long, slow breath. "I have no right to demand anything of you."

"You are frustrated and you want a purpose. There is no reason to ask forgiveness for that."

Truly, he was being very understanding.

"Perhaps there is something you can do that is more fitting for a viscount's daughter. I will think on it and ask our priest if he has any ideas or insights. And you must ruminate on it too."

"I will. Thank you." Audrey spoke more quietly, removing her hands from her hips. "That sounds agreeable."

"What languages other than French do you know? What have you studied in your education?"

"I know German. I am able to translate and copy Bible texts from Latin to English. I studied a smattering of science, particularly botany."

"How well do you know German?"

"Well enough to speak it. But not well enough to translate more complicated or academic texts."

"Would you be willing to teach German to me? I have been

interested in learning it but did not want to trouble with engaging a tutor."

How strange that he, a man and an earl, would be willing to be taught by a woman. Her father certainly never would have been.

"I would be pleased to study German with you."

"And to speak French with me? So I do not forget it?"

"Of course." Practicing languages with Lord Dericott would not keep her occupied for many hours in the day, but it was something at least, a way to earn her keep. And the prospect of spending extra time with him was appealing on another level; she enjoyed talking to him, and she was eager to try and figure out his character. Was he as honest and good as he seemed?

Perhaps they would even become friends. There must be very few people Lord Dericott could talk to, within an easy distance of travel. His brothers were all far away, training or engaged in their duties. He was pledged to be married to the daughter of an earl, but she apparently lived too far away for him to visit often.

Audrey sat down opposite him as they started speaking in French. At first it was a little awkward, trying to think of things to say, but soon they were having a conversation about the walk they had taken together after the badger caused his horse to throw him. She even corrected him once when he used the wrong word. They only stopped talking when one of his guards came into the room to speak with him.

"I shall go." Audrey took a book off the shelf and went toward the door. As she left, she peeked over her shoulder. Lord

Dericott's eyes were trained on her, watching her leave. He quickly looked away.

It was strange, but he was the first person, man or woman, who had ever treated her as an equal. She felt a peace when she was with him. But perhaps *peace* was not the right word. She felt . . . safe. Safe to say whatever she was thinking, safe that he would not ridicule or deride her, would not criticize or look down on her. But how did she make him feel?

She liked to think that even though she had caused him some trouble, perhaps he didn't mind. Perhaps he had little to trouble or interest him. Perhaps she added a bit of color to his life.

The thought made her smile.

Eleven

Edwin was sitting in his chair the next day, gazing out the window. The sky was so overcast there was not a hint of blue anywhere. Then he thought of Audrey. She would be entering the room any moment for their meeting together with the priest.

He suddenly realized how his spirit had lifted at the thought of her, as he anticipated the moment he would see her again. How could he be thinking so much of her when he was pledged to marry Lady Ophelia? Besides, no one as full of life as Audrey could want a man as broken and morose as he was.

His heart ached, but in a pleasant way, whenever he remembered something she said or the way she smiled. She was very conscious of her scars, but they did not detract from her beauty. In fact, she seemed not to understand how lovely she was, which was even more appealing.

Engeram, the priest, entered the room. He had been at

Dericott Cathedral for less than half a year, and Edwin liked him very much. He was young, and whenever Edwin talked to him he always seemed genuinely motivated to do and say good things.

Edwin stood, and they greeted each other. Before they could finish their greetings, Audrey arrived.

"Audrey, this is the Lord's priest, Engeram, who serves our village. And this is Audrey, the daughter of Viscount Engleford."

The two exchanged nods and polite words, then they all sat down.

Engeram spoke first. "Lord Dericott asked me if I knew of something a lady with an education such as yours might do, perhaps some good work that would benefit the community. I do not know if you will wish to do it, but I have an idea."

"Thank you. I would like to hear it," Audrey said with a smile, leaning forward in her chair.

"I teach the free villagers' sons to read and write. We have three hours of lessons in the morning five days every week. If you would like, you could teach the free villagers' daughters. You could have the girls' lessons in the afternoons at the church. But I understand if you consider this task too menial for you."

"I do not consider it too menial." She shook her head. "Not menial at all. I shall start as soon as possible."

"Very well. May I ask what you plan to teach them?"

"I shall teach them reading and writing in English, and perhaps Latin as well."

Engeram raised his brows. "Would it not be more practical to teach them embroidery and sewing?"

"I believe everyone should have the opportunity to learn to

read, girls as well as boys." Her gaze into the priest's eyes was unwavering.

Engeram fidgeted and glanced away. "Oh, well . . . hmm," he stammered.

"But I do have one more request. I would like to invite all the girls of the area to come to my lessons, even the ones whose parents are not free." She looked him straight in the eye.

"What do you mean? The villeins' girl children? You want to teach them to read?"

"Yes. It is my wish." She smiled as if she did not know what she was asking was strange.

Engeram looked at Edwin. His eyes seemed to beg for help.

"I see no reason why she cannot teach the villeins' children as well as the free men's."

Engeram stared at the floor, then took a long, deep breath and let it out. "Very well. If that is what you both wish." He looked slightly bewildered.

Audrey's smile was brighter than Edwin had ever seen it. "When may I start?"

Audrey hurried to the church and the room where her lessons would take place. Her walk took her down the lane from Dericott Castle, past a small forest, past fields and meadows, to the road that led to the village at the bottom of the hill.

She couldn't stop thinking about Helena, the only person she had ever taught, now that she was going to be teaching more girls. And how amazing that she would be getting to do what she had often imagined doing—teaching girls to read! And she had not even had to be married to someone powerful to do it. Lord Dericott and the priest, Engeram, had been God's instruments in making it happen, for indeed it seemed like a miracle from heaven.

As she was entering the village, she turned to look back at Dericott Castle. The enormous castle was an imposing sight sitting at the top of the hill, the entire stone structure just visible from where she stood. She could see the seven defensive towers, some round and some square, of various sizes, with a ring of crenellations around the top of each. The large square keep in the middle, with the rest of the stone castle connected to it, was where her bedchamber was located, along with Lord Dericott's, though she was not certain which chamber was his.

On her way through the village, the people she passed all stopped what they were doing to stare at her. Their stares made her pull at her hair to make sure it was covering her scars. Did they know about her scars? Were they staring because they'd heard about her? She should not assume the worst. Probably they were only staring because they were not accustomed to seeing strangers in their tiny village.

Still, they did not seem like other villagers she'd encountered on her way here. The Dericott people seemed happier, less fearful somehow. There was an air about them that conjured up one word—*hope*. Was it because, as she'd heard, Lord Dericott had given them a year of Jubilee from their obligations to their lord? Truly, it was a very generous thing he had done for the poorest of the poor. Was that not what Jesus had taught His disciples, to care for the poor? She felt as if, knowing Lord Dericott and seeing the fruit of his actions, she was witnessing something extraordinary, much like her miracle of getting the opportunity to teach.

She made it through the length of the village and came to the church, which stood down a lane a bit, away from the rest of the town.

She could hardly wait to meet her students. Engeram had only six boys who came consistently, but Audrey was hoping for more.

Engeram had been spreading the word about her lessons, offered to any girl seven and older, to learn reading and writing. Was this the fulfillment of her dream? Was this what would make her life a bright light in the world?

The children began arriving an hour early. Engeram tried to shoo them away, but Audrey protested. "Let them stay. It's all right."

Audrey gathered them in and played a game with them that Sybil had taught her when she was little.

There were ten of them, all wide-eyed and mostly quiet. The youngest was seven and the oldest fifteen. And when Audrey got them all seated and started teaching them the letters, she realized it would be a lot harder to teach ten children of such wide-ranging ages than it was to teach Helena alone, especially since Helena already knew some of the alphabet and how to read a few words.

No matter. They were all looking at her with respect and

eagerness, or at least with openness, so she was certain she could teach them. It was only a matter of time.

But besides wanting to see them read, something else tugged at her heart yet more—were they being treated well at home? Was someone hugging them every day? Providing them with enough food?

Audrey wanted to get to know each one and to know just what each of them needed. They were her students, and she felt a responsibility for them that she'd never felt for anyone before. And she already loved them. It didn't matter that she was just learning their names and knew very little about them; they were her students, they had come to her with humble hearts ready to learn, and she loved them on sight.

A few days later, Audrey and two of Lord Dericott's male servants carried baskets through the village to the church. Audrey couldn't help smiling as her students greeted her in front of the church door.

"What do you have for us, Mistress Audrey?" Lucinda, the youngest, was jumping up and down.

"Something I think you will like!"

The men set down the baskets and left. Audrey pulled back the cloth covering on one of them.

"Sweets!" Audrey handed out the sweet cakes, filled with apples and raisins and nuts, to the children.

Lucinda's eyes and smile were as big as the sky. All the girls

155

took a cake and ate it quickly, making delighted sounds of *mm* and sighing.

When they were all done and were talking of how delicious the cakes were, Audrey gave them each a little wedge of cheese and a roll of bread. They ate that as eagerly as they had eaten the cakes. Audrey felt her suspicions confirmed; these children either were not getting enough food, or the food they were getting was not very filling or tasty.

It took a bit longer than usual to get the children settled into a state where they were able to do their lessons, but they seemed to learn more than any day previous. Some of them were reading their first words by the end of the day.

When she announced it was time for them to go, three of the girls came up to her, doe-eyed and hesitating. Audrey instinctively knew what they wanted. She knelt down and put her arms around the closest one and squeezed her tight, feeling the child's little hands around her neck. She was smiling when she pulled away. Then one by one, the rest of them came and embraced their teacher, smiling and giggling.

"Thank you, Mistress Audrey," they said.

"You are most welcome. Now run home and I will see you tomorrow."

Audrey watched them go skipping away and tears filled her eyes. Was this how God felt when she came to Him and thanked Him for something He had done for her? "Thank You, God," she whispered. "Thank You."

Edwin watched Audrey, lighting the entire room with her smile, as she entered the library.

"Thank you for the food for the children. I wish you could have seen them." Audrey's voice was alive with fervency. A tiny sliver of her scar was visible, but she seemed not to realize it and did not pull at her hair to cover it. Somehow it made her even more endearing.

"They ate their cakes and cheese like they were the best things they'd ever tasted. I wish you had been there," she repeated.

"I am glad you had the idea. They probably learn better when they are not hungry."

"I believe that is true. They did seem to catch on to the lessons faster today. One little girl said, 'This cake tastes like manna from heaven.' She must have heard the story from the Bible about manna falling from heaven."

Edwin smiled at the way Audrey clasped her hands in delight. How unusual she was, to get so much pleasure from these villein children. Truly, he had never met anyone like this viscount's daughter.

"A group of Miracle Players were here last summer who acted out the story of Moses, and they demonstrated the manna from heaven as being like little cakes."

"Will you allow me to feed the children every day of our lessons?"

Edwin could imagine how his father would have reacted to this request. He'd once heard his father say that he fed the poor on holidays, and that if he fed them every day they would grow fat and lazy. He was not a ruthless man, but he was also not the most charitable. He certainly did not believe in thinking of villeins as equal with himself.

Once one of Edwin's brothers asked their father about the verse in the Bible that says God is no respecter of persons and that we should not treat a well-dressed man with more deference than a poorly dressed man.

Edwin's father had said, "Should we treat our servants and villeins as if they were dukes and bishops? Don't be absurd. That is . . . Well, it is treason, encouraging rebellion."

But Edwin was his own man. He could decide what to do, and the Holy Writ had a lot to say about never treating one's workers unjustly, never withholding wages, and showing kindness and mercy to the poor.

"Yes, you may feed them every day if you like. If Cook needs more servants, tell her she may hire another kitchen servant from the village."

"Thank you. That is very generous, and I am so grateful." Without pausing, she said, "I was also wondering if you had any books you would allow me to use to teach them. I noticed you have a copy of the Holy Writ in English. I can make copies of a chapter or two, if you have no objections."

"Of course. I will supply you with materials. But why not allow me to hire a scribe to make copies for you? Which books would you prefer to have?"

Audrey's eyes went wide. "Oh, thank you! That is wonderful. Let me think." She tapped her finger against her chin. "The Psalms would be good. But I think a story would be better. The Gospels have a lot of stories in them, stories about Jesus, but also parables." She paused a moment. "I believe the book of Luke would be best for the children to learn. It is written in a straight-forward way that will be easier for them to understand."

"Very well. I shall have copies made."

"Thank you. I am so grateful." Audrey clasped her hands in front of her chest again. The look in her eyes made his chest ache. "But I know the copies will take time, so if you could have them copy a few chapters at a time so that we can get them more quickly . . ."

"Of course. I shall find the scribes and it shall be done as soon as possible." At that moment he would have promised her anything.

"Thank you." Her face brightened again, her smile as wide as he'd ever seen it. "The children are so fortunate to have such a benefactor as you."

"And to have such a teacher as you."

She stared into his eyes from where she stood a few feet away. But then she blinked, lowered her gaze, and pulled on her hair, patting it down over her scars, as if she suddenly realized they had been showing.

"I shall go now," she said. "But . . . I know you said you would have some scribes copy the chapters from Luke, but I would like to copy something very short, if that is all right."

"Of course. Shall I send writing materials to your room?"

"Oh yes, thank you."

"And you may take the Bible that is there, on the shelf." He pointed.

"Will you not need it?"

"I have my own, and the scribes at the monastery will have one as well."

"Oh yes. Of course. Thank you again."

She hurried away, leaving Edwin with an odd ache in his chest. Something in her seemed to reach out and wrap around his heart, squeezing it. He longed to see her smile, and to know that her smile was for him.

But he was to marry Lady Ophelia. He could not think of Audrey in that way. Even though she had scars just as he did, scars that made her self-conscious, she was beautiful and a viscount's daughter. Someday she would marry.

Before he lost his arm, he'd been considered handsome, or so he'd been told by a few women, including the Duchess of Wymanton, whose flirtatious conversation had made him uncomfortable, especially since the Duke of Wymanton was only a few feet away, drinking and laughing with the sheriff of the county and the king's coroner. But he was well aware that most women would not view him now as they had before. Lady Ophelia might not either. But he would not imagine she would prove disloyal to him when so far he had little to no reason to think she would be, even if she still had not replied to his letters.

A good woman would not care as much about physical appearance as she did about character and kindness.

Perhaps Lady Ophelia was that good woman, and perhaps she was not. Perhaps instead of praying that Lady Ophelia would still want him, he should be praying for what was best. And only God knew that.

TWELVE

AUDREY CARRIED IN HER ARMS TEN COPIES OF THE FIRST five chapters of the Gospel According to Saint Luke as she walked to the church for the children's lessons. She was still amazed at how quickly Lord Dericott had produced the ten copies. She suspected he himself had copied one of them.

Once, she had walked into the library to ask him a question about the repast he provided for the children, and she had found him hunched over his desk with a pen in his hand. When he looked up, he bumped his inkwell, getting a splotch of ink on the paper. And now she saw an identical ink splotch on the edge of one of the pages.

She touched it reverently, running her fingers over the words and imagining him writing them with his own hand. How her heart expanded at the thought of Lord Dericott . . . Edwin. She allowed herself to call him Edwin sometimes, but only silently in her mind when she was going over their conversations in her head. Her heart grew inside her at the thought of him transcribing these holy words for her students to learn by. Who was he doing it for more? For her students? Or for her?

She was a foolish girl to think of him thusly. Indeed, it was wrong, since he was pledged to marry Lady Ophelia.

Tears stung her eyes. But that was ignoble of her. She should be happy for him, happy that he had made a love match, for she had heard that they had met at a ball and fallen in love. He was a wealthy lord, a powerful though young man, who enjoyed the king's favor and attention since proving his enemies to be the evil schemers they were. Yes, she knew he felt bad about losing his arm. She believed she could see it in his expression, in his eyes. Anyone would mourn such a loss and even be angry about it. But any woman would be fortunate indeed to marry him.

She felt a stab in her stomach at the thought that she would never marry Edwin, the young man whom her father had hoped to engage her to. It was wrong, though, to even think about such a thing. Lord Dericott had been so kind and generous to her, and she should pray for every blessing to be showered on him, including a happy marriage with someone who was his equal.

She was walking through the village when one of the girls asked excitedly, "What have you brought for us today?"

Several of her students greeted her before she could even enter the church. The servants carrying the baskets came into the schoolroom behind her and left the baskets on the table.

"Something delicious! Cherry pasties made with fresh cherries from Lord Dericott's own trees."

The girls gasped and "oohed" at this.

"And some cold pork with plum sauce and fresh bread."

The number of students had grown, and Audrey was fairly certain it was due more to the food than to her lessons and the enticement of learning to read. But she did not have the heart to tell Lord Dericott that she now needed more than ten copies of text. Rather, she would let the students pair up and study them together, as that seemed to help them learn faster anyway, one part friendly competition and one part helping one another. Most were already reading a few words, and the others were catching on to it a little more every day.

Today, near the end of her lesson, she glanced up to see Lord Dericott in the doorway, watching.

Her stomach fluttered as their eyes met and held. But she kept teaching, kneeling down to help two little girls who were sitting together on a low bench. When she looked up a few minutes later, Lord Dericott was gone.

The air went out of her. She refused to think about why she had felt so disappointed that he had not stayed until it was time for the children to go home.

"Thank you for teaching us." Rebecca, the fifteen-year-old, smiled shyly. "And please tell Lord Dericott we are grateful."

Audrey had made sure to tell the children that Lord Dericott was the one to thank for the food and texts from the Holy Writ, as well as the slates and soapstone they used for writing.

"You can tell him yourself, if he is still nearby."

"Oh no." Rebecca shook her head vigorously. "I could never speak to Lord Dericott."

"Whyever not?"

"He is the lord of this land. He is the Earl of Dericott." Her eyes were big and round, as if she could not fathom how Audrey could not understand that she could never talk to Lord Dericott.

"He will not frighten or harm you." But she understood. She'd probably feel the same if she ever had to speak to King Richard.

Nevertheless, Edwin—Lord Dericott—had such a gentle way about him, such a calmness in his demeanor. She couldn't imagine being frightened to talk to him. But she also knew how her father treated his villeins. He ignored them. If one were to fall across his path he'd probably either step on them or kick them. They might not be wealthy or know how to read, but they were humans, and Audrey had learned from reading the Holy Writ, both with her tutor and by herself, that Jesus did not treat people badly, no matter if they were rich or poor. And if the Son of God did not treat them badly, what right had any man or woman to do so, whether they be princes, earls, or viscounts' daughters?

The older girls helped Audrey roll up the Saint Luke parchments, and Audrey placed them in the empty baskets and hung them on her arms, as she normally did, and left from the back door of the church, out of the room they used for their lessons.

Standing under a tree was Lord Dericott, talking with her youngest students, Lucinda and Larissa.

"How did you lose it?" Lucinda was saying, staring wide-eyed at Lord Dericott's left shoulder where his arm should have been.

Audrey held her breath. Would Lord Dericott realize she was only an innocent child and did not mean any harm?

"My brothers and I were fighting with some soldiers and a soldier hit my arm with his sword."

"He cut off your arm?" Lucinda's eyes went even wider, if that were possible, her mouth a big O.

"Nearly. A surgeon had to take it the rest of the way off." Lord Dericott's tone was as matter-of-fact as if he were speaking about the state of the roads with one of his guards.

Lord Dericott turned to her as she approached. "Your delightful students have just been telling me what a great teacher you are."

Audrey felt her cheeks growing warm. If Lord Dericott was not accustomed to being around children, he might think they were being impertinent. But at least he was smiling.

"They are easy to teach, as they are eager to learn."

The children scattered, but some of them stopped several feet away and watched them.

"May I take your burden?" He stared at the baskets on her arms.

"Oh no, no." Her cheeks started to burn. It would be too unseemly for him, an earl, to carry baskets. And the fact that he only had one arm . . . Her face was positively in flames now.

Thankfully a guard was nearby, no doubt watching over Lord Dericott, and he strode forward and took her baskets from her without asking.

"I hope you don't mind if Daniel and I escort you home."

"No, of course not." Audrey's heart stuttered as they started walking toward the castle.

Audrey was careful not to walk too close to her lord. After

all, he was her benefactor as well as the children's. Probably he only wanted to see how his resources were being used.

"What do you think of the work you and Engeram have me doing? Is it a worthy endeavor?" Certainly no other noblemen she knew of would be pleased to spend their money on feeding and teaching poor girls from his demesne.

"I am pleased that you and I can do something for the poor. I am glad that you seem to be enjoying your work with the children, and that you are no longer working as a house servant—"

Audrey laughed at this.

"And that the children look so happy."

"I have always known how to read, since I was very young, as I learned from my older sister's tutor when Sybil—that is my nurse—said I was too young. Apparently I sneaked into the schoolroom and the tutor allowed me to stay. But it is hard to imagine not knowing how to read and write and add and subtract. I think it will give the girls a sense of confidence, and that will be good for everyone in the village."

"Confidence is a valuable character trait." Lord Dericott was nodding his head and staring at the ground.

Audrey stared sideways at him. Was he sincere?

"I like that you mention confidence. It is different from arrogance and pride, which inflates a person's view of themselves and makes them difficult to work with. But confidence is the very thing needed to accomplish any task. If a young squire has no confidence, he cannot succeed in training to be a knight. He cannot even raise his sword to fight. And the more confidence he gains, the more able he is to learn and the better he becomes. If he can stay humble rather than becoming prideful, then his confidence will increase and he can accomplish more and more."

"That sounds wise." She would have to ponder this, but it sounded quite true.

"I think that applies to others as well. If these girls have confidence in their abilities, they can do many more things."

She seemed to recall something in the Holy Writ about confidence, being confident in God and something about being bold.

And there was the part that said, "I can do all things through Christ who strengthens me." That certainly seemed like an expression of confidence in Jesus as well as oneself.

"I do care for my people," he said quietly. "It is not a very popular sentiment among lords, but I believe if I don't care for them, I am worse than an unbeliever in God's eyes."

He was correct; it was not a popular sentiment. As evidenced by the response to the Great Uprising, or Wat Tyler's Rebellion as it was also known, the lords of the land believed they had been given the right to own other people by God, that God had established them as wealthy lords and noblemen, and therefore their villeins, who had been born into poverty, were ordained by God to serve them. And they did not feel any obligation to care for those serving them in any compassionate way.

God judges the heart. Audrey seemed to recall reading that in the Holy Writ as well.

Audrey had never been able to see herself, in her mind's eye, being married to Sir Clement. But as similarly as she and Edwin seemed to think . . . The idea suddenly jumped into her mind of

Lord Dericott and Audrey living happily together as man and wife.

She thrust the thought just as quickly from her mind.

They walked the rest of the way to the castle, only speaking about the trees and commenting on the kinds of animals that lived in the forest, as they were near enough to his guard that he could hear their conversation. The guard still carried the baskets—rather stiffly and silently—now that they had passed through the village.

"I do like discovering new things about animals, learning how they behave," Audrey said. "I once watched a pair of beautiful blue kingfishers all summer. I knew where their nest was in the side of a riverbank, and I watched them catch fish and feed their babies."

"That sounds very interesting."

"Very! I could watch them swoop into the water and catch tiny fish. And they raised three sets of babies in that one summer."

"It sounds like you enjoyed that. I know of a stork's nest nearby, if you'd like to see it."

"Oh, I would love to. I have never seen a stork's nest. It must be enormous."

"It is very large. I will take you there sometime. Whenever you like."

"Thank you. I would like that."

They were walking across the castle courtyard when Audrey caught sight of a courier riding toward them wearing the colors of a nobleman. Lord Dericott saw him too, and nodded to Audrey. "Good day." Then he turned to meet the courier.

"Good day." Audrey was becoming accustomed to Lord Dericott's abrupt leave-taking. She would almost think she made him nervous. Or perhaps it was the courier who made him anxious, delivering an important letter he'd been waiting for.

Audrey took the baskets from the guard and went inside.

"Did the children like the food?" Mistress Wattlesbrook was standing in the corridor near the door.

"Yes, they did, I thank you. I shall go and tell Cook how much they enjoyed it."

"Did Lord Dericott walk with you all the way from the village?"

"He did. I think he wished to see the students he has been so generous with."

"The students. Hmm, yes." Mistress Wattlesbrook smiled but looked away, not meeting Audrey's gaze.

Did Mistress Wattlesbrook think Lord Dericott had other motives for walking to the church? But she had not seen the abrupt way he had taken his leave of her when they arrived home. And Mistress Wattlesbrook must know that he was to marry Lady Ophelia.

Audrey hurried away to return the baskets to the kitchen.

Edwin's heart jumped into his throat when he saw the courier riding up the lane wearing the colors of Lord Essex. The man dismounted and held out a rolled piece of parchment. "For Lord Dericott," he said.

Edwin took it, recognizing the seal and colored ribbons as also belonging to the Earl of Essex, then carried it with him to his library. He broke open the seal and unrolled the parchment.

A word jumped out at him. *Regret.*

He blinked and forced himself to focus on the letter and read the rest of the words.

> It is with utmost respect and regret that I write to thank you for your interest in marrying my daughter. I must inform you that Lady Ophelia has married the Earl of Cavendish's son Robert on Saturday last.
>
> Yours Respectfully,
> Essex

He was not surprised, but a pain shot through his chest anyway and his face burned. Of course a beautiful young woman such as Lady Ophelia would not want to be married to Edwin now that he had only one arm.

The only thing that had changed was that he was misshapen. Crippled. Lame.

But there was also the fact of his family's being falsely accused of treason and the time it had taken to prove they were innocent. Perhaps she did not wish to attach herself to his family's scandal.

In the end, not even his title of Earl of Dericott, nor his wealth and current good standing with the king, had been enough to induce her to marry him. Had she ever felt any love for him at all? The rejection was like a fist to the stomach.

No doubt this Earl of Cavendish's son had all four limbs intact. No doubt he was strong and capable of holding his wife in both arms.

He knew very little about her, truthfully. Perhaps it was for the best. Perhaps she would not have made a good wife.

Edwin wadded the parchment in his fist.

At least now he could allow himself to think the thoughts that came to mind when he was with Audrey, the thoughts that made him be so abrupt with her when he was feeling as if he was betraying Lady Ophelia. Now he was free to think . . . and pursue.

But would she reject him as Lady Ophelia had?

Audrey walked the next day to the church for the girls' lessons. The guards were carrying the baskets of food for her, as usual, when she caught a glimpse of a blonde woman in the village who looked like Maris.

Audrey slowed down and stared at the woman, who turned and walked in the opposite direction and disappeared around the side of the baker's shop.

Audrey felt sick down deep in her middle. The woman couldn't be Maris, could she? But Lord Dericott did say he would tell her father that she was at Dericott Castle. Had her father told Maris? He would not do that, would he? But Maris could be very persuasive. Or perhaps *calculating* and *manipulative* were better words.

Audrey's heart beat erratically as she thought about Maris coming here to do some terrible mischief to her.

She glanced to her right and her left at the tall, strong guards carrying her baskets. They would never let anyone hurt her. But they would leave her at the church for her lessons. Would Lord Dericott come back to escort her home as he had done the day before?

No, she would not allow herself to fret and worry. And besides, she had only imagined she saw Maris.

When she reached the schoolroom, Engeram was there, as he sometimes was, after the end of his lesson with the boys of the village. The guards set down the baskets and turned to leave. She opened her mouth to call them back, but she stopped herself. She was being childish. But the uneasy feeling in her chest grew heavier as she watched them walk out the door.

"Is anything amiss?" Engeram's brows drew together in a look of concern.

"No, no. All is well." She would have to explain about her sister, and that would take entirely too long.

The children began to arrive and Audrey barely noticed when Engeram left. She shared the contents of the baskets with the children, who delighted in the food as always. Lessons went better than ever, as the girls were learning and discovering more words.

By the end of the day, Audrey's head ached, as it sometimes did when she was tired. She glanced at the empty doorway, but Lord Dericott was not there. Her heart sank a little.

She gathered up her rolls of parchment and walked to the

door. It was only her foolish imaginings that made her wonder if Maris would be standing outside waiting for her. And just as foolish to wish Lord Dericott was there to walk her home.

Audrey stepped out and looked all around. A man was walking down the road at the end of the little lane leading up to the church. No one else was in sight. Her breaths seemed to come faster and the hair on her arms stood up.

She tried to breathe normally and shook her head. She needed to stop worrying about her sister. It had been four years since Maris had tripped her and caused her to fall into the fire. Audrey was safe now.

The lane was flanked by thick forest growth on the right side and a sheep-grazing meadow on the left. Audrey looked for the sheep and their shepherds, but the pasture was empty today.

A rustling sound came from the forest, but farther ahead where she could not see. She walked at a steady but measured pace. Then the woman she'd seen earlier stepped out of the trees and into the lane ahead of her.

Audrey screamed. It was Maris.

THIRTEEN

AUDREY'S HEART POUNDED AS SHE HELD ON TO THE rolled-up texts in her arms.

Maris sneered at her, and Audrey was ashamed of her scream, but it was all she could do to keep from screaming again. Maris was here. In front of her. With her lips curled in contempt. Just like the night she sent her into the fire.

"What are you doing here?"

Maris narrowed her eyes. "I was worried about my little sister."

"I am well."

"Oh yes, so I have heard. You and the young earl are quite comfortable and cozy together. All of the villagers are talking about it, how you came and now their lord is more cheerful and walks among them, sometimes even escorting the viscount's daughter home from her dubious occupation of teaching the village girls to read."

Audrey held the texts close to her chest as she stared hard at Maris, a few feet away.

"What do you want?" Audrey's thoughts were racing. If she ran across the meadow, would Maris catch up to her? She might have to throw down the parchment texts, but Lord Dericott would understand.

Or if she waited long enough, would Lord Dericott or Mistress Wattlesbrook send someone to look for her?

No, she must not allow Maris to make her a coward. She would not show fear. And she was more embarrassed than ever that she had screamed when she saw her sister.

"What do you want?" Audrey repeated when Maris did not answer.

"I want you to be as miserable as you have made me." Maris scowled, her face like a dark mask.

"I have not done anything to you."

"Because of you, Father won't allow me to marry. You're the reason he hates me. He always loved you more."

"That's not true. Father doesn't hate you, and if he did, it wouldn't be because of me."

"You're just so perfect, with your perfect little smile—always smiling at everyone, fooling them into thinking you're Father's meek little pet. Father always loved you and hated me, even though you're the reason Mother is dead."

"That's not true." Audrey's breaths were coming fast. Everything Maris said was a lie, but the accusation that she caused their mother's death felt like a knife stabbing straight into her heart. The guilt had weighed her down all her life, even though she tried to ignore it and tell herself it wasn't her fault.

"You have ruined my life. Now Father won't let me marry.

And you're going to marry an earl? No!" Maris took a step toward her, baring her teeth like an animal.

Audrey stepped back. There was no reasoning with Maris. She was not a rational person. But she couldn't help trying.

"I am sorry you feel slighted by Father, Maris. But I would never hurt you, and I don't believe Father wishes to hurt you. And as for me marrying Lord Dericott, nothing could be further from the truth. He is pledged to marry an earl's daughter, Lady Ophelia."

"Then come home with me, to Engleford Castle."

"Why?"

"Let us just say that I miss my sister and I want you to return home. And if you do not . . ." Maris's grin turned into a hard line. "I will cause great pain to every person you love, including that poor girl you made friends with, Helena, and your substitute mother, Sybil, and your new love, Lord Dericott."

Audrey felt sick. Surely Maris would not hurt them. She did not have that kind of power. She was only trying to scare her.

"You can't hurt anyone." Audrey's words were bolder than her voice, which sounded breathless. *God, help me.*

Maris tilted her head defiantly. "I lied to Father and said Sybil stole from me, and he sent her away. She's been gone a week now."

Sent away where? Sybil had no family. Audrey was her family.

"And I have someone helping me."

A crashing sound came from the bushes and trees just off the road, then a man, huge and hulking, came stomping out onto the lane.

"This is my new friend, Umfrey," Maris said, watching Audrey. "Umfrey, this is my sister, Audrey."

The hulking man, with a face twice the size of an ordinary man's, started toward Audrey.

"Not yet, Umfrey."

The man stopped and took a step back.

Audrey's knees felt weak. She needed to get to Dericott Castle to warn Lord Dericott's guards. If Umfrey got past them, Lord Dericott would be at the mercy of this giant.

She glanced toward the castle.

"Lord Dericott will not be coming here to see you, though I would not mind seeing him again. I remember him being very handsome. He is busy with something, a little distraction Umfrey and I came up with for him."

"What did you do? Lord Dericott does not deserve your cruelty. He is a good man, and he is not in love with me. He is in love with Lady Ophelia." The words hurt deep in her chest as she said them, but she had to protect Lord Dericott the best she could. She couldn't bear to be the cause of harm coming to him.

"That is sad, if you are in love with him."

"What did you do?" Heat rose inside her as Audrey clenched her teeth. If Maris had hurt Lord Dericott, she would never forgive herself for putting him in danger. Was she destined to cause trouble and pain for the people who loved her because of her sister's jealousy?

"Come home with me and you won't have to worry." Maris lowered her head and gazed at Audrey, her eyelids heavy. "No one has to die."

Audrey could not stand there and let her sister taunt and threaten her with the giant ogre, as if they were in a child's cautionary tale. And if Maris wouldn't tell her what they had done, Audrey would have to go and find out.

She let the parchment texts fall from her arms as she set out at a dead run. She ran, tucking her skirt into her belt just high enough that it wouldn't entangle her legs. She could hear Umfrey's giant footfalls on the hard-packed dirt behind her as she turned onto the road that led through the village and up to the castle.

Then she saw the smoke rising.

Edwin heard the yells and was on his feet before the guard entered his library.

"Fire! Behind the stables."

Edwin followed him outside and across the courtyard.

Dark smoke boiled up from behind the wooden stable. Horses were whinnying as they were being led out, while other men were running with buckets of water and disappearing around the back.

Edwin would be only half a man's help if he tried to carry water, so he ran into the stable.

He could barely see, it was so dark inside. The fire apparently had not yet broken through the wall. He hurried to find the nearest pawing, stomping horse. He grabbed a bridle and slipped it over the horse's neck, securing it and leading the horse outside. He tied its bridle to a hitching post that already had several horses tied to it, then hurried back in.

The stable was even hotter than before, and he could hear the flames licking at the wood.

"If the flames break through," Edwin shouted to the grooms, "just open their stalls and let them run for it!"

He hoped it wouldn't come to that, because some of these horses would likely be confused and get trapped. Others would be difficult to catch and might be stolen or lost.

Edwin and the grooms rushed to get the rest of the horses out. When the last horse was safe, he ran to the other side of the stable and saw that a large section of the outside wall was smoking, but the fire was out.

Blackened wood was scattered over the scorched ground. The fire had come very close to burning through in one spot. If the fire had taken a better hold, the stable would have burned to the ground.

His men were panting and sweating. The last two arriving with full buckets doused the smoking wood one last time.

"Good work, men. How did this happen?"

Several men started talking at once. All hushed but one of his older guards.

"Somebody piled some dry branches against the wall of the stable and set them on fire, or so it appeared."

"Did anyone see who did it?"

The men all shook their heads.

"Did you see anyone acting suspicious?"

"I saw a woman with blonde hair earlier this morning," one

man said. "I thought it was the viscount's daughter, but I wasn't sure. She was sneaking around in the tree line, looking at the castle. I only saw her for a moment, and then she was gone."

A strange feeling went through him that Audrey was in danger. He had an inexplicable urge to go find her and make sure she was safe. He glanced at the sun's position in the sky. Her lessons should be over now and she should be coming back to the castle.

He pointed to one of the guards. "Come with me."

Edwin led the guard toward the village. He was walking as fast as he could without risking losing his balance. But he'd already been moving faster than he would have been capable of a week ago. Every day he was getting stronger. And he had a feeling the future held the kind of trouble he would need his strength for.

On the road ahead he saw Audrey. She was running toward him with her skirt tucked up. She'd lost her head covering and her hair was flying back away from her face, running as if someone was chasing her.

His hand clenched into a fist. He suddenly knew he'd do anything—anything—to protect her.

Audrey glanced over her shoulder. Umfrey was falling farther behind, obviously laboring to breathe. Maris was hanging back, standing and watching.

Audrey kept running, more because she wanted to know if

Lord Dericott was safe than because she was scared for herself. And there he was, rounding a bend in the road, coming toward her.

There was soot on his face and streaking the face of the guard beside him. But at least he did not look injured.

As she ran she wondered what she would tell him. Why couldn't Maris give up trying to hurt her? And now that Maris suspected an affection between her and Lord Dericott, she would try to hurt Edwin as well.

Should she tell Lord Dericott she no longer wished for his protection and leave immediately to search for a new place to settle? That was the only way she could protect Lord Dericott. He wasn't safe as long as Maris was coming after Audrey. But what would she tell him? He would be upon her in a moment.

Tell the truth.

Of course God would want her to tell the truth. But what if the truth got Lord Dericott killed?

Tell him the truth.

Audrey remembered the story of Shadrach, Meshach, and Abednego. What was it they had told the king? That God was able to deliver them, and He would deliver them, but even if He did not, they would not bow to the king's golden statue.

Audrey would not bow to Maris and her schemes, even though it made her hands tremble and her knees weak.

When they were close enough, Lord Dericott shouted, "Are you all right?"

Audrey slowed to a stop and bent over, trying to catch her breath. "My sister."

"She's here?"

Audrey nodded. "She's behind me."

"Let us go confront her." Lord Dericott started to walk past her.

"No!" Audrey caught his arm. "Send for more men . . . before you talk to her." She was still gasping, still trying to catch her breath.

Lord Dericott looked confused.

"She has a giant with her."

"A giant?"

"A very large man. He is frightening, believe me."

"Golding is with us. He has his sword."

Audrey was doubtful even a trained guard with a sword could defeat Umfrey in a fight, but she did not want to insult Lord Dericott or his guard.

"Maris is very wily. You never know what she might do. What did she set fire to?"

"How did you know about that?" Lord Dericott asked.

Golding looked sharply at her.

"Maris said she had created a distraction. And you both have ashes on your faces."

"She set fire to some wood and tried to burn down the stables."

"She wanted to make sure you did not come to escort me back to the castle after the children's lessons. She wanted to force me into going back home with her."

Lord Dericott raised his eyebrows. "So that's why she did it."

"Was anyone hurt? The horses?"

"All is well. My men put out the fire before it burned through the wall."

"Thank God."

"Come. Let us find this sister of yours and her giant servant."

Audrey went with them. "Please be on your guard and do not turn your back on her. She is capable of anything."

"Trying to burn my horses in their stable, and for what she did to you, I verily believe you." Lord Dericott spoke quietly and with a serious tone.

As they walked back toward the church, everyone was sober. Some villagers stopped and stared curiously as they walked by, but no one spoke. Finally, when they reached the lane to the church, Lord Dericott stopped and squatted, looking down at the ground.

"This must be the giant's footprint." He pointed it out as his guard leaned down.

"And that is the sister's." Golding gestured toward the small footprint beside it.

"Where did they go?"

Golding followed the footprints while Lord Dericott stood and scanned the area. But Audrey saw no sign of them.

After losing their trail in the trees, Golding and Lord Dericott went into the village and asked some of the people standing about if they had seen a young blonde woman and a very large, strange man. Several said they had, but they did not know where they had gone.

When they had given up on finding them, they went to find the parchment texts Audrey had dropped.

"Forgive me for dropping them in the dirt," Audrey said.

"No harm seems to have come to them," Lord Dericott said, picking them up and holding them in his huge hand without crushing them. "It was more important for you to survive than the parchments. Your students could get new texts for their lessons, but they could not get another teacher such as you."

Audrey felt herself blushing. But perhaps he only meant that no one else in the area knew how to read or was willing to teach girls.

"You have not said what your sister—Maris, is it?"

"Yes."

"What she said to you?"

"She said if I didn't go home with her that she would do something to harm my old nurse, Sybil, my friend Helena, and . . . you."

"Me? Why me?"

"She does not want me to be happy, and she had surmised . . . Or the villagers were saying . . ." This was harder to say than she had imagined.

Lord Dericott and Golding were staring at her. Golding seemed to sense she was having a difficult time and he turned, walking a few feet away.

Audrey spoke very quietly. "Maris seems to think you and I have . . . tender feelings for each other and that we may get married. But I don't know why she would think that."

Her cheeks burned. Should she laugh and pretend to think it was humorous? Her face was on fire now, but she had no choice other than to finish her explanation.

"I told her that you are engaged to marry Lady Ophelia, but she thinks she can hurt me by separating me from you. And if I will not leave with her, she will hurt me by harming you and the people I love, Sybil and Helena."

"I see." Lord Dericott nodded. He opened his mouth as if he had something to tell her, not quite looking her in the eye, but then he seemed to change his mind and pressed his lips together. Finally, he said, "We should get out of the middle of the road. Come."

They started walking toward the castle.

What was going through his head? Did he realize Maris was right about her having tender feelings for him, or at least the beginnings thereof? It was so humiliating, since he was planning to marry an earl's daughter. He could not care for her in that way.

The situation was more painful than she'd realized. She'd made sure not to fall in love with him so that she could protect herself from the pain of rejection. But now he probably was as embarrassed for her as she was for herself. After all, he'd just seen her running as fast as she could down the road with her hair blown back, exposing her scars.

She'd snatched up her head scarf and pulled her hair down over her scarred ear, but not before he and Golding had seen it. Was there a nobleman in the world who would want to marry her? She was under no delusion that he would.

Perhaps he thought nothing of Maris's assumption. She had not confessed any love for him. Maris had only assumed that. But that was only her desperately wishing it to be so.

Once they reached the castle, they went into his library and he shut the door behind them. They sat, and he continued their conversation.

"Your sister is quite malicious. But I pray you not to believe her capable of harming me. I can take care of myself, and I have many trained guards. But you must always take a guard with you from now on when you go to your lessons, lest she try to take you by force. Unless you wish to go home?"

"No! That is the last thing I would wish. I am happy here at Dericott Castle. Everyone is very good to me, and I love teaching my girls and don't want to leave them. But I also don't wish to cause you any more trouble. Maris already tried to burn your stables. There is no knowing what she might attempt next." Her heart seemed to weigh a hundred pounds.

"You needn't worry about me. But you are probably worried about this Sybil and Helena, are you not?"

"Yes. I can't possibly protect them."

"As long as she and her man are here in Dericott, she cannot harm your friends, can she?"

"Perhaps not, but she already coerced Father to send Sybil away. I don't know where she is." Tears flooded her eyes.

Oh no! She could not let Edwin see her cry. She blinked furiously, unable to look at Lord Dericott.

After a few moments of silence while Audrey got herself under control, Lord Dericott said, "We can do something about that. I'll make inquiries with your father and find out where she is. And if she is willing, I will bring her here."

"You would do that?"

"Of course. It would be my pleasure and would be no trouble."

In spite of what he said, what he proposed to do would cause him at least some trouble. But she wanted Sybil to be safe and protected so much that she could not refuse.

"You are so very kind." The truth of her statement made her heart constrict. He was. So very kind. God could not have provided a better benefactor. Tears threatened again.

"And from now on the guards who walk with you to your lessons will stay and walk back with you. Or if you wish, we can set up a room in the castle for you to do the lessons."

"Oh no, you mustn't go to that much trouble. I am sure I'll be safe with a guard." He was already doing so much for her.

"I will send my guards to look for your sister and her henchman. In the meantime, I will write to your father telling him that his daughter is here and threatening you, and ask him the whereabouts of Sybil."

"Thank you very much." He seemed to be finished talking, so she started hedging toward the door. "Thank you again, and I shall let you get to your work."

"And please don't leave the castle without a guard, at least until we find your sister."

Her father had never cared so much for her safety. But it would mean a loss of freedom. She'd always run wild over the countryside of her father's demesne, picking flowers, watching birds build their nests, gazing at clouds drifting overhead. But she understood Lord Dericott just wanted to keep her safe.

"Of course."

Their eyes met and held, and something about the look on his face made her heart quiver. She could think of nothing to say, so she smiled and suddenly found herself leaving him abruptly, instead of the other way around.

FOURTEEN

EDWIN AND HIS GUARDS SEARCHED THE VILLAGE AND beyond for Maris and her giant henchman, but after two days, he deduced they must have gone elsewhere. A few days after that, Viscount Engleford sent a response to Edwin's letter.

And now Edwin finally had the time to talk to Audrey about her father's missive and ask her the questions that had been looming in his mind.

It was early afternoon, the sun was shining, and a cool breeze was blowing, though it was early summer. Since Audrey was not teaching lessons today, he found her outside with the house servants as they were doing the laundry.

He was approaching from the side, so Audrey did not see him yet. She was smiling, bending over a tapestry that was laid across her lap, working a needle and colored thread into and out of the fabric. The light shining on her hair made his chest fill with warmth. But her smile . . . Her smile was more radiant than the sun.

She seemed to have positioned herself closer to Joan than anyone else. He might not have expected Audrey to focus most on Joan, since Joan was rather different, speaking in a quavering, childlike tone, meeker than anyone he'd ever met. Some might even think her lacking in her mind. But as she had served his family since he was a young boy, Edwin knew she was only a bit eccentric but perfectly intelligent. And this was not the first time he'd seen Audrey single out Joan to converse with her.

Joan must have said something that made Audrey laugh, because she looked up at Joan and guffawed so loudly, the other servants turned to look at her.

How had she survived so much abuse from her own sister, as well as having no mother and a rather indifferent father, and still turned out so sweet-tempered and kind?

Every time now, when bitter thoughts went through Edwin's mind, when he thought about how unjustly he and his family were treated because of his stepmother, and when he thought of his missing arm and all the physical and emotional pain that had brought to his life, his mind went to Audrey. He thought of her scars, which must be both physical and emotional, and he remembered her smile and how cheerful she always was, and it made him ashamed of his angry, bitter, or vengeful thoughts. She made him want to be a better man.

Audrey looked up and saw him. Her expression changed, and she lowered her needle.

"Lord Dericott." Her smile was gentler now than it had been a moment before.

Looking into her eyes, he asked, "May I speak to you?"

"Of course."

"We'll put your work in your room for you," one of the servants said.

"Thank you." She left her unfinished tapestry on her chair and came toward him, pulling at the hair at the side of her face, covering her scars.

When she reached him, he said, "Walk with me, if you please."

She fell in beside him, and they walked away from the castle through a small gate in the rear wall and into the open area that led down the gentle rise on which the castle was built.

"Do you have news for me?"

"I do. As you know, I sent your father a letter about your sister being here, and he has sent this reply." Edwin handed her the letter. She unrolled it and studied it.

"This part is interesting. 'Forgive my daughter's strange behavior. She has long been a source of frustration and grief to me and to her sister.' Ha. That is understating the truth a bit."

She did not read any more aloud, but as Edwin knew, her father went on to offer the help of his own men to find Maris and bring her home. But most importantly, he told Edwin where he could find Sybil. The viscount believed Audrey's former nurse was in London with an aunt, and he provided the aunt's name and the street where she lived.

"As for Sybil," Edwin said, "I cannot imagine anyone who would rather live in London's smoky, congested streets than here in the country, so I wrote a message to your nurse and sent it by one of my men, offering her a position in my household and money to help her do whatever she needs to do so that she can come at once with my guard, who will bring her safely to Dericott Castle."

"Oh!" Her face brightened like a sunrise. "Thank you, my lord. I cannot ever thank you enough for your kindness. You are a true benefactor to me."

He was not sure how to deflect her praise, so he said, "I was pleased to help."

"Are you taking me somewhere in particular?"

They were entering a small forest when he stopped. "Forgive me for not asking . . . that is, I wanted to show you a few things I thought you might find interesting."

"The stork's nest?"

"Yes, the stork's nest, and a few other places. If you are agreeable."

"I am always happy to see interesting things. I am still unacquainted with this area."

"Very good. The first place is just on the other side of these trees."

They walked through the dense undergrowth of the forest, and when they came out on the other side, they were greeted by the sight of a large, grass-covered mound. He watched Audrey for her reaction.

"What is that? It looks man-made." Her mouth hung open slightly and her voice was hushed.

"It's a grave mound, where the ancient pagans who lived here buried their dead. I didn't know if you would like seeing it—"

"How intriguing!" She ran up to it and pressed her hand

against the side of the bank. "Doesn't it make you wonder who is buried here? If they were good or bad, what they looked like, what they died of?"

"I have spent some time ruminating over those questions, as well as wondering about their burial rituals."

She began to walk around the mound, every now and then plucking a wildflower. "I think I love wildflowers so much because nobody nurtures them but they bloom anyway."

Audrey was a wildflower, then.

"Can I get on top of it and look around?"

"I don't see why not."

He gave her a boost by bending down and letting her put her foot in his palm. He had to lean his opposite shoulder against the sloping side of the mound to keep his balance. But she managed to clamber up to the top.

She stood in one spot and pivoted all the way around, looking in every direction. "I can see so much from up here." She kept staring out, first in one direction, then another. "It's a sea of fields. That must be a stream over there." She pointed to the northeast. "I can see a line of bushes and trees, crooked like a snake's body."

"That would be the River Ivel."

"I see some strange-looking trenches over there." She pointed to the northwest. "I believe they are in the shape of a circle. A trench that makes a perfect round circle."

"Yes, my father believed it to be some kind of ring created by the same people who built the burial mound, probably a place where they practiced their pagan religion. He said his grandfather told him there were once tall stones inside the trench, but he had them hauled away so the men could plow the center of the circle."

"I would have liked to have seen those stones."

"He said they were too large and heavy for even ten men to carry."

She turned and looked down at him with that gentle smile of hers. Did she have any idea how appealing she was? Or that he no longer remembered—or cared to remember—what had attracted him to Lady Ophelia?

"We should have a picnic up here. It is so lovely." She went back to looking all around her, taking in the sights.

He didn't have the heart to tell her that he didn't trust himself to be able to climb up there anymore, now that he only had one arm. But he shouldn't pity himself. He did like the idea that she was wishing she could go on a picnic with him. He had worried she would be uncomfortable exploring the countryside with only him for company—and protection.

"I have another place to show you."

"The stork's nest?"

He nodded.

She scrambled down without waiting for him to help her. But of course it was much easier to get down than up.

"May I walk around the trench on our way?"

"Of course."

She walked around the mound with him beside her.

"Have you ever felt a longing for something but you don't know what it is you are longing for?" Audrey looked up at him.

"Longing?" He wanted her to explain, even though he was fairly certain he knew exactly what she was talking about.

"It's a feeling that you are missing something, a place or a person, but it's a place you've never been to and a person you've never met. Almost as if you dreamed about it and now you're longing for it. I asked my tutor about it once and he said the Germans have a word for that. *Fernweh*."

"I know the feeling you mean."

"Perhaps it sounds strange and unspecific, rather foolish, I imagine."

"Not at all. And if the Germans have a word for it, then you are certainly not the only one to feel it."

She smiled rather gratefully at him. "I had that feeling a lot before I came here, but I haven't had it since." She cocked her head to one side, staring at the ground, as if pondering this.

He felt longing every time he looked at her lately, but it wasn't *Fernweh*, because he knew exactly what he was longing for. He couldn't tell her that, so he said, "Interesting that we don't have that word but the German language does."

"I was supposed to help you learn German! I completely forgot. Why have we not started our lessons?"

"Because you were enjoying teaching the children and I did not wish to exhaust your patience trying to teach me."

"Not at all. You should have reminded me. I'm sure you are a very good student."

"I was not a good student when I younger. I would rather have been outside practicing jousting and sword fighting. But as I grew older, I liked reading and studying more."

"I always liked reading almost as much as exploring. And talking. I liked talking with my friend Helena even more than reading. I suppose that is the sort of thing that annoys men."

"Talking?"

"A girl's chatter. My father used to cover his ears and say, 'Don't chatter on so.'"

"I have never felt annoyed by you. That is, I do not believe I have the same disposition as your father."

Audrey smiled and shook her head. "No. I don't believe you do. My father is much gruffer and more impatient . . . and inattentive. I always feel as though he is not listening to me."

When they arrived at the trench, Audrey stepped into it and followed it all the way around, walking while looking down, a contemplative look on her face. When she came back around to him, she smiled.

"What were you thinking when you were walking the trench?"

"I was wishing I could hear the people who made the trench telling me why they did it. It seems such a strange thing to do, to dig a trench in a circle around some standing stones. I would like to know what they were thinking."

"Are you always so curious about what people are thinking?"

She appeared to ponder his question for a moment, then she said, "Yes, I suppose I am. I wonder what makes people do what they do and what it is they really want."

They started walking again as he began leading her to the stork's nest.

"For example," she went on, "I often wonder what you are thinking."

He waited for her to go on, fervently hoping she would.

"I wonder what it is you really want."

"What I want?"

She nodded.

"I want . . . I want to be able to take care of who and what I am responsible for—my land and my people, my castle and my horses and sheep, my servants. I want to be a good steward of what God has given me, to do good things and leave my demesne a better place when I die." And he wanted a woman to love and cherish, someone who would love him in return. But he couldn't say that.

She nodded slowly.

"And I do know what you meant by *Fernweh*. I often long for something, and I don't know exactly what it is. But yes, there is something inside that yearns . . . intensely."

"I also wonder about something else, but I am not sure I should ask you."

"You may ask me anything." Why did he suddenly feel nervous?

"How does it make you feel to have lost your arm?" She said the words very softly and gently.

Of all the things she could have asked him . . . He sighed. "It makes me feel . . . like a weak person who allowed his enemy to defeat him. And I always prided myself on my strength. It makes me angry and bitter, because the circumstances that led to it were caused by greed. Of all things, I think that is the most unforgivable sin."

"What is?"

"Greed. To wrong someone for material gain, to be so grasping that one would cause great suffering and hardship on another living person."

She nodded.

"And to lose my arm feels very personal, as if someone came too close and took something precious that never should have been taken." He could feel the heat making its way up the back of his neck. He took a deep breath while he calmed down. "But I am learning to be thankful that the injury was not worse, to be thankful that I lived, because one of the men I fought that day . . . did not. And the realization that I took someone's life has also been something I've had to think about when I wake up in the night and cannot go back to sleep."

Her eyes were full of concern when he forced himself to look at her.

"I always expected that I might have to kill someone in a battle or someone who was attacking me, but the soldier I killed was only doing his duty and defending himself. Still . . . it had to be done. I was defending myself as well as my younger brothers. We were set to be executed . . . But I do not wish to burden you with my burden. I am at peace with it—in the daytime at least."

"I understand. When I awake in the middle of the night, that is when fears attack me that I don't think about much during the day. That is when I start imagining Maris coming after me and doing more spiteful things to me."

The poor girl. She had truly been wronged, and by someone who should have been her closest friend, her own sister who grew up next to her.

"It is strange, because as much as I distrust and dislike her, I do feel sorry for her. I pity her because her thinking is so warped. I pity her because she always wanted me to pity her. She almost demanded it. Isn't that strange? She hated me but she demanded that I pity her. And even after she caused me so much harm, I still don't hate her."

She shook her head as they drew near to the stork's nest.

"Oh, I see it!" Her smile was as bright as the sun. "I never imagined it would be so big." She spoke in hushed tones now, watching as the mama bird swooped in and started feeding her babies.

And he knew now more than ever that he wanted to protect Audrey and gain her esteem, as much as he had wanted anything in this world.

It was evening. Edwin fidgeted with his knife, carving a sketch of a bird's nest into a block of wood he'd been using to blot his ink when he wrote letters. He was waiting in the library for Mistress Wattlesbrook to make her weekly report to him about the matters of the house servants and household expenses.

Mistress Wattlesbrook arrived in her usual bustling way, her hair a bit askew as it was wont to be at the end of the day.

"My lord, I trust you are well this evening," she said and sat in the chair near him.

"I am well. And you, Mistress Wattlesbrook? Is your leg still paining you?"

"God bless you, no, it is better today."

"I am glad to hear it."

They proceeded with the usual report, nothing out of the ordinary, and she presented him with the list of household expenses and needs for the following week. When she was finished, Lord Dericott launched into what he wanted to ask her.

"You know the lady, Audrey, a bit better than I do, I believe. What kinds of things does she like? Places she might like to go or things she might like to do?"

"Oh. Well . . . Has something happened? Forgive me for being impertinent, but . . . are you no longer pledged to marry Lady Ophelia?"

"I am not. She has married someone else."

Mistress Wattlesbrook's face brightened and she sat up straighter. Her smile was so big it put him even more on his guard than he already was. Should he try to contradict what she was thinking? No doubt she was already imagining his wedding to Audrey. But he had to win the lady's heart first.

"You asked about Audrey . . . I know she likes flowers. She went and picked a great armful of those common little blue and white flowers that grow by the stream bank and put them in a vase of water on her windowsill. And she loves to see the sun in the morning. Throws open her window shutters just as soon as she wakes up. She also loves teaching those children. You certainly gave her just the thing to keep her happy and occupied by allowing her to teach those girls at the church." Mistress Wattlesbrook lowered her head a bit and spoke more quietly. "And I've noticed her face lights up when you walk into the room."

He had known Mistress Wattlesbrook would react this way, but he hadn't expected her to say *that*. Her face did light up. That was true. But it probably had nothing to do with him. She was an enthusiastic person. She probably did the same when she saw Mistress Wattlesbrook.

He shouldn't have asked Mistress Wattlesbrook about Audrey. Now she would give him away, would behave suspiciously when Audrey was around, or even tell Audrey that he asked about her. He should have asked her himself.

"That will be all. Thank you, Mistress Wattlesbrook, and I pray you not to mention what we talked of tonight—my asking about Audrey."

"Of course. And Audrey is a very good sort of girl, the best kind of girl."

The woman was very slow to get up and leave. In fact, she took her time to scoot to the edge of her chair.

"She has a heart of love and goodness, that one. And honest. You could not find a better or a gentler lady."

He believed she was right about Audrey. Nevertheless, that did not mean the girl would want him. She hadn't wanted Sir Clement.

"Do you not believe me?"

"I do believe you. But what makes you think—" He stopped himself and looked out the window into the twilight.

"My lord, you must not think the girl would not admire and love you because of . . . because of what happened. She herself has scars."

"But she is not missing a body part, is she? I do not wish to speak of it. I bid you a good night."

Mistress Wattlesbrook stood. "Good night, sir. All shall be well." And with that she left the room.

He never should have brought it up to her, never should have spoken to her about Audrey. But at least now he could keep in mind . . . she liked wildflowers and sunrises.

FIFTEEN

AUDREY CARRIED HER PARCHMENT TEXTS TOWARD THE church. It had been over a week since she'd seen her sister, but she still could not pass the spot where she first saw Maris step out of the trees and into the road without shuddering.

But today she did not want to dwell on Maris. She was still thinking about the walk she had taken with Lord Dericott.

She had quite enjoyed Lord Dericott's company, and seeing the storks and their nest had been pleasant as well. The storks had built it in a tree that looked as if it had been struck by light-ning and the top of it had been broken out halfway up the trunk. The huge nest was nestled snugly in the hollowed-out space, and they'd been able to watch the adult birds feed the baby birds. But the most enjoyable part was talking with Lord Dericott.

Strange that he was the first man she'd ever been able to talk with as freely as she could with a woman. And yet he was very male and masculine. He was nothing like her father, who grew bored with her in a matter of moments, if he listened to her at all. And Lord Dericott was nothing like her tutor, who was fidgety and criticized many of the things she said.

In contrast, Lord Dericott was gentlemanly, attentive, and thoughtful in his responses. She could imagine asking him what he thought about a great many things.

She could also imagine the two of them becoming quite good friends, should she remain in Dericott for a long time. But how would she feel once he was married to Lady Ophelia? Surely they would no longer be able to walk and talk together. She didn't like to think about it.

How long could she continue teaching the village girls to read and write? She often wondered if Maris would leave her alone and stop harassing her. Would her sister return to Dericott and do violence to her? But she didn't want to think about that either. She was more content than she'd ever been, and she didn't want to drive away her contentment with wondering about the future. Besides, there was nothing she could do about Maris, and she thought about her a little less every day.

The guards accompanying Audrey left the usual baskets of food in her schoolroom. Then all but one guard left, the remaining soldier walking around outside keeping watch.

Now that most of the girls were reading at least a little, teaching them was even more enjoyable. She was surprised when one of the girls asked if it was time to go. Audrey looked out the window at the sun.

"Yes, you can be dismissed. You all are so clever, it makes

the time go by fast." Then she said, as she did almost every day, "Thank you all for working so hard. I will see you tomorrow."

The children filed out, talking among themselves, while Audrey gathered up her things to go.

"Trying to impress your young earl?"

Maris walked into the room. Her large friend, Umfrey, was just behind her.

"You must be trying to impress him. Why else would you be teaching the villeins' children to read? Though I do not know why Lord Dericott would care about a thing like that." Maris's expression was sneering but also confounded.

"What do you want, Maris?" Where was the guard? Why was he not there? Her heart pounded.

"I know what Lord Dericott told Father. 'Mad Maris is bothering poor little Audrey again.'" She made her voice sound both whiny and contemptuous. "But Father does not control me. And I will not be bested by you. You think you have won because you have your earl, but I will show you who has won."

"I don't *have* an earl, Maris. Lord Dericott is planning to marry someone else. I need you to stop being jealous of me for reasons that don't exist."

"It's very strange that you have not heard the news."

"What news?"

"That Lord Dericott is not marrying Lady Ophelia. She married someone else, the son of the Earl of Cavendish."

She didn't trust anything Maris said. But was it true? Her heart did a happy leap.

205

Foolish heart.

"That certainly does not mean . . ."

"That he will want to marry you? Everyone believes it but you—if indeed you do not believe it."

"Maris, please, just leave me alone. Please."

"Come home with me then. Or do what Father wanted and marry Sir Clement."

"But why? Why do you care? Why do you want me—"

"Because I hate you, that's why. I want you to be miserable, married to an old man who isn't even very wealthy. Why should you be happy? Father sent me to the convent because of you, to make you happy. Do you know what they did to me there? They forced me to pray a thousand times a day, to go days without speaking. They punished me by putting me in a room where I was not allowed to see anyone, and I was told to talk to God about my sins. I was not acceptable to them, and I was not acceptable to Father, and it is not fair!"

"I am sorry you were treated badly." Audrey's heart squeezed in pity. "It would be terrible to be shut away from people and—"

"Stop talking!" Maris covered her ears. "I can't bear to hear your mewling voice, pretending to care. It's all your fault anyway. Every bad thing that has happened to me is your fault!"

Audrey was afraid to say anything else. It seemed whatever she said would only incense Maris further. *God, please help me!*

"You will come home to Father or go to Sir Clement, because that is what Father wants."

"Why do you care what Father wants?"

"Father will see that I am the good daughter because I get

him what he wants. You are the rebellious daughter who is selfish and only wants her way."

God, help me.

"Now, will you come with me and Umfrey?"

Audrey shook her head. "I have an occupation here. I am a teacher. I need to stay."

Maris's eyes narrowed, her jaw flinching. Then she turned her head slightly toward Umfrey and said, "Get her."

Umfrey started toward Audrey.

Her heart beat hard and fast. She stepped back. "Stop. Stay away from me. What have you done to Lord Dericott's guard?"

"Get her!" Maris repeated, backing out of the way of Umfrey.

Audrey backed up a few steps, then darted toward the door, skirting around the lumbering Umfrey. But he was faster than she imagined him. He caught her by the shoulder before she could reach the door.

Audrey screamed. Umfrey's other giant hand clamped over her mouth, all but completely stifling her scream. She struggled and fought, but he gripped her tighter and tighter until he lifted her off the floor. She could hardly breathe, and she clawed at his hand.

God, help me. Please help.

Edwin sat at his desk writing a letter. The hair on the back of his neck prickled, and he looked out the window. Audrey should be coming back about now. The guards always went with her and one stayed behind to protect her, but he had an uneasy feeling.

It couldn't hurt to go meet her. Besides, they'd had a good time the day before. Perhaps he would walk her back to the castle and ask her if she'd like to go see a waterfall he knew about.

He stood and went outside. The uneasy feeling became stronger, and when he saw two of his guards he called to them.

"Mount your horses and go to the church to make certain all is well with Audrey and— Who was the guard that stayed with her?"

"Perrins, I believe, my lord."

"Go check on Perrins."

"Yes, sir." The two mounted their horses and rode off down the lane.

Edwin was halfway to the road that led to the village. When he reached it he could see down the slight hill to the village buildings and homes. All looked peaceful, and his guards were nearly to the church already, but there was no sign of Audrey. Had she come home early and he'd missed her? She usually stopped by his library to speak to him, to tell him a touching story about one of the children or something she observed on the way home.

He walked faster as his two guards turned down the lane that led to the church. As soon as they were out of sight, he heard them yelling.

Edwin started to run. A few villagers who were on the road nearby also heard his guards yelling and ran toward the church as well.

God, please don't let anything bad happen to Audrey. She is good and kind. She does not deserve bad things.

It seemed to take forever to get to the church. He stumbled a few times but managed to keep himself from hitting the ground. With every step Edwin was praying God would keep Audrey safe—and wishing he'd taken the time to get his horse.

One guard was running back down the road. The other was bent over a body lying on the ground next to the church.

"My lord," his guard said, hurrying toward him. "Mistress Audrey is gone, and we found Perrins unconscious on the ground. He's still breathing, but he's not waking up."

Edwin's hand curled into a fist as his mind went cold and calm.

"Get to the castle. Tell every man to go look for Audrey, except for two men who are to fetch Perrins and take him to Mistress Wattlesbrook. Go."

The guard mounted his horse and rode at a gallop toward the castle.

"You there." Edwin pointed at one of the men who had come from the village to help.

The man hurried toward Edwin.

"Did you see a woman and large man, very tall, both strangers, come through here?"

"Yes, Lord Dericott. We saw them walk toward the church an hour or so ago, but we have not seen them since."

"What about the children? Did they see anything?" Edwin's mind was sharp and alert, focused on the task at hand, even though he was more aware than ever that Audrey was in danger.

He was able to numb his emotions, as he'd been trained to do, and focus on the goal that needed to be accomplished and the actions that were required.

"I don't know. We can ask them."

The man trotted toward a group of people gathered in the road. "Do any of you have a girl child who was in Mistress Audrey's reading lesson today?"

One of them nodded, a plump woman with wrinkles at the corners of her eyes. "My girl goes to the lessons."

Edwin approached the group and heard the woman's response. "Would you fetch her so we can ask her a few questions?"

"Yes, Lord Dericott." The woman went into the baker's shop behind her and came out with a young girl, probably around twelve years old.

"Did you see anyone outside the church after Mistress Audrey's lessons?" Edwin tried to make sure he didn't frighten the child and kept his tone light.

"The guard. He was lying down with his eyes closed."

"Did you see anyone else?"

The girl shook her head.

The girl's mother took hold of her shoulder. "Go and ask the other girls if they saw anyone." Then she gave her a tiny shove.

"Yes, Mother." The girl turned and ran.

While they waited for her to return, Edwin talked with the other men and women standing about. A few of them had seen Maris and her large henchman in the village earlier, but they had not seen them in the last hour.

Edwin's guards came tearing down the road on their steeds, and the ones in the lead reined them in near Edwin.

"The woman Maris and her giant, Umfrey, have apparently taken Audrey from the church by force," Edwin told them. "Since no one saw them leaving, they may have gone through the forest. Six of you go search the forest. The rest spread out and search everywhere here in the village. We must find them. Quickly."

The men set out, urging their horses into a gallop.

Another guard came down the hill, too late to have heard the instructions. Edwin turned to one of the villagers who had been helpful.

"Fill this new guard in on what is happening." Then he said to the guard, "Give me your horse. You can go back and get another."

The guard's mouth fell open, but he only hesitated a moment before dismounting and handing Edwin the reins.

Edwin mounted the unfamiliar horse and set off at a fast trot toward the forest.

Edwin's horse bounded through the trees, crashing through the underbrush almost as fast as his own horse would have done. Branches slapped Edwin's arms and shoulders, and one even scraped his forehead, but he barely felt it. He focused on staying in the saddle and moving as fast as he could.

How dare they take Audrey? She was under his protection.

He had promised her she was safe. He'd sent his guard to protect her, and now his guard lay unconscious, possibly even fatally wounded.

Audrey had been so afraid of her sister. How could he not have taken her fear more seriously? Why had he not sent more guards to watch over her? If only he could find her before her sister and that man did something to hurt her.

He slowed his horse to a halt and listened. He heard the sounds of rustling and crackling leaves and twigs, like several horses moving through the trees and underbrush, then he heard men's voices, including the distinct sound of his captain's voice ordering the guards to spread out. It was coming from the southeast, so he turned his horse toward the northwest.

He rode a few minutes, then caught sight of something white in the distance, reflecting the light that filtered in through the forest canopy. He headed toward it.

As he got closer, he realized the white strip was a ribbon he'd once seen in Audrey's hair.

His heart pounded hard against his chest. He pushed his horse to go faster, and he began to notice signs that other horses and riders had been that way. A broken twig here and there, a crushed leaf or bush. Did Maris and Umfrey have horses? He should have asked that question, for then he would know if they could have made it this far.

If they were on foot, he could be close. But there seemed to be too many signs that they were on horses. Which meant it could be a long time before he caught up to them.

He kept going, every so often seeing a small piece of parchment that looked as if it had been placed deliberately into a bush where someone might see it. *Well done, Audrey.*

After riding for more than hour, he came to a slight rise. Edwin had not often been in this part of the forest. He pushed his horse to the top where there seemed to be a small clearing.

The top was rocky, more so than Edwin had expected. Before he could rein in the horse, it plunged down the other side, lost its footing, and fell forward onto its knees. Edwin went flying, clearing the horse's neck and head, and hit the ground before he could break his fall.

He turned and grabbed for the reins, but his hand missed and he fell forward onto his shoulder. The horse scrambled to its feet and darted away from him, whinnying.

Edwin pushed himself up onto his knees, but it was taking too long to get to his feet. By the time he was fully upright, the horse was running down the hill away from him.

He needed to catch the horse. He called it. He ran after it. He whistled for it and made clicking noises with his tongue against his teeth, but nothing worked. The beast did not know Edwin as his master and would not let Edwin get close enough to grab the reins.

Heaviness weighing him down, Edwin went back up the hill to the place where he had fallen. He looked for a sign of where Audrey and her captors had gone. Then he saw another white ribbon shining several feet away, lying on a bush. He hurried toward it.

He picked up the ribbon and noticed a brown stain in the shape of a thumbprint. Was that blood? Was Audrey bleeding?

Had they wounded her the way they'd wounded his guard? But no, she must be conscious if she was leaving him clues, signs of their trail so he could track them.

But the stain made his head hot, and he prayed out loud, "God, protect her. Help me find her. Jesus, give us a miracle and I will give You the glory and tell everyone that You helped me."

He didn't like to admit it, even to himself, but he had been angry at God for all He had allowed to happen to him, for the injustices done to him by his stepmother—that evil woman Parnella—and Baldric, the uncle of Delia's husband. But he was wrong to have felt that way. God did not do evil, people did. And sometimes God had purposes and reasons for the bad things that happened that were beyond the knowledge of mortals. Where was his faith if he blamed God for every bad thing? Should he not follow the example of Daniel's three friends who vowed to trust in God even if He chose not to save them? If God saved every Christian, there would be no martyrs to inspire the faith of others.

He squeezed his hand into a fist and got down on his knees.

"Forgive me, God, for my bitterness, unforgiving spirit, and lack of faith. But I beg You now to help me find Audrey. I am not trusting in horses or chariots, not running to Egypt for help. I am looking to You, Lord God, from whence my help comes."

He opened his eyes, half expecting to see Audrey standing in the distance. But she was not there.

"Very well, God, but lead me to her. I have faith that You will."

He stood and continued to walk. While he was among the

dense trees, he was actually able to see more signs of their trail now that he was on the ground and not on horseback. But once he came into a clearing, there were fewer ways for them to leave a trail.

In the distance a flash of color—dark green—disappeared into a small copse of trees on the other side of the grassy hillside he was standing on.

Edwin hurried toward it, careful to watch the ground for rocks so that he would not stumble and fall. He made his way through the tall grass and plunged into the cover of the trees.

Just ahead was a horse tied to a tree. Edwin looked carefully, squatting to give himself a smaller profile. Two more horses, both standing still and grazing. He started walking carefully toward them, trying to make sure his footfalls were quiet.

As he drew near, he heard muffled voices. He crept closer but made a wide path around the horses lest he spook them, causing them to announce his presence.

The giant—he was indeed quite large—was making a fire in a small pit dug out in the earth. Maris was standing over Audrey, whose mouth was covered by a cloth tied around her head. Her wrists were tied together in front of her.

Heat rose into his head again. But he forced his emotions to go cold. He had to save Audrey, and it would be much easier if he did not let anger scramble his thoughts. He needed his head clear to think and plan.

He moved over so that he was squatting behind a large tree trunk. The late-day sun was shining through the trees to his right, and Audrey was sitting very still. Maris bent down and yanked the cloth down away from her mouth. The blonde woman turned to her giant.

"What do you think I should do with her?"

"I can snap her neck. It would be easy," Umfrey said.

Maris turned to Audrey. "What do you think, dear sister? It would be a quick and painless way to die, I would imagine."

He saw the flicker of sadness, rather than fear, that passed over Audrey's features.

"What makes you treat me this way?" Audrey rasped. "You are my sister."

Maris turned to walk away, but then she whipped her body around and shook her finger in Audrey's face. "You ruined my life!"

The woman was clearly mad.

If Edwin did not do something to get Audrey away from her sister, and very soon, it might be too late.

SIXTEEN

AUDREY SAT LISTENING TO HER SISTER, WHO SOUNDED increasingly agitated, ramble and rant while Audrey studied the bonds constraining her hands, examining the knot. If they tied her ankles together tonight, as she anticipated they would, perhaps she could figure out how to untie it.

She'd tried to leave little bits of evidence so Lord Dericott and his men could follow her trail and find her. But they had gone so far and no one had found them yet, so it seemed unlikely that she would be rescued. No, she had to escape. Tonight she would do whatever she had to do to get away. In the meantime she had to survive.

Was this how Edwin felt when he was a prisoner at the Tower of London? Falsely accused. She could imagine how that felt, as Maris constantly accused her of things she had not done.

"Are you listening to me?" Maris fairly screamed.

Keep screaming, Maris. Maybe Lord Dericott's men will hear you.

"I'm listening."

"What are you to the Earl of Dericott? Are you his concubine? His betrothed?"

"No, neither. He is a kind man who is letting me stay at Dericott Castle."

"Why didn't Sir Clement want to marry you? Lord Dericott must have told him not to, that he wanted you for himself."

"Why would he do that? You're always telling me how ugly I am."

"You are ugly, as you well know, even uglier now that you have those disgusting scars." Maris's expression twisted.

"But perhaps you bewitched Lord Dericott somehow. There is no predicting how men will behave. When a woman is determined to have him, she can turn his head and make him do whatever she wants."

How would Maris know such a thing? She had been in a convent for the past four years. Had she even seen a man in all that time? But some monasteries were less strict and chaste than others, Audrey had been told.

Perhaps she would be wise to play along with Maris. Could she say that she was sorry for trying to turn Lord Dericott's head and lure him into marrying her? For trying to bewitch him? But she wasn't sure she could lie like that. Helena and Sybil both had told her she was very bad at lying the two or three times she had tried in jest.

Audrey kept her head down, trying to look defeated in the hope that Maris would leave her alone. And Maris did indeed wander over to Umfrey's fire and gaze down at it. Then she started asking him about how he would cook the pheasant and the two hares he had killed and had been carrying with them, tied to his saddlebag.

Audrey lay down and closed her eyes. She should try to rest and sleep as much as she could if she hoped to be able to untie the bindings and put some distance between herself and her captors during the night.

After waiting, still and quiet, until night had fallen, Edwin crept carefully through the forest toward Audrey.

Thankfully he always kept a knife strapped to his belt. He paused to take it out of its sheath and held it in his hand as he moved slowly around bushes and trees.

Maris and her giant lay close to Audrey, but they both appeared to be sleeping. Poor Audrey was lying still too. The girl had been through so many injustices, and he knew just how she felt. But he was a man. She was soft and vulnerable, like his sister, Delia—though Delia could be strong, now that he thought about it. But Audrey was smaller than Delia, shorter and more delicate. She was sweet and feminine and caused an ache in his chest, his longing to protect her.

He despised the loss of his arm even more now that Audrey needed him fight for her. Nevertheless, he would save her, since his men had not yet arrived. He had to.

He crept closer, carefully watching Maris and Umfrey. But

they hadn't moved for what he guessed was at least half an hour. Now that he was closer to Audrey than to her captors, he could see she was working at the strip of cloth that bound her ankles. She was actually trying to free herself, even though her hands remained bound.

He crept still nearer, checking where his feet would go, making sure there was nothing that would make any noise when he stepped on it, checking to make sure Umfrey and Maris remained motionless, their eyes closed, all the while clutching the knife handle in his hand.

When he was about ten feet away from where she lay on the ground, he took a step, looked up, and she was gone.

He glanced around, frantically searching the darkness for her. Not seeing her, he closed his eyes and listened, detecting a slight crunching of dead leaves to his right. He turned in that direction. A low-hanging tree limb moved. Then another limb a little farther away. He headed toward it. Then he heard a rather loud crackling, as if she had stepped on a large twig and it broke.

Edwin looked back to see if Maris or Umfrey had heard the noise.

Umfrey rolled onto his side, then used his hands to push his torso up, looking at the spot where Audrey had been lying.

"She's gone!"

Edwin's blood jolted through his limbs as he sprang forward. He had to protect her.

Audrey stepped onto the twig and felt it—and heard it—break into pieces. Her heart trembled. Was that as loud as she thought it was?

She held still, listening, afraid to move. Then she heard Umfrey say, "She's gone!"

Audrey started running, crashing through the brush, no longer paying attention to where she was stepping or how much noise she was making. Her heart pounded so hard it hurt her chest.

She heard sounds that were not coming from her own footsteps, and they were very close. Had Umfrey grown wings and flown? He seemed to be right behind her.

She put every ounce of her strength into moving faster, running harder. She leapt over bushes and fallen trees, holding on to her leather slippers with her toes. Still the noises behind her grew louder and closer.

Suddenly, her foot caught on something unyielding. She pitched forward at such speed she was not able to catch herself with her hands. She hit the ground on her shoulder and the side of her face. She lay, too stunned to move.

A strong hand grabbed her upper arm and yanked her to her feet, almost as swiftly as she'd fallen.

Audrey sucked in a loud breath.

"It's me," Edwin's voice came in her ear. "We must run."

Her heart soared at his presence. She put her hand on his back and started running, intermittently touching him so she wouldn't get separated from him. Did he know where he was going? It was so dark. Was he familiar with this place? She wanted so much to ask him, but there was no time. And for the moment it hardly mattered. They had to keep running.

A partial moon hung overhead, thankfully, so there was a bit of light, but a tree trunk was suddenly in front of her, and Edwin pulled her to the side just before she ran headlong into it. He must have lost his balance because he suddenly fell to one knee. But he was up again in a moment.

"I know a place where we can hide," he said, talking so low she barely heard him. "Follow me."

"Come back here!" Maris screamed from somewhere behind them.

At least she wasn't as close as Audrey had feared. But where was Umfrey? No doubt with his enormous legs he was leaping over bushes and pushing aside the small trees.

Lord Dericott made a sharp right turn. She caught the back of his shirt and followed him.

They scrambled down into a ravine, sparsely occupied by small trees. Then Audrey realized the slight roaring sound she was hearing was water, and they were getting closer. Audrey did not know how to swim. Was his plan to cross a river? Most waters she'd encountered in this part of England were not deep, but if it was moving as fast as this sounded, she could get swept downstream.

Perhaps she should just trust him not to let her come to harm. They were running too hard, and the danger behind them was too great, to ask him to explain his plans.

The way was a little rougher now, with large rocks in their path. Then Audrey saw it—a waterfall shining in the light of the moon. Only about thirty feet away, the water rushed down some rocks and went over the side of a ledge, plunging into the darkness.

Edwin headed straight for the waterfall, then toward the ledge. Two feet away from stepping out into the water, he sat down on the grassy slope and began making his way down. Audrey followed right behind him, mimicking him.

When they were halfway to the bottom of the six-foot waterfall, Lord Dericott stepped to the side and disappeared behind the water that was flowing straight down.

Her heart in her throat, Audrey strained her eyes to see where she would be stepping. Would she be dropping down into a river or a lake? Should she tell him she couldn't swim? The water was making so much noise, he probably wouldn't hear her.

Just as she was trying to decide if the darkness was a rock she could step on, Lord Dericott's hand came out from behind the waterfall, palm up, as if he was waiting for her to grasp it. She did, and put her foot down on solid rock.

"It's wet, so take care not to fall," he said, leaning so close to her she could feel his breath in her hair.

Still holding on to his hand, she looked into his face. It was so dark she could barely make out more than the whites of his eyes.

She was breathing hard. Perhaps she looked frightened, because he squeezed her hand and leaned down to speak into her ear again.

"We will wait here until they have had time to pass us by."

Audrey nodded, then they both stood facing the water that

was falling in front of them. She could see less than a foot in front of her, but the water racing downward was splashing her with tiny droplets of water. And she recalled holding his hand once before, when he saved her from the snake that was about to strike her.

"Move back." Lord Dericott gently pulled her as he moved two steps back.

Audrey stepped with him and her back bumped against uneven rock—as far away from the water as they could get.

She started to shiver. Her whole upper body shook, and she didn't know if it was more because she was getting cold from being wet, or because she was reliving the shock and fear of the past several hours, culminating in running for her life in the dark.

She became aware of Lord Dericott looking down at her. He let go of her hand and unbuttoned the front of his outer tunic, then shrugged out of it. He wrapped it around her, and it engulfed her much smaller frame. Underneath his tunic he'd been wearing a white linen shirt with laces at the top.

"You'll get cold," Audrey said, her teeth chattering. "You shouldn't give me your clothes. I think I just g-got sc-scared." The tunic was wet on the outside but was made with two layers, and inside it was warm and dry.

"Come, we can sit down and get comfortable while we wait."

The overhang was narrow but long, and he moved farther into the rocky recess behind the waterfall, bending over as the overhang got shorter, and sat down. When she stood gazing down at him, he repeated, "Come."

224

Audrey moved to sit beside him. What would happen now? She was still shivering, her teeth knocking together.

"Forgive me if this suggestion offends you," he said, "but you should sit close against my side to get warm. It's the only way I can help you, and I promise not to do anything untoward."

Audrey took comfort in the sincerity in his voice, so she slid closer to him until she was pressed against his side and her head was resting against his shoulder—or the place where his arm used to be. Why did she not cringe at his missing arm? Not only did she not cringe, but she felt safe, warm, and comfortable beside him.

After what was probably a few minutes, he said, "Your teeth aren't chattering anymore."

It was true. She hadn't noticed, but he had.

"I hope I'm not making you uncomfortable," she said. Then she noticed how near his face was to hers. Her breath began to come faster. Was her nearness affecting him the way it was affecting her? She suddenly remembered what Maris had said about him being no longer pledged to marry Lady Ophelia. Was she telling the truth?

"You're not bothering me at all. I'm quite comfortable, but I'm afraid we need to move again, to get out of the spray from the waterfall."

Audrey had been holding herself stiffly, trying not to lean against him too much. Now he reached out to feel around and she leaned away from him.

Lord Dericott seemed to be searching around the rock where they were sitting.

"There is a space under the outcropping here. We need to get out of the wet so we don't freeze. It gets cold at night."

There was indeed a space where she'd thought there was a wall of rock. Lord Dericott crawled on his knees, using his elbow and forearm to move along the wet surface.

Audrey followed him. It was drier there than where they had been sitting. But there was no way to sit in the small space without being quite close to him. She hesitated to touch him as he maneuvered himself as far back against the rock as he could go.

Audrey moved closer, her face once again coming quite close to his.

"Do not worry. I won't bite."

Audrey laughed, a nervous little sound. She kept her elbows tight to her sides and her hands clasped in front of her chest.

"Do you think they will give up looking for us?" Audrey said, more to break the awkward silence than anything else.

"I don't know, but I do not think they will find us here."

The way they were sitting—almost facing each other in the confined space—her hands were just touching his chest. But she was warmer and suddenly her eyelids were quite heavy. A thought came to her.

"This is the second time you have come looking for me." She smiled.

"And I found you. Both times."

"How did you do it this time? Did you see my ribbons and the pieces of parchment?"

"I did. It was very clever of you to leave a trail for someone to find. They led me straight to you. Where did you get the parchment?"

"I had a piece in my pocket, and since my hands were tied in front of me, I could still get the parchment out and tear off a piece of it. But they did eventually catch me and took it away."

"They did not hurt you, did they? I saw a bit of blood . . ."

"Oh no. I cut my thumb on a thornbush." Her heart skipped at the thought of him being concerned about her. She looked at him closely and saw that he had a bloody scratch on his forehead. She wanted to mention it, to help him clean it. And she wished she had some of Mistress Wattlesbrook's ointment to put on it, but that was not possible at the moment.

"They did injure my guard."

"I know. He was not seriously injured, was he?"

"I don't know. He had not awakened yet when we discovered him."

"Oh no. I'm so sorry."

"It is not your fault, and he still may be well. Time will tell. What did they intend to do to you?"

"My sister said she wanted to take me to Sir Clement. She was so adamant about me marrying Sir Clement. She was trying to talk me into going to his home and begging him to marry me. Which I never would have done, of course. And I do believe they would have killed me eventually."

"Does she know that Sir Clement gave up all claim to marrying you?"

"I told her, but it didn't make a difference to her. I even explained that he deserved to marry someone who at least *wanted* to marry him." Audrey almost laughed, but ruefully. "I left him with no doubts about my unwillingness, I suppose. Poor Sir Clement."

"Do not worry about him. He is well. Besides . . ." He was quiet so long, Audrey almost asked him if he was all right. "I don't believe a woman should have to marry someone she does not feel love for."

Audrey absorbed this in silence. It was not a popular sentiment. In fact, she did not think she'd ever heard anyone say such a thing—except herself.

"That is just what I think," Audrey said quietly. It was strange how well she could see his face in this dark place, at night, behind a waterfall. The moonlight must be reflecting off the water as it fell. And maybe it was that moonlight that was making them both say things, more open and expressive things, than they'd ever said to each other before.

She grabbed her hair and pulled it down over her scars. She'd almost forgotten about them.

"You don't need to worry about your scars," Lord Dericott said.

"I like to keep them covered." Her cheeks burned.

"Your scars don't detract from your beauty at all."

She held her breath. Why had he said that? Did he think she possessed . . . beauty?

"Maris always said I was ugly, even when we were little girls." She hoped he didn't think she was trying to manipulate him into giving her a compliment.

"She was very wrong. I am quite confident you have been a

beauty all your life. She was only jealous of you, no doubt. You are so much more beautiful than she."

"But she is the one with perfect skin and big eyes."

He shook his head. "She does not have half your beauty."

Audrey could hardly take a breath as she dwelled on his words. Could he truly mean them? Could he know they made her heart soar and then quiver with fear that he didn't mean them?

"But what is better is the way you care for others, the way you teach the children every day and feed them and dote on them. And you're always cheerful, always eager to help the servants, or to laugh and talk with them."

"Oh."

"I wanted you to know that I admire those things about you."

Was he telling her this because he thought they were going to die? Whatever the reason, he made her feel warm inside. His words made her want more, and that frightened her. She mustn't imagine she could have more than this moment, that Edwin's words meant he would fall in love with her. They were friends, that was all.

"Thank you. I admire a lot of things about you too. You are steady and kind. You don't treat your people badly. And you gave me an occupation by letting me teach girl children to read. You allow me to live in your castle and coerce you into feeding my students."

That made him smile.

"You didn't have to coerce me. I was pleased to do it."

Truly, he was a good man. She drew in a long breath and let it out slowly. Good and kind and handsome. Could he possibly be thinking and feeling the kinds of things about her that she was thinking and feeling about him? She was scarred. But he was also scarred. Would he ever consider marrying her?

She suddenly wanted him to, so much so that tears filled her eyes.

I am ridiculous.

SEVENTEEN

Edwin sat facing Audrey. Even after all that he'd said, Audrey still did not seem to understand how he felt about her. Or perhaps she understood exactly what he meant by his words and was only pretending not to know because she did not feel the same about him. Lady Ophelia rejected him. Audrey might not want him either.

"Do you think Maris and Umfrey have moved on and lost our trail?" Audrey asked, interrupting his thoughts.

"I don't know, but it's unlikely they will find us here, especially in the dark. The only way I knew about this hiding place is because I've been here before."

"Shouldn't we leave while it's still dark? To make our way back to Dericott Castle?"

"We could do that. But I'm concerned about the wolves in this area. If we run through the forest at night, we will attract their attention. And as I didn't bring my sword with me, a pack of hungry wolves could kill the two of us easily."

She didn't speak for several moments, and he regretted being so honest about the wolf threat. He'd probably frightened her half to death.

"You don't think we're going to die, do you?"

"No." He waited, and when she didn't speak, he said, "At dawn we will be safer. We can head back toward Dericott. Without horses we will have to take care not to let Maris and Umfrey see us. My hope is that my men will capture them once it is light. They will surely have tracked them by then."

Perhaps he was overstating his confidence a bit, but he did not want her to worry. He'd already frightened her enough.

"The wolves can't find us in here?"

"They probably wouldn't be able to smell us behind the waterfall. Besides, we are not doing anything to attract their attention."

A shudder went through her.

"You are cold. Come closer. We need to keep warm, and we need to lie down and try to sleep."

"Are you certain? My clothes are wet."

"I am certain. Come." He motioned her closer.

He didn't want to make her uncomfortable, and getting so close would have been unseemly in normal circumstances, but if they got too cold and fell asleep, they might never wake up. And if he was honest with himself, he was not sorry that their situation warranted such closeness.

They both stretched out their legs and lay in the narrow space under the overhanging rock. She scooted near, tucking her head down so that the top of her head was just barely touching his chin. Her hands were clasped in front of her chest, and soon they were pressed against his chest.

"Is this all right?" she asked.

"Are you close enough to get warm?"

"I believe so." She kept her head down now, no longer able to look into his face.

Her knees were pressed against his legs and her hair was tickling his face. But he did not mind. He stayed as still as he could. And for the first time, he could think of a reason why it was good that he had only one arm—because it wasn't getting in the way. He was lying on his left side, and there was no arm to come between his body and hers. His right arm rested against his side. If he dared, and if she wished it, he could put that arm around her and pull her a little closer. But of course, he did not dare, and she probably would not wish it.

Ideally, she would need to take off her wet clothes and let them dry. But he did not think it would get cold enough tonight to require such drastic measures.

Soon Audrey's breathing was steady and deep, indicating she had fallen asleep. It filled his chest with warmth knowing she trusted him so much. She might have panicked at the prospect of hiding here with him. She might have been indignant, or even afraid to stay there, and might have rather tried to run back to Dericott in the cover of darkness. Or she might have dissolved in terrified tears, fearing the worst, afraid of being captured or getting eaten by wolves. But Audrey was brave. She'd borne this threatening situation as she seemed to bear everything, with fortitude and maturity.

Watching the water fall across the opening in their little hiding place, and knowing Audrey was as safe as he could make her, and also knowing she felt safe enough to fall asleep, he was beginning to feel drowsy himself. Their mutual body heat was also creating a more comfortable warmth, and he felt himself drifting.

"The sun is coming up." Lord Dericott's voice came from just behind her.

Audrey opened her eyes. Her back was pleasantly warm as she stared at the waterfall for a moment before she remembered where she was. In the middle of the night she had turned over and was now facing the water as it rushed down endlessly before the opening in the rock where she and Lord Dericott lay. Then she realized the pleasant firmness and warmth on her upper back was coming from Lord Dericott's chest.

She rubbed her eyes at Lord Dericott's words and pushed herself up—and pain shot through her head as it hit the rock overhang.

"Are you hurt?"

Audrey put her hand on her head and tried not to groan. "I am well. No blood. How silly of me not to remember that rock was there."

"It is not silly to sit up when you awake in the morning. I should have warned you to watch your head."

They both squirmed and crawled their way out of their rock hideaway until they were able to stand.

Now that they were not in such close proximity to each other, Audrey shivered. She hadn't realized how much warmth Lord Dericott had provided. The faint light of dawn was showing through the watery curtain.

Her stomach rumbled. Fortunately, the sound of falling water drowned it out. In spite of needing food and water and wanting to escape from Maris, she was reluctant to leave this place. Lord Dericott had said such complimentary things to her, things she hadn't realized she'd been hungry to hear. Her father rarely spoke to her, and certainly never said thoughtful and kind words.

She loved Sybil, but she was more likely to scold her good-naturedly than to praise her, though she did often tell her that she was more beautiful than Maris. But Sybil only said that because she disliked Maris so much.

Helena often said kind things to Audrey, but Helena was a bit in awe of Audrey due to her having read so many books and because she was a viscount's daughter.

But Edwin—Lord Dericott—shared none of those reasons for praising her and pointing out the good things she had done. And even the fact that Lord Dericott thought those things were good made her want to get closer to him.

Lord Dericott reached his hand into the waterfall. "We should drink some water before we start out."

She followed him out of their hiding place, climbing down the rocks and walking down to the river. He lay on his stomach on the bank and put his hand in the water, cupping it and bringing it to his mouth. Audrey did the same.

The water tasted fresh and cool.

"Normally you should not drink from a stream or river," Lord Dericott said. "Better to find a spring at its source and drink from there. Spring water is less likely to make you sick. But since we don't know where to find a spring and we need to get moving, we have to take the chance."

Audrey remembered her father's guards telling her something similar.

"We will make our way under the cover of trees whenever possible," Lord Dericott said quietly. "We need to get back to Dericott without being seen by your sister and Umfrey."

They made their way back up the hill, with Lord Dericott moving slowly, obviously struggling to keep his balance. Nevertheless, she could see that he was better at balancing than he had been when she first met him. But she sensed he would be embarrassed if she mentioned it.

"We will be moving in a northeasterly direction, but we need to make a wide path around the place where your sister and her henchman slept last night, since they may go back there, or may be there now."

Audrey resisted the urge to grab his hand. Instead, she used words to express the gratitude that had been welling up inside her.

"Thank you for coming after me and helping me. I would have been so frightened last night if you had not been with me, and I never would have found that hiding place behind the waterfall. You should be safe and comfortable right now in your home instead of walking throughout the countryside in danger from my mad sister. So I thank you. I am so grateful."

He had a pained look on his face. Did he regret coming to search for her? But of course he did. She was only reminding him of what he already knew—that he could be at home doing whatever he wished instead of out here with her. Her heart ached while she waited for him to speak.

"It is my privilege to help you. I only wish . . . I wish my men had found you instead of me."

Her heart twisted painfully inside her chest. He glanced back at her.

"Do not misunderstand. I am thankful to God for letting me find you. I just know that my men could have taken better care of you than . . . than I could, a broken man with only one arm."

Her heart constricted again, but this time in compassion for him.

"You are not broken, and you are the best man I've ever met." She hurried to get in front of him so she could look him in the eye.

He raised his brows but looked away from her.

"I do my best, but I could not even stay on top of a horse. I fell off and couldn't grab the reins because my balance is gone. I cannot even walk at a normal pace."

"But you are getting better at balancing, and you will get stronger and—"

"Please don't pity me." He held up his hand, palm out. "I cannot bear it." He still would not look at her.

"Forgive me. I didn't mean to—"

"I will get you back to Dericott Castle, Lord willing, but if anything happens, do not worry about me. Save yourself."

As they walked on in silence, she cast about in her mind for the right thing to say.

"Truly, you have saved my life. I would not have found a hiding place, and Maris and Umfrey would have caught me and killed me, if not for you. You are a good and kind man who bravely saved a woman far beneath you, and—"

"You are not beneath me. I will not allow you to say that."

"Very well, but I am a woman. And I am beholden to you."

"You owe me nothing. I only wish you had someone better to protect you."

"Why are you being so stubborn?" The words came out of her mouth before she thought about them.

He turned toward her, finally looking at her. Then he continued on his way, as they were walking through a meadow of tall grass and heading toward a stand of trees. Had she angered him?

"What I mean is, you should simply accept that you helped me and that I am grateful to you. There is no need to reject my gratitude or pretend you did not save my life. You are whole and good, and you helped me."

She immediately worried she had spoken too vehemently and had overstated her point. Would he say something cold and harsh, as her sister would in this situation? Or would he ignore her as if she mattered not a whit to him, as her father would?

"You are right. I am stubborn. And I'm sorry for burdening you with my gloomy thoughts. You are very welcome for my help. That is the truth, and it is what I should have said. I am very glad God used me to help you."

"Good. Thank you."

He looked her in the eye, finally, and stopped walking. Then he smiled. "I have never known anyone like you."

She smiled back, relieved and surprised at his reaction. "I have never known anyone like you either."

"Come. We must get out of this open field before someone sees us."

Lord Dericott continued walking but then suddenly stumbled and fell forward.

Audrey's heart leapt into her throat. "Are you all right?"

Lord Dericott rolled over and kicked at something on the ground. "Stay back."

"What is it?" Audrey suddenly saw it—a wolf lying on the ground, bloody and unmoving. She gasped. "Is it dead?"

"Yes." He got to his feet and stared down at the animal. He kicked at it again with his booted foot. It was stiff. "It looks fairly fresh. Probably your sister's friend killed it last night."

"Do you think the wolves chased them while they were trying to find us?"

"That is possible. And we might actually find that the wolves . . . Well, I will just say that wolves run in packs, and they attack their prey in packs, and they may have greatly outnumbered your sister and her henchman."

"You mean, they may have killed Maris and Umfrey?" Audrey felt slightly sick but also a little relieved. *God, please forgive me.*

"It is possible. But we cannot depend upon it. And it is even more likely that your sister and her henchman killed this wolf, which means they came through here in the last several hours. We must take care."

They walked to the shade of the forest, and Lord Dericott proceeded cautiously, looking hard into the trees. Audrey stayed close by his side, again thinking how it would feel to take his hand in hers. She'd felt the comfort of it twice before. But if she grabbed his hand now, would he be horrified at her boldness? But of course, she would not do it. She was only wondering what it would be like if he cared for her and if she were ready to declare her feelings for him.

She wished she had the courage to ask him if he was still pledged to Lady Ophelia.

They made their way through the trees, cutting a very wide path around the place where Maris and Umfrey had bedded down and from where Audrey had escaped.

Audrey's heart was beating fast. She slipped on a large root sticking out of the ground, making her stumble forward.

"Are you all right?" He turned and waited for her to catch up to him.

She nodded. She walked beside him, making her way through the thick bushes and vines and thorns.

Something moved about six feet from where they were standing. Audrey sucked in a loud breath, clamping her hand over her mouth to stifle a scream. As it ran away, she saw it was a rabbit.

Audrey pressed her hand to her chest. Then she realized she had grabbed Lord Dericott's arm with her other hand.

"It's only a small rabbit," he said in a quiet voice.

She let go of his arm, thinking he was annoyed at her silly fear over something as insignificant as a rabbit. But when she did, he put his arm around her shoulders. And when he did that, she leaned into him, pressing her face against his chest. He tightened his arm around her and she slipped her arms around his back.

Her breath went out of her at how she felt when he pulled her close to him, in the vulnerability of embracing him.

It did not mean anything. He was simply comforting her . . . as a friend comforts a friend. And perhaps he needed a bit of solace and comfort too.

But did she dare to let herself enjoy it? To draw strength from his solid chest and his strong, muscular arm around her? To imagine that they might mean more to each other than mere friends? She tried not to move, wishing the moment never had to end.

"Audrey." He said her name as if he was enjoying the way it sounded.

"I am sorry. The noise startled me and I . . ." She pulled away to look into his face.

He leaned down and pressed his lips to her forehead. Her breath went out of her at the tender look in his eyes and the way he kissed her, letting his lips linger. The emotions going through her were nearly overwhelming. He did feel for her the way she did for him! He was kissing her forehead even though she was a mess. Her hair was tangled, her clothes were dirty and wrinkled, and she probably did not smell very good after running around, terrified, through the woods for almost a day and a night.

She wrapped her arms around him tighter and buried her face in his shirt. For some reason he did not smell bad at all, even though he'd been running around the same as she had. In fact, she liked the way he smelled—warm and masculine.

She squeezed her eyes closed even as she tightened her arms around him. Was she in love with Lord Dericott? Was he falling in love with her? Would he try to kiss her mouth if she pulled away again? Her heart stammered and stuttered. What had she done by simply grabbing his arm?

But she wasn't sorry. No, she did not regret it. His arm felt perfect around her. How could she ever want another man? She would never, could never.

She pulled back, stood on the tips of her toes, and pressed her lips to his.

Edwin must be dreaming. The most beautiful, most good-hearted woman he had ever met, the woman he'd been admiring for the past two months, was kissing him. Ophelia had rejected him, and he was suddenly very, very glad she had.

He held her as tightly as she was holding him as they kissed. He'd been kissed by girls before, though only a few, and he'd tried to extricate himself from them before anything else could happen. He knew he would need to marry someone his father approved of, and it would be wrong to dally with a woman's affection or take advantage of her. He'd thought he was in love with Lady Ophelia and was looking forward to making her his wife. But then his father had died, and Edwin had been entangled in the web his stepmother had woven for him and his brothers and sister. He had wondered if any young woman, beautiful or otherwise, would ever want to kiss him again after he lost his arm.

These thoughts passed quickly through his mind. He needed all his senses to revel in this kiss, this wonderful moment with this amazing woman.

When their kiss ended, her eyes were still closed, her face still tilted up toward his, her lips slightly parted. She took his breath away.

Her eyes fluttered open. She looked slightly embarrassed, so he bent and kissed her again, but briefly. He took her hand in his, squeezing slightly, and said, "We should go."

She nodded.

Just then he heard a crashing sound. Edwin spun around and held out his arm to make sure Audrey was behind him. Umfrey ran, lunging at him.

Edwin reached for his knife. Too late.

Eighteen

Umfrey slammed into Edwin, knocking him to the ground, his meaty hands wrapping around Edwin's throat.

Edwin fought to stay conscious, as his head slammed into the ground. His vision went dark for a moment. He was aware of Audrey screaming very close by. He wanted to tell her to run, but the giant's hand blocked his airway. He couldn't take in a breath.

He could see now. Audrey had a stick in her hands and was beating the man's bald head. Blood was running down onto his neck.

Umfrey roared, letting go of Edwin's throat. The large man stood up and reached for Audrey.

"Run, Audrey!" Edwin pushed himself up, sucking in air and coughing. His vision was narrowing, but as he breathed in more air, his vision cleared.

Someone held Audrey from behind. A knife was pointed at her neck and her arms were being twisted up behind her, forcing her onto her toes.

Umfrey grabbed the back of Edwin's neck and squeezed hard, while the giant's other hand was holding Edwin's knife, pointing it at Edwin's nose. He must have taken it when Edwin was gasping for air. But it was the knife sticking into Audrey's pale skin, the sensitive spot below her ear, that made him mad to reach her and protect her. Umfrey's huge hand held Edwin's neck with an iron grip, his other arm wrapped around Edwin's shoulder, his elbow digging into Edwin's chest while he held the knife in his face.

God, give me the strength of Samson. But even without his hair, Samson at least had two good arms.

Audrey was still while her sister pressed the knife point into her neck. Her eyes were wide, and she looked afraid but calm. And maybe a little angry.

What kind of man was he—what kind of knight—to let one man capture him? A year ago it would have taken at least two or three men to subdue Edwin, more if he had a weapon.

Oh God, if I can't save Audrey, how could I ever forgive myself? She doesn't deserve to die this way. Let me give my life for hers. She can marry someone else and be happy, but I . . . I could not live if she dies.

He felt a strange quietness in his spirit, an assurance that God had heard him.

"Look what you did!" Maris fairly screamed. Her hand holding the knife shook. "Umfrey is bleeding. And we had to chase you last night. Did you know that wolves attacked us? We had to kill one of them just to get away. And it's all your fault!"

"I'm sorry, Maris. I'm sorry you had to fight the wolves. That was not my intention, I—" Audrey was trying to reason with her sister, but Maris's face just grew redder, her expression more tense.

"Be quiet! Let me think." Maris was breathing hard.

Audrey was doing her best to lean away from the knife pointed at her neck.

Maris glared at Edwin. "Why are you here? You are keeping my sister from her duty to our father."

"Your father has released her from whatever you claim is her duty."

"What do you know about my father? Or my sister's duty? Father sent me away, but it wasn't my fault that my sister is clumsy. He sent me away for an accident, but Audrey defied Father by running away and refusing to marry the man he chose for her, and he never punished her at all."

"Your father is probably very concerned for you right now. He is probably worried and looking for you. He knows where Audrey is. It's you he is searching for."

"You don't know." Maris was silent, morosely staring with a glazed look. "I never could please him. I tried so hard, but he was always displeased with me and pleased with Audrey. He tried to marry her off to you, but he sent me, the oldest, who should have been married first, to a convent." Her face screwed up like she was about to spit out something hard and bitter. "I cannot let her get what she wants. She always gets what she wants, and I never do."

"How did you get Umfrey here to help you?"

Umfrey grunted and tightened his grip on him at the sound of his name.

"He worked at the convent where Father sent me. He understood me and wanted to help me." Her expression softened when she spoke of her henchman.

"He is loyal to you, then?" Edwin would keep asking questions and getting her to talk. Maybe his guards were tracking them and were nearby and would hear them. And though it might be foolish, he was also curious how her mind worked.

"He is very loyal to me. Shall I show you how loyal? Shall I tell him to kill you?"

Umfrey again grunted and tightened his hold.

"No, no. I believe you."

"Do you know what it's like to feel you can never get your father's approval?" Maris's voice was tight and a bit hoarse. "Umfrey approves of whatever I do, but my father . . . I wanted *his* approval. I had no mother and I would never be anyone or anything, alone and cast out as soon as my father died. And while I was forbidden from marrying, I had to watch my father plan for my younger sister to get married and have her own home and family. Do you have any idea how that made me feel? Well, I might not be able to stop her from marrying, but I thought at least I could watch her marry someone old and ugly so that she would be as miserable as I am.

"Of course you don't know anything about the injustices I have faced," Maris continued. "You are the firstborn son of an earl. You were a knight and in control of your future. You knew you were the favored one, destined to a life of power and wealth."

"I rarely saw my father, and my mother also died when I was a young child," Edwin said. "I can imagine you had a very hurtful childhood, from what Audrey has told me. My brothers and sister and I had a cruel stepmother, so I can imagine how you felt. I am fortunate in many ways, but you are as well. You were brought up by a father—you are no orphan. You have servants to care for you, I assume, and food to eat and clothing and a home."

Maris scrunched her brows, as if thinking. "I am no villein, if that is what you are saying."

"No, you are not a villein, and therefore you are blessed. You were cared for, were you not?"

Maris glared at him. "Do not distract me. You do not know what you are speaking of. No one has ever cared for me. Our nurse loved Audrey and hated me too. She used to beat me and starve me even though I didn't do anything wrong. She never treated Audrey that way. But now it is my sister who is doing wrong, and I have to take her to my father so he can see that she is the one who is guilty of wrongdoing, not me, and he can punish her."

Edwin said, "But your father might not react the way you think. If you force your sister to go home, he may be angry with you and feel compassion for her."

"Then I will kill her instead." Maris's face grew a strange reddish-purple color. "She deserves to die for the ways she has ruined my life. And then my father will love me again."

"Again, I do not believe you will achieve the reaction you are hoping for. Your father may love her more in death than in life and hate you for killing her. No, it will not go well if you kill your sister."

"I hate her. I will kill her. Father will never know I killed her." Her eyes were wide, and she was literally spitting as she talked, tears starting to spill down her cheeks.

"You don't want to do that, Maris." He tried to make his voice low and soothing. "You should kill me instead."

"Why would I do that?"

"Because you can make up a tale about how I was abusing her, and you killed me to save your little sister. You can take your sister to a convent and tell your father that she wished to go there. Then you will be your father's favorite. He will be so grateful for what you did to save Audrey. And because I am an earl, your father will be forced to defend you. He will come to your defense in ways you've only dreamed of."

Her eyes cleared, her face losing its strange color. He could see she was liking the idea. But then her face clouded over again.

"Why are you saying this? Why would you want me to kill you? You're trying to trick me."

"I'm trying to help you get what you want."

"Why would you want to help me? Why would you want to die?"

He had to take care he did not say the wrong thing. Audrey was a wonderful, amazing woman, so very dear, and he couldn't bear to see harm come to her. But Maris would not appreciate him saying that, and she was mad but not necessarily daft.

"I am willing to die because I will be remembered as a man who lost his arm saving his brothers, and Audrey will know I gave my life for her. That will be enough for me."

"Perhaps Umfrey will kill you and then we will kill Audrey anyway."

He had thought of that. But if she truly had no qualms about killing her sister, she probably would have already killed her. He was offering her a way out, a reason not to take Audrey's life.

"You could kill her, but you would be wasting an opportunity to win your father's approval. Just think how he will feel when you tell him you rescued her. And you can bribe someone at the convent not to send any of her letters to her father. That should be a simple thing to accomplish. You can write letters for her, telling your father what a courageous and loyal sister you are."

It was a strange way for him to save Audrey, an outlandish scenario, but Maris was an outlandish person, bitter and spiteful and clearly not right in her head. He couldn't help feeling some pity for her, but he was more concerned with saving Audrey.

"This sounds like a plan that I . . . but I will have to think about it." She nodded her head. "Umfrey, tie him up so he can't escape."

At least he had bought them some time. How was Audrey faring? She hadn't spoken. Her face was a bit pale, but she otherwise looked strong. Now he just had to pray. God was their only hope.

Audrey wanted to weep at Edwin's suggestion that Maris kill him and let her live. But instead of crying, she chose to pray silently, as fervently as she ever had in her life.

She watched Umfrey tie Edwin's ankles together and then tie his torso to a tree, while Maris did the same to Audrey.

Her sister tied the hemp rope so tight it cut into her skin on her ankles and her wrists, and the rope squeezed her stomach uncomfortably as she secured it around the tree.

"This time she won't be able to untie her bonds," Maris said with a smile, talking about Audrey as if she weren't there. But Audrey remained silent, sensing her voice and her words would only incense Maris.

All the ways God might rescue them were going through her head. *God, You could send Edwin's men here to save us. You could cause Umfrey to disobey Maris and set us free.* She kept praying, until she realized what she was doing—suggesting to God how He might help them.

Of course God had already thought of the same ways they might be saved, and more. She didn't need to tell Him what to do. But thinking about how they might get away seemed better than imagining all the terrible things that might happen, how it would feel to die, and worse, how it would feel to watch Edwin die.

Thinking about his kiss made her want to cry. What if she never got to kiss him again? What if she was never able to discover all the things about him that made him so unique and wonderful? What if they were perfect for each other but never got to be together?

She had to stop thinking about such things. But it had been so heavenly to see the tenderness in his eyes, to know that he wanted to kiss her as much as she wanted to kiss him.

But perhaps she shouldn't have kissed him. If she hadn't, they might have noticed Maris and Umfrey sneaking up on them, might have been alert enough to get away from them and not get captured. *I'm so sorry, God, for getting us captured.* God would forgive her, and perhaps He would save them.

She gazed over at Edwin—Lord Dericott. Would he let her call him Edwin? She always imagined calling her husband by his given name, the way his family would. If she wasn't closer to her husband than his parents and siblings were, then that was not a man she wanted to marry. Her marriage would be loving and close and intense or she would not be happy. She knew that much about herself. After all, she'd been waiting all her life to feel loved and cherished.

Edwin's face was so dear, so very dear. And since he had not been able to shave for a day, the lower half was covered in short dark stubble, giving him a manly, rugged look. He was so handsome, a good man, full of courage and integrity. He hated that he had lost an arm, hated the way it made him feel weak, but it also made him vulnerable, and she liked that. How could she tell him that without offending him? If he were perfect, if he never needed help, how could they grow closer? Because she was not perfect and she often needed help.

Having two arms did not make a man good or strong. Surely he would see that.

"I have decided," Maris said suddenly, nodding to Umfrey and walking toward Edwin. "I will do what Lord Dericott proposed. I will kill him and let Audrey live."

"No!" Audrey gasped. "No, please." She couldn't bear it. She strained against her bonds, pulling at the rope that tied her wrists together, even though it was cutting into her skin. She leaned forward against the rope around her stomach, but nothing gave way.

She should probably pretend not to care, but she'd done that and it hadn't worked. *God, please! Please help.*

"It is all right," Edwin was saying.

She turned and looked into his eyes, even though it hurt so much to see him, knowing he was sacrificing himself for her.

"I want to do it. Let me do this one last thing to protect you."

The intensity of his gaze wrung a sob from her throat.

Maris laughed. Such an ugly sound. How could she laugh? How could she be so cruel? But Audrey would not spend her last moments with Edwin worrying about Maris. She had to tell him how she felt. She couldn't let him sacrifice himself without knowing . . .

"I love you, Edwin."

"And I love you, Audrey."

He loved her! Her tears came faster.

"And now," Maris said, looking at Audrey but motioning to Umfrey, "we have to decide how to kill your love." Her lips twisted as if in anticipation.

Was Maris only saying these things? Would she truly kill an earl, a wonderful man like Edwin? But she'd relished tripping her own sister so she would fall into the fire. She'd just laughed at Audrey's distress over Edwin being killed. And Umfrey seemed to follow Maris blindly, obeying her every whim and wish.

Umfrey lumbered closer to Edwin.

"Not yet," Maris said, folding her arms over her chest. "I'm thinking. We could make it quick and relatively painless."

Audrey went numb all over. Surely this was not happening.

"Or we could make it slow." She tapped her chin. "What do you think, Umfrey?"

"I break neck." Umfrey demonstrated with his hands how he would do it. "Like chicken."

Maris laughed. "Just like breaking a chicken's neck. Very good, Umfrey. Any other ideas?"

"I cut." Again he demonstrated, this time drawing his finger across his own neck.

"Also very effective," Maris mused.

Audrey knew it was worse than pointless to argue with Maris or to beg her to have mercy. But she had to try. She had to.

"Please, Maris, don't do this. Father would not approve. Please."

"Don't speak to me about Father." Maris glared at her.

She had to think of a different tact. "Lord Dericott has never done anything to harm you. He is good to his people, and they need him."

"They don't need him." Contempt oozed from Maris's expression. "His next brother will simply take over for him."

Audrey frantically searched her mind for something else. "But if you kill a good man, God will not approve. He will let Satan get control of your mind and you will never be free from his grip."

Maris half frowned, half smiled. "Try again."

"Please don't, for my sake, Maris. We were friends when we were children, were we not? I loved you as my older sister. I would never hurt someone you loved."

"You ruined everything! You turned Father and the servants against me. You were the perfect one, doing everything right, and I was 'Mad Maris,' the strange and unpredictable one. I know what they called me, Father and all the servants. And I hated you for it. It was your fault. Even as children, I was despised and you were loved."

"I'm sorry, Maris. I never meant to hurt you. I have never turned anyone against you." Audrey could feel the tears welling up. Nothing she was saying was helping Edwin's cause. She was making it worse! *God, help me!*

"Your sniveling entertains me. What other arguments do you have?"

"There is no priest to speak the final rites." *O God, please save us.* "And it's me you hate. Not him. Kill me instead." How could she live knowing he died trying to save her?

"Audrey, no." Edwin's voice was deep and gruff.

"It's not right for you to die because of me." Audrey was on the verge of sobbing. She had to control herself and let the numbness take over her mind and heart. But Edwin was looking at her so intently, she could not look away.

"I want to do it. Let me prove I'm a knight, courageous in death. I want to do it for you."

Her heart swelled at the love she saw in his eyes. She had never dared believe he could love her, but he'd said it, and now he wanted to die for her. It felt so good to be loved—and so horrendous to think of him dying. Good, kind Edwin.

"This life is but a puff of smoke, and heaven awaits us. Don't cry, Audrey."

Rebellious tears dripped down her face. How she longed to wipe them off, but her hands were bound.

"This is truly sickening." Maris frowned. "But at least I will have the pleasure of knowing I hurt you as much as you have hurt me."

"Please, Maris. I never meant to hurt you. We can all change. We'll show Father that we are different now, that you are able to get married, and I will go to the convent and you'll never have to see me again. Just please don't kill him."

She hardly knew what she was saying. She only knew she had to stop Maris. And words were her only resource.

"I am growing weary of all your false promises and begging. Umfrey, let us consider together how we will take care of the earl."

Maris and Umfrey walked away, so far Audrey could barely see them through the leaves of the trees. Then she turned her head toward Edwin.

"I am so sorry. Please forgive me."

"Forgive you? There is nothing to forgive."

"I am the cause of . . . this." She swallowed, unable to speak the words "your death." It was too dreadful, too painful.

"You are not the cause. Listen to me." Edwin's face was so dear, so intense. If only they could have more time. "You did nothing wrong. Your sister and her henchman are the only wrongdoers here. And I was trained as a knight. I know my duty to those under my protection, and it is my privilege to die for you. Not only because you are under my protection, but because you are the woman I want to marry."

Her heart soared even as a sob wracked her chest.

"You are good and kind and loving. You are everything I could wish for. And you are beautiful . . . the most beautiful woman I have ever beheld." His intense expression was transformed by a slight, gentle smile.

"There must be some way to escape. I cannot bear it if they kill you." Her heart hurt so much; perhaps she was dying. What a blessing if she could die with him.

"You will be strong. Do it for me. Be courageous. And if she puts you in a convent, you will escape. You will have a good and happy life if God allows me to have anything to do with it. I will watch over you and beg God night and day to bless you."

"You are too wonderful. I don't want you to leave me alone. Please . . ."

"Remember how much Mistress Wattlesbrook adores you. She will tell my brothers to watch over you. And remember your friends, Sybil and Helena. You can bring them to Dericott Castle and live there when you are free."

He was so kind. How could he be thinking of her when he was about to die?

"Do not worry or lose heart," he said, "no matter what happens. I want more than anything for you to be happy."

"I know that I shall always love you. You will forever be in my heart. My dearest Edwin, I shall never forget you or stop loving you or stop thinking you are the best man who ever lived." More tears squeezed from her eyes, even though she did her best to blink them back.

Maris and Umfrey were coming toward them.

NINETEEN

EDWIN KEPT HIS EYES ON AUDREY, REFUSING TO LOOK AT his executioners as they walked back toward him.

She was so pretty, even when she was crying.

In his training to be a knight, he had imagined being killed many times for a good cause. And just as he'd been prepared to die for his brothers and sister several months ago when they escaped the Tower of London, he was prepared to die now for Audrey. He did not even feel much fear; instead, peace bloomed inside him. He was determined to die with courage so that Audrey could tell the tale without shame of the man who saved her life.

Audrey's lips were moving and he discerned that she was praying, but she focused her eyes on him. Tears streamed down her face as her lips kept moving.

Poor girl. He felt worse for her than he did for himself. She would be so traumatized. He only hoped she would hold fast to her courage and strength through whatever Maris did to her.

"Stay alive, and stay strong," Edwin told her.

Umfrey was looming over him holding a knife. So it was to be throat slitting. At least Edwin felt calm, a bit numb, at the prospect of dying. It was not as frightening as he had imagined. Umfrey grabbed the rope that was tied around Edwin's middle, and he sawed at it with the knife he was holding, finally breaking through.

The large man then took Edwin by the arm and lifted him from a sitting position to standing.

Edwin's ankles were still bound together and his wrist was tied to his ankles, the rope so short he could barely stand upright. He felt like a trussed pig. He'd heard stories from other men who had been in battles and wars and minor crusades about getting captured by the enemy. He felt as if he were in one of those stories, as if his own imminent death were a dream and not real. "God bless and save you," he said to Audrey, suddenly feeling very spiritual. He imagined he could hear angels' wings as they came to carry him to heaven.

But he gradually realized the sound he heard was more like several horses' hooves from far away. It grew louder, and Umfrey and Maris apparently heard it too, because they lifted their heads and stared at each other.

This sound of horses . . . Instead of taking him to heaven, was God about to deliver them?

"Help us!" Audrey shouted.

He was surprised her small throat was capable of such a large sound. Maris stepped toward her with a menacing look.

"We go," Umfrey said, grabbing Maris's hand and pulling.

Maris pointed a skinny finger at Audrey. "Curse you! May you be forever cursed! I'll get you yet!"

She and Umfrey ran to their horses, mounted up, and were just disappearing from sight when the horses and riders came into the small clearing where he and Audrey were.

"Gerard!"

His brother was there in the front of the group, urging his horse faster in his direction.

"Father!" Audrey's face was bright, her eyes wide and her mouth open. "Thank God. We are saved."

Gerard dismounted quickly and ran to Edwin, pulling a knife from his belt.

"Send some men after them," Edwin said.

"Which way did they go?" Gerard quickly set about cutting his bonds.

"They went north. A woman and a very large man."

Gerard pointed and yelled at the men accompanying them, "Find them and bring them back!"

Viscount Engleford went straight to Audrey and cut her loose from the tree as the rest of the men galloped away. "Thank you, Father. You came just in time."

"How'd you find us?" Edwin asked as Gerard finished cutting the ropes from his wrist and his ankles.

"I was riding home to surprise you, as the marquess had given me a few months to do as I wish, and I came upon the viscount looking for his elder daughter, who had gone missing and was possibly plotting harm. So I decided to join him in the search. I did not realize you were in danger as well. We discovered your trail and followed you here." He looked long and hard at the bloody skin on Edwin's wrist. "Are you all right?"

"I am well. But they were just about to kill me."

"Kill you? What did you do to make them so angry?"

"I? Nothing. I shall explain later."

Just then he saw Audrey coming toward him. He turned and hurried to meet her. He couldn't kiss her again; there were too many people around, one of whom was her father. But he was happy enough to embrace her. She threw herself into his chest as he wrapped his arm around her. He pressed his cheek against her hair and closed his eyes.

How good it felt to hold her. Never again would he be careless enough to let that sister of hers get near her.

"Thank God you're safe," he said.

"Me? You were almost killed! Oh, thank You, God," she said, burying her face again in his shoulder, her arms wrapped tight around him.

They were alive. Not so long ago he'd been so bitter, he hardly cared if he died. There were moments when he had wished for death. But now, with Audrey holding on to him . . . he was so glad to be alive.

Father put Audrey on his horse and rode away on another horse with the group of guards to go try to capture Maris and Umfrey. Meanwhile, Edwin rode beside her on his brother Gerard's horse. Edwin's brother seemed kind and pleasant, but Audrey barely glanced at him, since she couldn't tear her eyes away from Edwin.

"As soon as we get back to the castle," he said, "I'll have Mistress Wattlesbrook tend to your wrists."

"Yours as well." She stared at his wounds as he held his horse's reins. She took in a slow, deep breath and let it out. "I'm just relieved beyond words that we escaped, relatively unscathed."

He gave her a crooked smile and winked. She couldn't help but smile back. And couldn't help but remember how willing he had been to die to give her a chance to one day escape the fate Maris planned for her. And the kisses they'd shared—that was unforgettable as well.

Had Edwin meant it when he said he loved her and that he wanted to marry her? Her heart still fluttered thinking about it. Loving him was so easy, and the truth had been dawning on her, gradually, for some time now. But she had not dared to let herself dwell on her feelings as long as she believed he was pledged to another—or to let herself believe he could love her.

As they rode through the village of Dericott, people came out of their homes and stared at them. They began to recognize Edwin and Gerard, and smiles broke out on their faces. A few called out, while others cheered. Three of Audrey's students were playing together and saw her. They called out, "Teacher! Teacher is home!"

Gerard moved his horse closer to Audrey. "They're more delighted to see you than Edwin or me!"

Audrey laughed, then shook her head.

Edwin raised his brow at her. "It is true." He smiled, as

if it pleased him that the villagers loved her more than they loved him.

They made their way up the hill to Dericott Castle.

"Do you think my father and his men have captured Maris and Umfrey?" she asked Edwin, who rode close to her.

"They should have by now. I would not worry. His men are experienced trackers, no doubt, and Maris and Umfrey could not outrun them for long."

She couldn't help but feel a bit uneasy until she heard they were captured.

Mistress Wattlesbrook met them on the front steps of the castle. She clasped her hands, her eyes watery. "Thanks be to God for bringing you safely home."

The guards began to inform Lord Dericott of the happenings at the castle while Edwin's brother, Lord Gerard, helped her down from her horse.

Edwin called up to Mistress Wattlesbrook. "See that her wrists are bandaged."

"I shall attend her, never fear." Mistress Wattlesbrook whisked Audrey inside and Gerard followed, leaving Edwin outside to talk to his men.

"Lord Dericott also has some injuries," Audrey said, trying to look over her shoulder for him.

"Very minor," Gerard said, winking and shaking his head.

"And what a surprise to see you!" Mistress Wattlesbrook called to Edwin's brother, even as she hurried down the corridor with Audrey.

"I thought I would surprise you," Gerard said in his pleasant manner. "But I was the one surprised when I came upon this young lady's father, searching for her and her sister. It seems quite a lot has been stirring around here."

"Indeed," was all Mistress Wattlesbrook said.

They went into a small room, and Mistress Wattlesbrook reached for a roll of bandages and a flask.

"Now, I must hear all that has happened with the both of you. Who shall begin?"

Audrey and Gerard exchanged looks.

"I believe the lady should go first. Her story is much more harrowing."

Even as tired as she was, Audrey was rather eager to tell the tale to a sympathetic ear, and she knew Mistress Wattlesbrook was just that sort of listener. So she began from when she was finishing her lesson at the church the day before and told of her experiences, although she made sure to leave out the detail of her and Edwin's mutual kisses and declarations of love.

When she got to the part where Edwin persuaded Maris to kill him and spare Audrey, she got choked up. She had to stop and take deep breaths while Mistress Wattlesbrook made encouraging noises such as "There, there," and "*mm, mm,*" and "*tsk, tsk.*"

Audrey cleared her throat. "When they were about to do something horrible, my father and Lord Gerard came to our rescue. If they had come one minute later, it would probably have been too late."

Unbidden, tears flooded her eyes and she had to take deep breaths again to chase them away.

Mistress Wattlesbrook patted her shoulder very gently. "All

is well. God provided help when you needed it, and we are all so grateful to the Almighty." The good woman clasped her hands together and closed her eyes for a moment.

"I thank God we came when we did," Gerard said. "I can hardly believe a woman . . . Well, I can believe a woman could be so heartless." He frowned and met Mistress Wattlesbrook's gaze over Audrey's shoulder.

He must have been referring to their stepmother, who had falsely accused him and had ultimately cost Edwin his arm.

"I am very sorry," Gerard said to her, looking so sincere and reminding her a bit of his brother—though Edwin's face was infinitely dearer.

"Thank you. Maris went through some horrible things when she was a small child and I was a baby. It greatly affected her and made her terribly jealous. And Father . . . I believe he could have handled the situation better." Though perhaps they would think her unseemly to criticize her own father.

Mistress Wattlesbrook squeezed her shoulder comfortingly. "Do not worry. Everyone is safe now. And we expect your nurse, Sybil, soon."

A sudden thought came to her. What if Sybil was intercepted by Maris and Umfrey? That would be grave indeed. But it was very unlikely they would meet, as Maris was fleeing her would-be captors and Sybil was coming here. Besides, Sybil had Lord Dericott's guard to protect her.

Just as Audrey was wondering about Edwin, she heard footsteps coming down the corridor, then he appeared in the doorway. His eyes met hers.

"Thanks be to God you are safe and found." Mistress Wattlesbrook pressed her hands together with a huge smile. "And, Audrey, you can put some ointment—this one right here—on the lord's wounds and bandage them."

"What wounds?" Edwin said, frowning at her.

"On your wrist. I can see the bloody marks without even looking. Come, Lord Gerard. I must help the servants draw water for you and Lord Dericott and Audrey to bathe yourselves." Mistress Wattlesbrook motioned to Edwin's younger brother as she shuffled out the door.

Gerard looked confused, but Edwin raised his brows. Gerard's eyes went wide and he gave his brother a quick, knowing nod, then hurried away.

When they were gone, Audrey sat back down and Edwin sat on the stool Gerard had just vacated. Edwin stretched out his hand to her. "Mistress Wattlesbrook must always have her way."

"Yes. We had better do as she says." Audrey smiled. She opened the flask and poured out a bit of ointment onto her fingers.

She cradled his hand in hers and began to smear the ointment on his wrist where the skin was flayed and starting to scab over.

"It does not smell very good, does it?" she said. "But it is not as bad as the salve my nurse used to put on my cuts and scrapes."

Their eyes met as they gazed at each other. She drew in a deep breath and let it out, finally looking back down at his wrist.

His hand was very large, with long, strong-looking fingers. There were small scars here and there on his hand, probably from his training as a knight. His skin was warm, and she felt quite comfortable sitting so close to him, touching his hand. He never did anything to make her uncomfortable, even when they had lain behind the waterfall trying to stay warm and hidden from her sister. He had never blamed her for their misfortunes either, though he could have—the way her sister did.

"I'm glad you didn't die today." Audrey was trying to make light of what had happened, but it was too soon for that, because she felt the tears dam up behind her eyes again.

Edwin leaned toward her. Was he wanting to kiss her? She stared into his eyes and leaned toward him. She closed her eyes and let her lips touch his.

When the kiss ended, he said, "Will you let me take you somewhere tomorrow morning?"

"Take me somewhere?"

"Yes. I want you to accompany me to a place I think you will like."

"Of course."

"At sunrise. I shall come to your room and knock on the door, and we will go."

"Very well."

He kissed her again, briefly, as they heard heavy footsteps in the corridor where anyone might walk by and see them. Then she let him kiss her again, and he kissed her until a servant called out that food was being served in the Great Hall. And it had been too long since either of them had eaten to ignore that.

Audrey was ready to go when she heard the knock at her door the following morning. The sun would rise at any moment.

"Good morning, Audrey." Edwin was wearing a white linen shirt that laced up at the top. His dark hair looked freshly washed, and his smile was gentle and respectful. Indeed, he looked very handsome.

"Good morning, Lord Dericott." Her voice sounded breathless. She did not dare call him Edwin—not yet.

"Are you wearing your sturdiest shoes?" He glanced down at her feet.

"I am. I thought you might be taking me somewhere like the burial mound and the stork's nest, so yes, I put on my sturdiest shoes."

"Good." He held out his arm to her and she took it without hesitation.

Holding on to his arm felt simultaneously natural and thrilling as they made their way down the stairs. The corridors were quiet, and he headed toward the Great Hall.

"Have you heard anything from Father? Have they found Maris?"

"Not yet. But I am sure we will hear something soon."

Audrey nodded, telling herself, *Don't worry. All will be well.*

"I did ask some guards to follow us and be nearby, just to be doubly safe."

"Of course." Audrey smiled to show she was not worried.

"Mistress Wattlesbrook has packed us some food." He took

the basket from a small table by the door and they made their way outside.

They walked a short way as the sun was making the sky yellow and pink, even though it had not topped the horizon yet. On a rise, she helped Lord Dericott spread a thin blanket on the ground, and they sat and watched as the sun made its appearance.

"What a beautiful sunrise," she said, not wanting to miss a moment of the radiant color God was painting in the sky.

"It is beautiful. I'm so glad it isn't cloudy or rainy."

"It is an ideal morning," Audrey agreed. "A few clouds, which gives the sun somewhere to show off the colors."

"But it is not as beautiful as your smile." Lord Dericott was staring at her now.

"You are flattering me." She felt herself blushing, her mind flitting to their kisses and his declaration of love for her the previous day.

"It is not flattery but truth. I think your smile is more beautiful than the sunrise."

"And I think you are the bravest and best man I know." *And I love you*, she couldn't help adding in her mind, not courageous enough to say it aloud again, not yet. But oh, how she loved him, this man who would have given his life for her.

They gazed into each other's eyes for a few moments, then went back to looking at the sunrise.

"This is a perfect spot to see the whole sky. I dearly love to see the sunrise—and the sunset too." Audrey leaned back on her hands and gazed all around, then came back to the eastern sky.

"I thought it would be a good place to break our fast." He opened the basket. "Take whatever you like."

Rather than let Lord Dericott hear her stomach rumble, she reached inside and took out a fruit pasty. "Your cooks make the best cherry pasties," she said.

He smiled and took a bite of one, then nodded.

When the sunrise had faded and the sun was shining brightly, he said, "Shall we wander and see if we can find some wildflowers?"

"Oh, I love wildflowers!"

He offered her his arm. She took it and they walked quite close together. It was strange, but whenever she was with him, she felt safe, peaceful, and less impulsive. He made her feel as if she had nothing to fear and that all would be well, no matter what happened.

Perhaps she should tell him that, but it felt so good and comfortable walking close by his side that she didn't want to spoil the moment. Whenever she glanced up at him, he was either looking very serious as he led them on a narrow path down the side of the ridge or he was gazing down at her with a gentle smile.

They were at the bottom, walking through some trees, when they came to a shallow stream about six feet wide.

"So pretty!" Audrey loved the sound of the water spilling over the smooth rocks that lined the bottom, perfectly visible through the clear, clean water. The bank was rather steep, but there was a tiny dirt path that led to the water's edge.

"Come. We will cross it." Lord Dericott started leading her down to the water.

"How? We will get wet."

"Do you trust me?"

"Of course, but our feet will get wet. Should we take off our shoes?"

"Just trust me."

When he got to the river's edge, he reached for a piece of wood, which had been sawed lengthwise to form a flat surface. It was tucked against the side of the bank. When he laid it across the water, it reached from one side to the other.

He held out his hand to her and they crossed slowly, he slightly ahead of her, on the piece of wood. They only had to step off on the other side and climb another little path up the other bank.

At the top of the bank, Audrey gasped. All around her, in a meadow of green grass, were hundreds of wildflowers in every shade of blue and pink and purple.

"This is the most beautiful place I've ever seen." She couldn't take her eyes off of it.

"I thought you would enjoy it."

"I do! I've never seen so many beautiful flowers. So many colors." Audrey bent and started picking the flowers. Mistress Wattlesbrook and the other servants, even though they never seemed to adore the flowers she picked as much as she did, would have to admit that these were beautiful.

Lord Dericott had grown quiet. The last time she'd seen him, he was behind her. With her flowers gathered to her chest, she turned and saw that he was down on one knee just behind her. And he was holding out something in his hand—a ring.

"Audrey, you have made me glad to be alive. I have admired your spirit and your sweet temper ever since you came to Dericott Castle. I know I want to spend the rest of my life with you beside me, waking up with me to watch the sunrise, picking wildflowers, or whatever we choose to do. Will you marry me, Audrey?"

Audrey started to sob. Still holding the flowers to her chest, she raised her hands to her face as the tears leaked from her eyes. "You don't mind my scars?" she asked in a shaky, tear-filled voice. Her heart was soaring out of her chest, but she had to ask.

His shook his head, his own eyes looking a bit misty. "Your scars are what make you beautiful, the things you have overcome, the way you have stayed gentle and kind and compassionate in spite of what has been done to you. Do you not mind my missing arm?"

"No, of course not. You are the best man I know—good and strong and courageous. I could never want anyone but you."

"Then you will marry me? Are you saying yes?"

"Yes, yes, I'm saying yes."

He stood to his feet. They were both smiling as Edwin brushed the tears from her cheeks with his fingers, caressing her jawline. Audrey let him slide the ring onto her finger, unable to tear her gaze from his blue eyes. How good it felt to be looked at with so much openness and tenderness, to see the emotion there.

He took her face in his hand and kissed her, a sweet, gentle touching of lips that made her forget where she was, even made her forget the flowers she was holding. They all spilled onto the ground as she put her arms around him and they kissed again and again. How beautiful his face was, so infinitely dear. And the way he kissed her made her stomach flip.

Edwin kissed her one last time before pulling away. His eyes gazing into hers told her everything she wanted to know. She was loved.

TWENTY

LATER THE SAME DAY, AUDREY HURRIED DOWN THE STAIRS where Edwin was waiting for her.

"Is she here?"

"Just dismounting from her horse." He was smiling, amused at her excitement, no doubt.

She took his hand and squeezed it and forced herself to walk, not run, through the castle to the door and across the bailey.

Sybil stood talking to the groom, who was taking a large bundle off the back of a horse.

"Sybil!" Audrey called.

Sybil turned to her and covered her mouth. Her face was crumpling up like it did when she was about to cry. She met Audrey halfway, and they wrapped their arms around each other.

"Why did you have to go and leave me like that? I didn't know where you were or if you were alive or dead." Sybil's voice was high pitched while tears continued to fall from her eyes.

She put her hand up to her face to wipe them away. "But you are well, I see, thanks to God watching over you." She raised her brows at Audrey with a questioning look.

"I am very well. But I am so sorry Maris had you sent away. How did you fare?"

"I was with my sister in London, and I must say, I despise the place. A body can hardly stir around in there. So many horses and carts and men yelling and women pouring out pots from their windows right into the street. The smoke from the chimneys and the stench from the excrement . . . But you don't want to hear . . . I am so grateful for being able to get out of that place. Thank you, my sweet Audrey, and to you, Lord Dericott. I am most grateful to you, my lord." She stepped back and bowed to Lord Dericott.

"You are very welcome here."

"I don't expect to be treated like a guest," she said quickly. "Put me to work. I can do anything."

"We can discuss that later," Audrey said. "For now you can sleep in the little room next to my chamber." Then Audrey leaned closer to Sybil and said softly, "Lord Dericott and I are to be married."

Sybil's eyes flew wide and her eyes filled with tears. "I am so happy."

They embraced each other again, Audrey with a little laugh and Sybil with a squeal. But she soon recovered herself and turned to Edwin.

"Lord Dericott, Audrey was always the sweetest child. She used to kiss my cheek every morning and every night and tell me that someday I was going to marry a knight with a purple feather in his helmet." Sybil laughed.

"That was a very long time ago." Audrey glanced shyly at Edwin.

"Perhaps you will," he said.

Once Sybil had gone into her chamber to rest, Audrey and Edwin went for a walk to the lake where the swans lived. She squeezed his arm.

"How glad I am that Sybil is here safe."

"Yes, and my steward is finishing the letters to the rest of my brothers and my sister, inviting them to our engagement ball and wedding."

"I am so excited to meet them. I love your stories about them, and Gerard is so pleasant. Do you think they will like me?"

"Of course they will. Delia always wanted a sister—she will adore you."

"Also, are you sure we should have an engagement ball? It seems so . . . public."

"We don't have to invite many people—mostly just my brothers and my sister and her husband. And I will hire some singers and players, of course. My steward always takes care of the details. You can speak with him and make sure he doesn't invite too many people."

"But if my father is invited, I'm afraid Maris will hear about it somehow and cause trouble."

"I'm afraid we cannot avoid inviting your father."

"I suppose not." Audrey was worrying her lip with her teeth when Edwin bent and kissed her cheek.

"All will be well. Your father's men and some of mine are still out looking for her. I received word that they found a fire they thought may have belonged to her and her henchman. They will soon locate her and capture her."

"I am glad you feel that way, because I was hoping to have lessons tomorrow with my students."

"I've been thinking about that." Edwin took a deep breath and let it out.

"Uh-oh. You have that look on your face."

"What look?"

"Your lordly look."

He shook his head. "I just want to keep you safe."

"Please don't tell me you're not going to let me teach the children anymore."

"No, but I want you to do your lessons here at the castle."

"But that's too far for the children to walk."

"No, it's not that far. And you walked that far when you went to the church for the lessons. They won't mind."

"But I must at least go one more time to the church so they will know—"

"I will send a man to tell them."

"A man and me?"

He sighed. Waited. Then said, "A man and me and another man and you."

She smiled and leaned forward to kiss him.

He had been giving her control, letting her decide when and how much affection to show. But now when she kissed him and pulled away, he leaned toward her and pulled her closer, his eyes reluctant to open. Her heart jumped and she kissed him again.

How good it was to love and be loved by someone as gentle and attentive as Edwin, someone so completely unlike her father.

Audrey took Edwin's arm, squeezing it tight, as they started down the hill toward the village.

Edwin exulted in the feel of her hugging his arm while they walked. In the past month, his balance had improved so much that it was no longer as difficult to walk or ride as it had been, although he would probably never gain back the stability he'd enjoyed when he was a knight.

But Audrey was helping him realize it wasn't brute strength or his ability to sit a horse or wield a sword that made him a man. Self-sacrifice and courage were what defined the best kind of man.

Instead of riding to the church for her lessons, Audrey had asked to walk with him. So he sent a guard ahead of them to make certain Maris and her henchman were not there threatening the children or lying in wait for Audrey. Two more guards, fully armed, rode beside them at a slow walk. He did not want to regret once again not being adequately protected. Besides, Audrey was worth any measures it took to keep her safe.

"I am so thankful you are allowing me to continue my lessons with the children," Audrey said softly.

He kissed her hair. "I want you to be happy."

"Ever since I was a child I wanted my life to be extraordinary, to be a bright light in the world. I know that sounds daft."

"Not daft at all."

"I didn't know what that extraordinary thing would be. I just knew I wanted my life to matter and to make a difference. But when Maris caused these scars on my face, I was afraid I'd never be able to do anything remarkable. Father stopped trying to marry me off to a nobleman with a title. I felt ugly. I felt I was damaged."

His heart expanded inside his chest. He knew exactly what she meant.

"You are not ugly or damaged. You are beautiful, the most beautiful woman I have ever seen."

She squeezed his arm. "I'm so glad you think so."

"You know you are beautiful, do you not?"

"You make me feel beautiful." She squeezed his arm again, gazing up at him in a way that made his chest ache. "And as long as people cannot see my scars . . . I don't feel ugly anymore. And my students tell me I'm pretty." She smiled up at him again.

"I'm glad. You are lovely. The fairest maiden in all of England."

"You are just seeing me through the eyes of love." She laughed, a soft sound.

"I am in love with you."

She squeezed his arm again. "And I am in love with you." After a few moments she went on.

"I have been thinking a lot about what God would want me to do with my life. I don't think I ever would have found my purpose had I married Sir Clement."

"I'm very happy you did not marry Sir Clement."

She rewarded him with another squeeze and a smile. "When I started teaching the girls, I felt as if that was the significant thing I had been hoping to do. These children have become so very dear to me, and I enjoy teaching them. I couldn't bear to give that up because of Maris. Does that make sense?"

"Yes. I understand." But his heart felt a little heavy. He had to think about why.

"Do you feel that way too?"

"I was told I would one day be the Earl of Dericott, but I was glad I was able to train as a knight. I always wanted to be a strong fighter and do courageous things and fight for the oppressed. But the only fighting I did was to save myself and my brothers from our stepmother. That doesn't sound very noble, does it?"

"Of course it was noble. It's always noble to save your own life from someone who is trying to harm you. That's what you told me."

She always knew just what to say.

"And it's noble to save your younger brothers. What could be nobler than that?"

She smiled up at him in that endearing way of hers. If they weren't walking down the village street, he would kiss her.

"And you saved me from my sister and her henchman. But now, let us hope we don't have any more attacks from people who wish us harm. We've had enough for a lifetime, I think."

"We have had our share."

They were nearly to the church, and he was reliving the sinking feeling of discovering that Audrey had been taken by

Maris. The sight of his guard lying unconscious on the ground. Thankfully his guard had recovered from the head injury. He was still having some vision problems, but he said even that was improving.

Was Audrey also reliving the trauma of what had happened that day?

"Are you well?" he asked.

"I am well. I feel safe with you."

At the church, they found several of the children already there. Once they had all arrived, Audrey and Edwin and the guards led the children back to Dericott Castle and to the storage room on the first floor that his servants were cleaning out and making into a classroom. The children seemed content with the new arrangement. They obviously believed that wherever their teacher was would be a good place for them.

He could not have agreed more. And he could keep her close to him now.

TWENTY-ONE

AUDREY SIGHED HAPPILY AS SHE WATCHED EDWIN OUTSIDE the window. He was talking to the captain of the guard on the grassy bailey below.

The invitations had been sent out for the festive ball Edwin was giving to celebrate their engagement and their wedding, which would follow the day after the ball. The guests would be arriving in a few days. Clothes had been ordered for Audrey, finery more impressive than anything she had owned as a viscount's daughter. And she had been teaching her children every day at the castle.

Sybil had made herself quite useful helping Audrey prepare things for her students and getting ready for the ball. But best of all was having her there for Audrey to talk to, a woman who had known her all her life.

As she was getting ready for her students to arrive, she heard Sybil greeting them at the front door.

"See that you clean your feet on the rug before you come inside," Sybil said, no doubt pointing at the plaited hemp rug she had laid in front of the door for that purpose. Many of the children did not own shoes, but the twisted hemp was good for rubbing off dirty, dusty feet as well as shoes.

The first girl to run into the room was Clarice. She was adorable, with her wide, eager eyes. She held out a rolled-up piece of paper with a string tied around it.

"Here, Mistress Audrey. I didn't read it. The boy told me not to read it and I didn't."

"What is it?" Audrey asked, untying the string and feeling a prickling sensation on the back of her neck.

"I don't know."

Audrey unrolled the paper and felt like she'd been punched in the gut.

> Call off your wedding and the engagement ball. Tell Lord Dericott you changed your mind and you will not marry him. Have you forgotten about Helena? Have you forgotten what I can do? Don't show anyone this missive or tell anyone about it. Leave Dericott now and no harm will come to Helena or your students.
>
> Maris

Audrey's hands shook as she rolled the paper back up and tried to smile at the children filing into the room.

"I shall be back in a few moments," she told them, feigning cheerfulness. She hurried out of the room and encountered Sybil.

283

"What is the matter, child?"

"Do you know where I can find Lord Dericott?"

"No, my dear. But he may be in his library."

Audrey thanked her and rushed down the hall.

Should she tell him about the letter? Maris had ordered her not to. But what could she do? And how dare she threaten Helena and her students! Helena was in Engleford, but where was Maris? Was she here or was she in Engleford? Would she send Umfrey to harm Helena?

O God, what should I do?

The last thing she wanted to do was endanger the children or Helena, or anyone else. How horrible not only to be unable to do something significant with her life but to actually cause harm to innocent people, people who were so dear to her.

She stared down at the paper in her hand. What would Edwin say when she showed it to him? No doubt he would send men to look for Maris. What had Clarice said about the person who had given her the letter?

Audrey hurried back to the schoolroom.

"Clarice!" she called from the doorway, getting the little girl's attention. She hurried toward Audrey.

"Yes?"

"Clarice, who gave you this note?"

"A boy."

"Did you know the boy? How old was he?"

"I never saw him before. Did I do something wrong?"

"No, Clarice, of course not. You are a good girl. I just wanted to know about the person who gave you this."

"He was about John's age."

"Who is John?"

"John is my brother and he's twelve years old."

"But the boy . . . what did he say?"

"He said to give this to Audrey, my teacher. He said not to read it. That's all. Then he turned around and ran away."

"Where was this?"

"Outside my house. He ran away through the woods."

"Was anyone else around?"

She shook her head, her eyes wide and her expression fearful.

"Thank you, Clarice. I did not mean to frighten you. All is well." She gave the little girl a hug, which put a smile back on her face. "You may go back in the room with the other children. I'll return shortly."

Clarice went inside. Audrey watched as she started playing a rhyming game with three other little girls. Then Audrey went to the library.

Edwin was sitting by the window in his usual chair, reading something.

"My lord?"

He shook his head. "Edwin. You have to call me Edwin now."

"Of course. Edwin."

"What is the matter?"

She hurried over to him. "I hope I am doing the right thing by showing you this. One of my little girls, Clarice, gave me this a minute ago."

Edwin took the paper from her and read it, his brows lowering. He looked up. "Where did she get this?"

"From a little boy, she said, about twelve years old. He gave it to her in the woods by her house. He told her that she was to give it to me and not to read it. Then he ran away."

He reached out and she came to him, wrapping her arms around him as he pulled her close.

"We have to learn where this little girl lives. Will you find out her parents' names and where her house is? I will get some men to go with me to look for Maris."

"I will."

"Don't worry, darling. This could be a good thing. It seems likely she's still in this region, and if she's here, she has not done anything to harm Helena. I believe we have a good chance of finding her soon." He looked so confident and capable.

"Thank you. I know all will be well."

Yes, Edwin was capable. But she also knew he was not invincible. He would do his very best, but ultimately she—and Edwin—had to put their trust in God to take care of them. And no matter what happened, they would both be brave in the face of it.

Edwin took five of his men and went in search of the little girl's house once Audrey found out where she lived. It did not take them long to find it. They looked for any evidence of a strange boy who could have come from a neighboring village, and for Maris and Umfrey. They questioned anyone they saw about whether they had seen them, but no one had any information.

They could be hiding anywhere—in an abandoned house, in a hollowed-out tree trunk, in an abandoned wolf's den, or somewhere he hadn't thought of. Perhaps they had disguised themselves, or they were simply staying hidden and living off animals they were able to kill and eat.

Every minute he did not find and apprehend Maris and Umfrey, he felt as if he was not protecting Audrey. He was failing her. And that was his worst fear—that his weakness would keep him from being able to protect her. That he would be unworthy of her.

He also knew that if she could not teach her little girls, she would be devastated, but it was continuing to prove dangerous for her to teach them, providing Maris a way to get to Audrey. But he could not ask her to give up her lessons. She had said herself that it was the one thing that made her feel as if she was making a difference in the world.

He and his men searched the woods on foot, particularly the wildest part where no one traveled or hunted, overgrown with ferns and bushes and vines, where trees rotted where they fell, mosses and lichens covering them, and where every manner of creature lived—except people.

"I found something," one of his men called out. Edwin and the other men turned their horses in that direction, leading them by their reins, since the trees were too thick and branches too low-hanging to navigate on horseback.

A tiny area had been cleared out, just big enough for two people to sleep, with a small fire pit in the middle where someone had cooked an animal and left the bones.

"We can stay hidden," one of the men said, "and watch to see if they come back here."

"Better if only one or two of us stay, lest they see us and get suspicious," said another.

Edwin agreed and had two of them stay while he and the others went back to the castle.

The sun had gone down by the time they dismounted in front of the stable. Edwin hurried inside to find Audrey waiting for him.

She embraced him. "I'm so glad you're back safely."

"Of course I'm back safely." He caressed her shoulder. "All is well. I left two of my men to spend the night in the forest. We think we may have found their fire."

"What makes you think it was them?"

"It was a fresh clearing where two people had slept, and it was not near any roads, so it probably was not travelers."

"Come. You must be tired."

"We can sit in the library, unless you want me to change my clothes first."

"No."

He must have looked puzzled, because she added, "I like the way you smell when you've been riding—like leather and fresh air."

She said such surprising things. He never had to worry about life with her being dull. She was everything he'd always wanted in a woman, as well as things he didn't know he wanted.

When they were seated he asked her, "How did your lessons proceed today?"

"Well enough. But I kept thinking about how Maris was able to get that letter to little Clarice. I don't like that she was that close to her, or to any of my students."

"I am sure it was very disconcerting for you."

"Do you think she will harm my students? Or Helena?"

"I don't know, but she has only herself and her henchman. Your father and I have a lot of men between us, and my brothers will be arriving very soon for the ball and the wedding. That is a lot of trained men determined to find her and stop her."

"I know, but . . ." Audrey's eyes were filling with tears.

"Please don't cry. I will protect you." He put his arm around her where they sat on the cushioned bench side by side. She leaned into him, pressing her cheek against his chest.

"I am sorry. But . . . what if she succeeds in hurting someone? How will I forgive myself?"

"Forgive yourself? You have done nothing wrong. It is Maris who needs forgiveness, not you."

"But what if she hurts someone just to avenge herself on me?" She was quiet for a moment. "Perhaps we should postpone the wedding, just until she's caught. Is it too late to tell the guests not to come?"

He felt a stab straight into his heart. "Do you not want to get married?"

"I do, I do."

Was she crying? She was clinging to his shirt, her body turned toward him on the bench.

"I want to marry you, very much." Her voice kept cracking. "I am just afraid of what is going to happen. She has ruined everything that seemed good in my life. And she seems so determined to hurt me. She wants me to suffer. And you and I both know she is capable of violent and despicable things. I couldn't bear it if something happened, if someone else was harmed because I was too selfish to give up a little bit of my happiness. But I don't want to hurt you either."

She began to sob quietly, almost silently, her body shaking.

He held her as tightly as he could. *God, give me the words to say.* He wanted her to trust him, to believe that he could keep her and everyone else safe. But she obviously didn't. And how could he blame her? They had both nearly been killed, only saved by his brother and her father and his men. And as far as he knew, her father was still out looking for Maris.

The sobbing subsided as she began to sniff and take deep breaths.

"I don't want to, but if we postpone the ball and the wedding for a short time, perhaps Maris will be caught by then, do you not think?"

"Yes, I think that is very possible, but what if she is not caught? Should we postpone the wedding again? I do not like the idea that we are giving her what she wants. She has had far too much power over you for too long."

Audrey pulled away, wiping at her face with her hands. "You are probably right. I just don't want to see anyone get hurt."

"And I think it may be too late to stop the guests from arriving. The invitations were sent a few days ago. The ball is in five days, the wedding in six."

They were both silent as she rested against his chest.

"But if you wish to postpone the wedding, I will certainly honor that and do my best to prevent the guests from coming." He said the words quietly and sincerely, even though they seemed to tear his heart in two.

"No. No, I don't wish to postpone the wedding. I was just giving in to fear. I was so afraid that you marrying me, you loving me, was too good to be true. But I don't want to wait any longer than we have to. I want to live with you and love you and be your wife as soon as possible."

"Let us not worry. I will send men to make sure Helena is safe—and I will have them bring her here for the ball."

"I would like that very much." Her face brightened.

"Let us have faith that Maris will be found and all will be well. Indeed, she could be found and captured this very night." He was putting every effort into assuring her that Maris would be apprehended. But if he was honest with himself, he'd had the same thoughts she was expressing.

God, help me find Maris and get her somewhere she cannot harm anyone. It would be too cruel to have to postpone the wedding because a woman was so jealous of her sister that she would do anything to hurt her.

The next day a letter came for Audrey. Edwin paid the courier and looked with concern as Audrey opened it.

"It is from the abbess of the convent where Maris was living." Audrey commenced to read it out loud.

The Honorable Audrey of Engleford,

Please excuse my forwardness in writing to you, but it has come to my attention that your sister, Maris, who was lately a resident here at the abbey, has been causing trouble of a serious nature. If she can be found, I have a proposition.

I am the new abbess here, and it has been related to me by Sister Delores, one of our most respected servants of the Lord Jesus, that she had enjoyed some success with helping Maris while she was here. It seems Maris enjoyed gardening and this sort of work was helping Maris to find peace. But the abbess did not understand the kind of calming influence this work had on her, and there was another resident who tormented Maris and said incendiary things to her. Sister Delores believes that the lack of freedom from the abbess, along with the taunting from this other resident, was what caused Maris to become unhappy here.

And now I come to the purpose of my letter. The abbess and this resident, who was unhelpful in Maris's progress, are no longer here at the abbey and will not be returning. If Maris is found, Sister Delores would like to be put in charge of her care and will make sure she is allowed to spend as much time as she wishes in the garden. Sister Delores, who has an interest in helping troubled young women, will attempt to help her make peace with the past that has created such chaos in her thoughts and actions.

Thank you for considering this as an alternative to having Maris locked away when she is captured. And I do pray that she is found soon, for the safety of all.

May God grant His grace and peace to you and all who are with you.

God's humble servant,
Abbess Agnes

"This would be ideal, if it would work." Audrey glanced up at Edwin.

"But your sister is not to be trusted." Edwin's brows drew together. "She wants to kill you. Growing cabbages and turnips will not change her."

"But what if she becomes gentler at the news that the people who did not treat her well are no longer living at the abbey? And that she will be allowed to stay with this Sister Delores?"

"I don't know, darling. It seems quite farfetched to me. Besides, first we must find her."

"But if it is possible, if Maris seems agreeable to it?"

"Possibly. I don't know. Possibly."

At least it was a reason to hope that things could be better for everyone.

TWENTY-TWO

"Helena!"

Audrey ran to her friend and embraced her. "It is so good to see you. Are you well? Are you exhausted from your trip?"

Now it seemed everyone she and Edwin loved was safe from Maris.

Helena smiled. "I am well. But what is this about Maris threatening to harm me?"

Audrey took her inside and explained what Maris had done and said the last few weeks. Helena was aghast. But the joy of her wedding to Edwin, and Helena's awe of him, quickly overshadowed any sad tidings.

More guests had arrived the day before. Her father sent word that he would not make it to the ball but hoped to be at the wedding, as he was following the lead of a possible sighting of Maris. All of Edwin's brothers and his sister, Delia, and her husband, the Duke of Strachleigh, had arrived and been installed in rooms. She hadn't thought it possible to fill up all the bed-rooms in Dericott Castle, but they had accomplished it. Helena would have to sleep in Audrey's room.

Audrey let Helena rest while she went to teach her students. Even though the castle was so full, she had not told the children to stop coming for their lessons. So at the regular time, she greeted them in their classroom.

She had been so nervous meeting Edwin's siblings, it was good to see the children's loving, familiar faces. Not that Edwin's family wasn't kind and gracious to her—they were. But she had been so afraid of saying or doing something wrong and she had needed a respite.

The children were a little distracted, however, and the lesson did not go as well as usual. They could hear the hustling and bustling about and knew the engagement ball was taking place the next day, with the wedding the day after that.

"Are we having lessons tomorrow?" Clarice asked, and all the children turned their faces toward her.

"Tomorrow will be a busy day, and the day after that, so we will not be having lessons. In fact, because I am getting married, we will not have lessons for two weeks. Lessons will resume two weeks from tomorrow. Please tell your parents. Two weeks from tomorrow."

The children looked a little sad at the postponement of lessons but giggled happily when she said she was getting married.

"Aren't you excited to be marrying Lord Dericott?" Dorcas asked.

"Are you nervous?" asked the oldest girl, Rebecca.

"I am excited and a bit nervous about the wedding, but not about getting married to Lord Dericott." She made an effort not to let herself blush. "He is a good man, and I am happy. But if you ever have doubts that the man you are marrying is not a good man, then promise me you will not marry him."

She looked hard at each one of them.

"We promise," they all chimed.

"There are a lot of preparations for a wedding and a ball, so I am a little apprehensive about those things." As well as about Maris, who still had not been captured, but she would not share that with her students.

"Have you ever been to a ball?" Susannah asked.

"I actually have not." When she'd been fifteen, her father often mentioned throwing a ball, inviting several unmarried noblemen or noblemen whose sons were unmarried and not betrothed. But after Maris caused her scars, her father never brought up the ball again.

"I did have dance instructors who taught me how to dance." Although it had been a while since she'd practiced. Would she embarrass herself in front of everyone Edwin knew and loved?

Yes, if she was honest, she was very nervous.

Perhaps she could get Edwin to practice the dances with her tonight. That could be enjoyable—a wonderful excuse to get close to him, as they'd hardly shared even a hand squeeze the last few days with so many guests around.

She waved fare well to the children from the door of the

castle. A few of them had parents waiting to walk them home. They never did that before Maris started causing so much trouble. Audrey's heart sank at the fact that they felt the need to do so, but she was also glad the children would have some adults walking with them. There were also more guards than usual, as Edwin had his brothers, as well as his brother-in-law, the Duke of Strachleigh, and some of his men patrolling the area to keep watch for Maris and her henchman. With so many guards, how could she not feel safe?

While Audrey was watching her students walk down the lane toward the village, her youngest student, Lucinda, who had not been in class that day, came walking up from around the side bailey.

"Lucinda! I missed you today."

The child came closer. By the expression on her face, Audrey could tell that something was wrong. Then Audrey saw it—the rolled-up piece of paper clutched in her little fist.

Audrey's heart jumped into her throat as her breath shallowed. She took the proffered paper, held on protectively to Lucinda's shoulder, and glanced around.

Guards milled about the bailey. The other children and their mothers were walking together, getting farther and farther away. A groom was brushing a horse.

She quickly read the message.

Sister dear, please come to the burial mound north of Dericott. I am holding this little girl's sister. Come with only this little girl. If I see anyone else with you, I will kill her sister. I have a knife to her throat even as you're reading this.

You do not need guards, as I have sent Umfrey away.

Your sister,

Maris

Audrey's hand trembled as she finished reading the note. She glanced around again. No one seemed to be paying any attention to her and Lucinda.

God, I can't let Lucinda's sister die. She happened to have a knife in the chatelaine purse hanging from her belt. Would that be enough weapon against Maris, if it was only her and not Umfrey she had to fight?

Of course, Maris could be lying about Umfrey no longer being with her. But how else was she able to evade all the guards who were out looking for them?

It could also be a trap, but if she told Edwin about it, he would never allow her to go alone. She had to go and save Lucinda's sister. Her heart was pounding. She couldn't let the child die, but Edwin would be so disappointed in her for running off by herself. Still, she couldn't tell him. Besides, once Maris released the little girl, she could run back home and tell the guards where Maris was, and they could track her from the burial mound.

Her thoughts were spinning and contradicting each other, her head pounding almost as hard as her heart. Part of her wanted to run inside and tell Edwin everything. She wanted his help, his approval of her plan, though he would never approve of her going on her own. She was taking a big risk. Maris could release the child but harm Audrey, which was no doubt what she wanted.

"Teacher, please." Tears were running down Lucinda's cheeks, leaving a clear track through the dust on her face. "The woman said I had to bring you back or she would do something bad to my sister."

"Let us go, then."

Audrey held tightly to Lucinda's hand and hurried down the steps. They walked quickly toward the back of the castle but did not run, not wanting to draw attention.

She was being impulsive, just like when she ran away from home, and just like when she ran away from Dericott Castle when Sir Clement came looking for her. But how could she refuse Lucinda's desperate eyes, her tears, her pleas to save her sister?

They took the path that Edwin had taken to show her the burial mound and the trench. Was she doing the right thing? *God, help me. Keep me safe. Help me keep these children safe.* She would proceed carefully. *God, tell me what to do.* If only she could hear God's voice instructing her. But her thoughts were so loud, twisted, and tangled, she probably could not have heard God if He had spoken to her.

As she neared the field that bordered the burial mound, she slowed, still holding on to little Lucinda's hand. She had been silent since they left the castle.

"Are you all right?" she asked the little girl, bending to look into her face. Her heart constricted in pity at the poor child's terrified expression.

Lucinda nodded, her thin blonde hair hanging down over one eye, as she got a better grip on Audrey's hand.

Audrey pushed the strand of hair off her face. "All is well. Just hold on to me and do what I say."

She nodded more vigorously this time.

They walked closer, slowly crossing the fallow field. Audrey's eyes were trained on the burial mound. She thought she saw something flash in the sun, like a polished piece of metal.

She glanced all around. Someone could be watching them from the forest nearby. Would Umfrey suddenly come running out at them?

What would Edwin say? He'd be so disappointed in her for leaving without telling him where she was going. But if she survived, she would tell him she was sorry. He would understand.

Her eyes darted from left to right to the burial mound ahead. Finally, two people came into view—Maris and a young girl probably around five years old. Maris was standing behind the girl and held a knife near her face. The girl was very pale.

"That's my sister," Lucinda said and burst into tears.

"Don't worry," Audrey said softly. "We will get her back."

"Audrey, I see you came." Maris's voice was strangely cheerful and animated. "That was not so hard, was it?" She whispered something in the child's ear, then lowered the knife.

The little girl hurried away from Maris, scrambling down the side of the grass-covered mound, then ran. The two little girls tearfully embraced.

Audrey bent to the children's level. "Go on back home now," Audrey said quietly. "I shall see you later."

The two set out at a trot, hurrying across the field, back the way they had come.

"Audrey, I just wanted to talk to you. I know you must be very angry with me. Everyone is looking for me." She laughed, a sound that grated on Audrey.

How dare Maris laugh? How dare she enjoy being the focus of everyone's attention and worry? How dare she frighten children and control Audrey, forcing her to come out to this place to help a child Maris had kidnapped? How dare she enjoy making her life hard, threatening people's lives, including hers and Edwin's?

Audrey would not give her what she wanted, which was her time and attention. She turned and started walking back the way she had come, her fists clenched.

"Wait!"

The children were not very far ahead. Perhaps Audrey should occupy Maris a bit longer to make sure they were able to get away. She turned to face her sister, who was now scuttling down the side of the burial mound.

"What do you want, Maris? I need to get back. If anyone followed me, you'll be captured."

"I just want to tell you that I'm sorry Umfrey frightened you and Edwin."

She wanted to tell her she wasn't allowed to call him that, that he was Lord Dericott to Maris and always would be.

"I believe it was you, more than Umfrey, who frightened us. Your hatred and your murderous urges."

Maris's expression suddenly changed, going from contrite to dark and angry.

"You always did hate me," Maris said in a cold voice. "Because you were ugly and I was prettier than you."

Audrey resisted the urge to roll her eyes. "I need to go back. Father is looking for you, Maris."

Her sister moved toward her slowly, taking a few steps, then stopping, then taking a few more steps. Audrey stepped back when Maris moved forward, matching her step for step. Hopefully the two little girls would run into a guard and tell him about Maris and send him to apprehend her. Audrey just needed to keep Maris from trying to harm her or running away.

"What do you want, Maris?"

"I want you not to marry Lord Dericott."

"He wants to marry me. Why should I not marry him?"

"Because you are supposed to marry Sir Clement."

"Why don't you marry Sir Clement?"

Maris's face turned dark again. "How dare you taunt me?"

"I was not meaning to taunt you." Audrey tried to sound meek. "I simply wondered if you wanted to marry Sir Clement. He has released me from our marriage agreement he made with Father. Or perhaps if you tell Father you're sorry, he will find you someone else to marry."

"You know Father doesn't want me to marry."

"He could change his mind."

"You're taunting me again. You want me to rot in that convent with all those nuns who hated me and tried to tell me there was something wrong with me. Well, there's nothing wrong with me."

"The new abbess, Agnes, says the woman who used to torment you has left. She is not at the abbey anymore. Sister Delores wants you to come back so the two of you can work in the garden together."

"She said that?" Maris narrowed her eyes even as her mouth went slack.

"She did. Abbess Agnes wrote me a letter and said if you come back, she will allow you to do as much gardening as you wish, and you will not be forced to have periods of silence. Sister Delores will have charge of you. Would you like that?"

"I'm afraid you are only saying this to trick me. Because you don't want me to marry."

"You could marry if you wanted." Audrey said, still walking backward. "Everyone always says how pretty you are."

"I am pretty."

"You can marry if you wish."

"I could marry if I wished to."

"Yes. And if you asked him, Father might even give you a dowry." Of course, he probably would not. But she prayed God would forgive her for being deceptive.

"You didn't ask me what happened to Umfrey," Maris said.

"What happened to Umfrey?" They were nearly to the other side of the field. Should Audrey turn and run?

"He did not understand what I wanted, and he was too eager to kill someone for me. I would not have really killed you, Audrey. But Umfrey wanted to. He argued with me about it, and I did not like that. Sister Delores would not have been happy with me if I had let him harm you, would she? And I was afraid he was going to get me caught. He was too big. Everyone noticed him. So I sent him away."

"I see." Audrey was only half paying attention to her. She was thinking about how to escape from her sister. "Would you like to come to the castle tomorrow for our ball? You will enjoy the music and the food."

Maris looked confused for a moment, then she stopped walking. "You're taunting me again. Do not expect me to be happy about your wedding. I will not be, and I will not forget how you refused to do as I asked."

"I want you to be happy, Maris."

"No one lets me be happy. I was happy in the garden when I had Sister Delores to talk to. But no one wants me to be happy." Maris looked as if she might cry. "Go on!" she said, shooing Audrey with her hand. "I don't want to see you right now. Leave me alone."

Maris always did hate for anyone to see her cry, and her face was scrunching in that way that said she was about to start sobbing.

"Fare well." Audrey turned and walked quickly instead of running, fearing that Maris, like a wild animal, would be attracted by her running and would be that much more determined to catch her.

TWENTY-THREE

EDWIN SEARCHED FOR AUDREY EVERYWHERE AND COULD not find her, either in the castle or outside it. He asked Sybil and Mistress Wattlesbrook if they'd seen her, then went into the bailey and asked a guard there. No one knew where she was.

His heart pounded against his chest. Could she be in danger? Why had she left the safety of the castle?

He went back inside and found Mistress Wattlesbrook again. "Audrey is missing. Have the servants search every nook and corner of the castle until she is found."

Mistress Wattlesbrook looked alarmed. Good. If alarm was what helped him find Audrey, so be it.

He went outside and spoke to the captain of the guard. "I need some men to go and look for Audrey. Search in every direction until she is found."

Edwin thought he heard someone calling him. He spun around. Audrey was hurrying across the bailey. He rushed toward her, relief flooding his veins.

"I am so sorry for worrying you," she said.

He blew out a pent-up breath. *Thank You, God. She's safe.*

"Where were you? I have all the servants and the guards searching for you."

"Maybe not all." Audrey nodded at someone behind him.

Edwin turned and saw three of his men staring at them.

"She has been found," he said loudly enough for anyone in the bailey to hear. He turned back to Audrey. "What happened?"

Audrey lifted her hand and stared at the paper clutched inside it, as if she'd forgotten it was there.

"My littlest student, Lucinda, came to me after the lesson today and gave me this."

He opened the wadded-up paper and read it. Then he looked at her. "You didn't." He immediately turned to yell at his men. "Go now to the burial mound. Maris was there a few minutes ago."

They all hurried to mount their horses and rode away.

He gazed at Audrey. *Thank You, God, that she is alive.* But how could she have been so foolish?

"Forgive me. I know it was impulsive of me, but I was very careful, and apparently she did send Umfrey away. It was only her, and she was calmer this time."

"I cannot believe, after she nearly murdered us . . ."

"I couldn't bear the thought of one of these precious girls being frightened or getting killed. I thought I could save her. Do you forgive me?"

"Yes," but his reply sounded grudging.

She gazed up at him with so much contrition, but his heartbeat still had not returned to normal, and he could still feel the effects of the blood pumping extra hard through his body, preparing to do battle, if need be, to get his lady back.

"I know it must have been very upsetting to find me gone. But you did not look for me long, did you?"

"That is not the matter under discussion. It is the amount of danger that you were in, the risk you took. Did you not trust me to look after you? Did you think I could not have found a way to save the girl?"

She looked sad. "I am sorry. But all is well now."

He took a deep breath and let it out slowly. "Do you not know what you mean to me? How much I love you?" He spoke in as low a voice as possible, but part of him wanted to yell at her.

"I do know. You tried to give your life for me. I was there. I remember." She pressed her palm to his cheek and looked deep into his eyes. "And I am sorry for worrying you."

He still didn't think she actually understood. But he was so relieved that she was alive, he might end up embarrassing himself in front of his men. So he took her hand and led her inside the castle.

Audrey let Edwin lead her inside. Her heart beat extra fast as she wondered how angry he was with her. But at least he was holding her hand.

They found Mistress Wattlesbrook looking quite frantic. Then the woman's gaze alighted on Audrey.

"Sweet saints and angels, she is found." She smiled, clutching her chest. "I shall go and tell the others." She bustled off, calling to the servants, "She is found! All is well!"

Still holding Audrey's hand, Edwin continued down the hall to the library. He closed the door behind them. He didn't even look at her, just stood with his head down.

"Are you angry with me?"

He ran his hand over his jaw, taking another deep breath and letting it out. "No, I'm not angry with you."

"Perhaps it was foolish, certainly impulsive, and I wasn't sure if I was doing the right thing, but I just wanted to stop Maris from hurting her." She put her arms around him and buried her face in his chest.

"The important thing is that you're safe." He wrapped his arm around her and she could feel his breath in her hair. He took another deep breath and let it out, holding her even tighter.

"Tell me everything that happened," he said.

At least he seemed calmer.

They sat on the bench and he watched her face while she talked. Her heart beat fast and her breath shallowed as she recounted the events and thought about how much danger she had put herself in, and no one even knew where she was.

When she finished, he squeezed her shoulder and said, "You were very brave. And I am thankful God watched over you. But don't put yourself in danger like that for someone else. Your life is just as important as anyone's, and it's time you learned that."

"You are angry with me."

"No, I am trying to make you understand that you are

valuable. For too long you have believed you were damaged and didn't deserve loving care, and that is not true. Your sister is mad and malicious, and she has not treated you well. It would be good if we could help her, but I will not allow her to hurt you again. She's out there terrifying children, for heaven's sake." He ran his hand through his hair and sighed.

"But that's not what I wanted to discuss. What I wanted to say is that you matter just as much as she does. And to me, you matter more than anyone else." He looked intently into her eyes. "Your father didn't protect you as he should have. He even pretended not to believe you when you told him about her. I want to protect you, but I need you to cooperate with me and not leave the castle without me and at least two guards. It does not matter what Maris does or says or what messages she writes to you."

Audrey gazed into his blue eyes, her heart fluttering. She leaned forward and their lips met in a long kiss, as intense as the look he had been giving her. When the kiss was over, it took her a moment to collect her thoughts and be able to speak.

"I promise not to leave the castle without you and two guards."

He squeezed her shoulder. "Thank you."

Though his kisses were exciting, he made her feel content and peaceful at the same time. She had never felt so loved.

But that made her wonder . . . Did she make him feel loved?

"Do you forgive me for running off and not telling you?" She laid her head against his shoulder and let her hand rest on his chest.

"I forgive you, darling. It was a moment of crisis and you did what you thought was best."

"But I won't do that again. I love you, and I don't want to hurt you."

"I know. All is well."

She looked up at him and he was giving her his gentlest smile. And somehow it felt so good to know they'd had their first almost-fight, and they'd resolved it peacefully. He wasn't angry with her, he wasn't ignoring her, and he had forgiven her.

She let out a long breath. She was so fortunate to be marrying this man.

Audrey sat in the Great Hall at the end of the table with Edwin at the head and Delia, his sister, on her other side. Sybil and Helena were sitting farther down the table. She had met all of Edwin's brothers and they were all polite and kind. Even the youngest brothers were able to come for the wedding. But it was Edwin's sister, Delia, whom Audrey was most hoping would like her.

"I always wished for a sister," Delia said. "Can you imagine having seven brothers? But they were not so bad. They were only home until they were six or seven, and then they were sent away. I suppose if they'd been home all the time I would have fought with them more."

"Seeing you interact with your brothers makes me wish I had one," Audrey said shyly.

"I hope it is not wrong for me to mention it, but Edwin told me about your sister. I am so sorry she has given you so much grief and hardship. She sounds perfectly terrifying. I hope I am not offending."

"Not at all. Terrifying is a good description of my sister."

"I think Edwin minimized the danger he was in when Gerard and your father's men found you. Gerard told me your sister's man was about to kill Edwin."

"It is so."

"But all is well now? She has been captured?"

"No. Not yet."

"Oh. Well, with so many brave men around us, we are perfectly safe."

Of course Delia was trying to reassure Audrey, and probably herself as well. But it was true. They did have many brave men around them.

"I hate to say it," Audrey confided, "but Maris's advantage is that she is a woman, and no one suspects a woman of such vengeful intentions as trying to harm others and even kill them."

"I know exactly what you mean. My stepmother—Edwin has probably told you about what she did?"

"Yes, a little. I don't think he likes talking about it, though."

"Edwin is quiet. But he is capable of talking about himself and about how he feels, so don't let him get away with not telling you what is on his mind."

"I won't. He is a good man, and I am so very thankful he loves me." Tears stung her eyes at the truth of what she had just said.

"And I'm so grateful my brother found someone as kind and good as you. I couldn't be happier."

Why did Delia have to say that? It did not help her teary-eyed situation.

"Delia, what are you saying to the poor girl?" Gerard asked, suddenly coming up behind them. "She looks fit to cry."

He could have said the words in a way to embarrass her, but he said them so gently and with so much compassion in his voice, it only made it worse. Audrey had to flick away two tears that made their way out of the corners of her eyes. But she was determined to dry them up and took deep breaths while wiping her face.

"No, I am well."

"Don't worry." Another brother came up beside Gerard. What was his name? Berenger? "Edwin is not so bad when you get used to him. He can be useful, if not very amusing."

"Amusing like you?" Edwin had been listening to the conversation, and she suspected Berenger knew it, which was why he said it. But Edwin smiled, which put Audrey more at ease, and she smiled too, her tears completely gone.

"Can we tell the players to play and sing now?" a third brother said, one of the younger ones—David, she thought. Roland, the youngest, was picking at the cake that had just been set in the middle of the trestle table. He pulled off a sub-tlety, which the cooks had made with almond paste and sugar in the shape of a bird, and bit its head off, then smiled while he chewed.

Delia laughed. "Roland, you should at least wait until

everyone has had a chance to admire the cake before taking some."

"It's been out here for at least two minutes," he said with his mouth full. "It's not my fault everybody is too busy talking to look at it."

Delia shook her head, but Audrey laughed. How good it was to be with people who reacted in a friendly fashion to what was said and done by those around them. She did not wish to be gloomy thinking of Maris. Besides, she should not envy Edwin's sister and brothers. They had been through their own troubles, which had obviously made them closer.

Lively music began, and Edwin was suddenly standing beside her holding out his hand.

"Shall we dance?"

Audrey took his hand, and they and their guests stood up from the tables as the servants took away most of the food, moved the large cake to the dais, and pushed the trestle tables against the wall to make room for dancing in the Great Hall.

Audrey had more confidence in her dancing since she and Edwin practiced some of the dances he thought they'd be doing tonight. She found she remembered dances she thought she'd forgotten, and Edwin gained a bit of confidence too. He confessed he'd been worried he wouldn't be able to dance at all or that dancing would be awkward. So they'd practiced and reassured each other.

Audrey learned to notice when Edwin was starting to lose his balance and help him compensate for it. She worried that might hurt his pride, but he reacted instead with patience and humility, even letting himself lean on her in certain steps. And that touched her heart more than any amount of prideful competence.

Their scars were not things to hide and be ashamed of. Their scars kept them humble, which was pleasing to God, and kept their hearts soft. And it was a bond between them that she was confident would never break.

Lady Delia danced with her husband, Lord Strachleigh. Gerard invited a young woman, one of the guests who was related to Lady Delia's husband, to dance. Several other guests also danced, but Audrey was enjoying herself too much and was too focused on her own partner to pay much attention to who was partnered with whom.

Edwin was wearing a white linen shirt that laced up at the top. The sleeves were generous, and he wore a brocaded, sleeveless velvet tunic of dark green over it that also laced up the front and allowed his sun-browned skin to be contrasted against his white shirt.

His blue eyes focused on her while they danced, and her heart thrilled at his gaze and the touch of his fingers on hers. They danced line dances and chain dances, hopping, twirling, and even skipping to the music, until Audrey was winded and giggling at the way Edwin was holding her.

Suddenly, Audrey heard shouting. It seemed to be coming from the corridor outside the Great Hall. Edwin tightened his grip on her waist and looked toward the sound. People all around them stopped dancing and stared at the doorway.

Someone holding out a torch in front of their face came into the Great Hall. It was a woman, and Audrey knew immediately who it was.

"Stay away from me," Maris said, waving the flaming torch in front of her. "Your men tried to grab me. Is that any way to treat the sister of the bride?" Maris was fairly screaming the words.

Audrey's heart pounded. Edwin nodded at a guard who was positioned nearest to Maris, then moved toward her, even as all the guests were backing away.

Edwin's brothers Gerard, Berenger, and Merek were also moving toward Maris, flanking her on both sides and the front, along with Edwin's guards, even as more guards came in from behind her.

"You need to put down the torch, Maris," Edwin said loudly but evenly.

"I need to put down the torch?" Maris sneered, her teeth showing white in the torchlight. "I will burn anyone who comes near me. I have something to say!"

"Then say it."

"My sister and my father sent me to a convent where I was shut away and forced to be silent. But I won't be silent anymore. My father betrothed my sister to a knight, and she refused to marry him, like the spoiled child that she is. She ran away from home. Why was she not sent to a convent? She has always hated me. She and my father both hated me. But it was my sister who caused my mother's death. So why was I hated instead of her?"

Maris let out a strange wailing sound, while Audrey's cheeks burned, wishing she could defend herself but not knowing how.

Most people would understand that Audrey had done nothing bad, wouldn't they? She wanted so desperately for Edwin's family and friends to love her, and here was her own sister making an unholy scene with a torch in her hand, yelling and accusing her.

Edwin had moved past her, putting his body between her and Maris.

Someone touched her shoulder. Audrey turned to see Delia just behind her.

"Don't worry," Delia whispered near her ear. "The men will capture her."

But what if one of them was burned by her torch? Maris had always enjoyed burning things. She was capable of anything.

"She should not be marrying you," Maris said, pointing at Edwin. "She should be marrying Sir Clement. He is the one she was pledged to."

The guards and Edwin's brothers were drawing closer and closer to her. Audrey's stomach twisted into knots. How could she bear it if Maris hurt them? Maris, who blamed Audrey for all of it.

"Get back!" Maris held the torch out like a sword, pointing it first at one brother, then another.

Why were they getting closer? Did they not know Maris would burn them? *O God in heaven, please don't let Maris hurt them.*

She felt turned to stone, holding her breath.

Someone caught Maris's arms from behind her. Maris screamed and clutched the torch, which shook perilously. But soon several men had taken hold of the torch and Maris's arms.

Berenger closed in from the side and was able to pry the torch from her fingers.

Maris made a strange sound, almost like a wolf's howl, as the guards and Edwin's brothers dragged her away.

"Fire!" someone yelled from somewhere in the corridor. Another voice said, "Come quickly! . . . burning!"

Several of the guests, as well as Edwin, went running out of the Great Hall.

"What has she done?" Audrey whispered. Would Maris have her revenge by burning down Dericott Castle?

Twenty-Four

EDWIN FOLLOWED HIS BROTHERS DOWN THE CORRIDOR and up the stairs. Before he lost his arm he would have been the one leading the charge. But he wouldn't do anyone any good by getting in the way of able-bodied men trying to put out the fire.

When he reached the top of the stairs, smoke was billowing out of Audrey's bedchamber. His heart stopped. He had to remind himself that she was downstairs. She was not in the burning room.

Men were running in with tapestries with which to beat the fire out, and coming out again coughing, their faces covered in soot. Finally, some men came with buckets of water. After what must have been only a few minutes, someone said, "The fire's out."

More guards were hurrying in and Edwin ordered them, "Go and search the whole castle and the outbuildings. Make certain there are no other fires."

Edwin went back downstairs and found Audrey sitting with Delia. When she saw him walk in, she stood and hurried toward him.

"Someone said the fire was in my room."

"I'm afraid so. You should probably let the smoke clear out before you go in. I'm so sorry."

"You can sleep in my room tonight," Delia said.

"Thank you."

"I'm sorry about your room," Edwin said again.

"That is all right. I did not have anything very sentimental. Although I am very sorry to say that my dress I planned to wear to the wedding was in there."

"I can loan you a dress if you need one," Delia said. "I'd be honored if you wore one of my dresses on your wedding day."

"That is very kind." Audrey smiled at Delia.

How good it was to see them treating each other like beloved sisters.

But this never should have happened. Poor Audrey, to be traumatized yet again by her sister. He'd promised to protect her.

"I don't know how Maris got inside without the guards seeing her. I'm so sorry, Audrey."

"Perhaps she covered her head or used a disguise," Audrey said. "But it is all right. No one was hurt, I hope."

"I believe everyone is well, just smoky and dirty."

"I am thankful for that." Audrey caressed his arm. But there was a haunted look in her eyes. "Where is Maris? Do your men have her secured somewhere?"

"I had a room cleaned out in the cellar for her, in case she was caught. She is locked up there with guards to watch over her."

"No one will harm her? She will be taken care of?"

"I shall make sure of it. She shall have food and anything she needs, but every precaution will be taken to make certain she does not escape."

"Thank you."

"And after the wedding I shall send a few of my brothers and the captain of my guard to take her to the abbey and Sister Delores. I'll pay for a guard to watch over her there and make sure she doesn't leave. We will ask for a report every month to let us know how Maris is progressing. But if she escapes or recommences her violent behavior, we shall take her to London to have her tried by the king's court. I mean to make sure she does not threaten you again."

Audrey nodded, her expression grim.

"I am sorry the engagement ball was ruined," he added.

"It was not ruined. We ate well, and we even danced."

"Why should we not dance some more?" Delia asked. "The singers and players are still here. We need not stop the music yet."

Edwin had the musicians begin playing again. Perhaps the sound of music would draw the guests back and beguile them into dancing some more.

And the guests did return. They seemed even more festive than before, talking and laughing and glad to be alive.

Edwin was certainly glad to be alive so he could marry this beautiful woman who was smiling up at him.

Audrey stood talking with Delia while Sybil, Helena, and Mistress Wattlesbrook dressed her for the wedding. The sky outside the window was bright blue, with a few white fluffy clouds for contrast. And she was marrying the best man, the gentlest, kindest, most responsible man she had ever met. The fact that he was handsome made it even better. He was not prideful or arrogant. If he had ever been so, his troubles and losing his arm had made him humble. And she loved him humble, just the way he was.

"You look very happy," Sybil said, her eyebrows raised, a little smirk on her face as she plaited small braids into Audrey's hair with pink and lilac ribbons.

"I am very happy." Audrey realized she needn't be ashamed of her joy. She did not have anyone withholding love from her, or a sister treating her like she wished she didn't exist, scheming vengeful things to do to her. Best of all, she was marrying an upright, good-hearted man, and she was in a home with people who cared about her. And it felt wonderful.

"You look beautiful," Mistress Wattlesbrook said. "We are all proud to have you for our lady and thankful Lord Dericott found such a good wife."

Her words made Audrey's breath catch in her throat. "That

is so kind of you to say. And I am thankful for you, for everyone at Dericott Castle. I have never been so happy. It feels like a wonderful dream."

"And you are making Edwin very happy too," Delia said, gently squeezing her arm.

Truly, it felt like a miracle to be marrying Edwin. She had half expected Maris to escape her cell and try to murder Audrey in her sleep, but she was awake and alive and the wedding was happening. It was really happening.

As they made their way down the stairs, she caught sight of Edwin walking past. He looked up and his expression changed. He stopped and turned toward her, watching her come down the steps.

"You are beautiful," he said in a soft voice.

"You look beautiful too," she said, her voice choking up. But he might not think *beautiful* was the right word. "Handsome. You look handsome." And he did, his blue eyes bright against the bright blue coat he was wearing.

He took her hand, neither smiling nor frowning, but the look on his face seemed to convey many things—awe, love, humility, gratitude, tenderness, and admiration. He lifted her hand to his lips and kissed it.

They walked through the castle and outside, down the lane toward the village and all the way to the church. All the while she hugged his arm and listened to the cheerful well-wishes of the villagers.

Her father and several of his men had arrived the night before, just as the ball was ending and everyone was going to bed.

"I will take Maris to Sister Delores at the convent," he had told her and Edwin.

"Father, you will take care that she doesn't escape, won't you?" Audrey couldn't help asking.

Father's face turned red. "You insult me. Of course I won't allow her to escape, not after all the trouble she has caused."

Edwin finally agreed to let her father and his men escort her, though he insisted on sending one of his own guards who would stay at the convent with her.

Audrey only hoped Maris somehow would be able to make peace with her past, with the cruelty she suffered as a child, and be able to get rid of her violent thoughts and find a better purpose in life.

Audrey thrust her sister from her thoughts. She wanted to remember every detail of this cherished day. She waved at every person who waved at her, her heart expanding at the joy on their faces. She saw her students lined up along the street and blew them kisses, laughing and waving back at them.

As they drew near to the church, Edwin leaned down and said in her ear, "You are an amazing woman. I am so fortunate to find you."

He had told her that before, but it once again took her by surprise that he thought so much of her.

"I am the fortunate one," she whispered back, kissing him on the cheek.

As the priest was already waiting for them on the top step of the church, she took Edwin's hand and let her chest fill with love so big it threatened to carry her away.

She may not have known what her life would look like when she was a girl in Engleford, dreaming of being a shooting star, but making sure the girls of Dericott learned to read and write gave her purpose and joy.

And if anything made her feel like she was living a life of vivid color, it was loving and being loved by her students, God, and her beloved Edwin. Giving and receiving love was the best purpose of all.

ACKNOWLEDGMENTS

In finishing this, my twentieth published book, I want to thank all the people who helped me accomplish this goal as a writer of fiction. I'd probably leave out quite a few if I attempted to list them all. But I am grateful to all the people who helped me on this journey. God has blessed me so much, in many ways surpassing what I imagined for myself, and I'm so thankful.

I want to thank my agent, Natasha Kern, who continues to help me on this journey. I want to thank my editors, Kimberly Carlton and Julie Breihan, who are so directly involved in the process, as well as everyone else at my publishing house, Thomas Nelson and HarperCollins Christian Publishing. You all add a sparkle and shine that is beyond my ability.

I want to thank my daughters, Grace and Faith, my husband, Aaron, and all of my friends who encourage me and occasionally brainstorm ideas with me or listen to me "talk out" my story while I'm writing it. I love you and appreciate you all so much.

I especially want to thank my readers, without whom I would not be able to see my novelist dreams come true. You are so dear to me, more than you know, and I can never appreciate you enough. I pray that God speaks to you and helps you in the exact ways you need him to. God bless you.